THE GIANT
AWAKES

THE GIANT AWAKES

A JAKE KRUSE NOVEL

OLIVER NORTH

AND BOB HAMER

FIDELIS
PUBLISHING

Fidelis Publishing, LLC
Sterling, VA • Nashville, TN
www.fidelispublishing.com

ISBN: 978-1956454048
ISBN: 978-1956454055 (e-book)

THE GIANT AWAKES
A Jake Kruse Novel

For information about special discounts for bulk purchases, please contact BulkBooks.com, call 1-888-959-5153, or email - cs@bulkbooks.com.

Cover designed by Diana Lawrence
Interior layout by Lisa Parnell
Edited by Amanda Varian

Manufactured in the United States of America

10 9 8 7 6 5 4 3 2 1

FIDELIS
PUBLISHING

For Betsy

who embodies Proverbs 18:22

*He who finds a wife finds a good thing
and obtains favor from the Lord.*

GLOSSARY

ADIC	Assistant Director in Charge
AG	Attorney General
ASAC	Assistant Special Agent-in-Charge
AUSA	Assistant United States Attorney
BAU	Behavioral Analysis Unit
CACO	Casualty Assistance Calls Officer
CART	Computer Analysis Response Team
CAS	Chinese Academy of Sciences
CHS	confidential human source
CCP	Chinese Communist Party
CCW	concealed carry weapons permit
CIA	Central Intelligence Agency
CPAP	continuous positive airway pressure mask
DACA	Delayed Action for Childhood Arrivals
DHS	Department of Homeland Security
DOJ	Department of Justice
EEO	Equal Employment Opportunity
FBI	Federal Bureau of Investigation
FCI	Foreign Counterintelligence
FEC	Federal Election Commission
FFL	federal firearms license
FISA	Foreign Intelligence Surveillance Act of 1978
FISUR	foreign intelligence surveillance (wiretap under FISA authority)
FMM	Forma Migratoria Multiple card

FSA	Flores Settlement Agreement
GED	graduate equivalency diploma
GPS	global positioning system
ICAC	Internet Crimes Against Children (task force)
ICE	Immigration and Customs Enforcement
I/O	intelligence officer (foreign)
LAPD	Los Angeles Police Department
MARSOC	Marine Corps Special Operations Command
MMA	mixed martial arts
MPP	Migrant Protection Protocols
MS-13	Mara Salvatrucha
MSS	Ministry of State Security (China)
NSA	National Security Agency
OPR	Office of Professional Responsibility
PAC	political action committee
PC	probable cause (legal term) or politically correct
PRC	Peoples Republic of China
RCT	Regimental Combat Team
RF	radio frequency detector
RPG	rocket propelled grenade
SAC	special agent-in-charge
SEC	Security Exchange Commission
SWAT	special weapons and tactics
TSA	Transportation Security Administration
UC	undercover
UCLA	University of California, Los Angeles
USC	University of Southern California

China is a sleeping giant. Let her sleep
for when she wakes, she will move mountains.
Let her sleep for when she wakes, she will shake the world.

NAPOLEON BONAPARTE

✕ ✕ ✕

A great civilization is not conquered from without
until it has destroyed itself from within.

ARIEL DURANT

Chapter One

Within the hour, it would all be over. There was little else Jake Kruse could do but wait. Everything was set and now it was all up to Fat Willie. Hard to believe life revolved around a corpulent, middle-aged white man with a prison record, but much of Jake's life depended upon those who flaunted their multi-page rap sheets. Fat Willie was only the latest in a long line of outlaws betrayed by Jake, a government-sanctioned Judas.

The undercover agent leaned back in his chair, propping his well-worn Tony Lama ostrich-skin boots on a marred and battered pine desk. With penetrating hazel eyes, perfect for UC work since the color seemed to change with the lighting, Jake stared out the window, watching several semis rumble out of the industrial complex. A target once described Jake as having "killer eyes" and Katie liked to joke it was his most attractive feature: "nondescript killer eyes."

Overcast skies portended a storm lurking in the distance, providing the perfect backdrop for this afternoon's felony fiesta. The air draped over the city like a sweat-saturated towel following summer football two-a-days. As the advance element in the weather front, winds whipped up trash and debris from the homeless camp in the ravine just off the main entrance to the multi-use business facility.

For Jake, inside the warehouse was the quiet before the storm. The TV was off, and he shut down Pandora: no more Charlie Daniels or

Johnny Cash. It was time to put on his game face: his pure vanilla game face. He was no Hollywood pretty boy undercover agent. You might label him "rugged," but few would call him "ruggedly handsome." A nose—broken in fights, both in and out of the ring—listed slightly to one side, and his hair—which for this assignment hung almost to his shoulders—was mousey brown. Five days of stubble surrounded a face far from centerfold material.

Because of a COVID-induced backlog at the grand jury, the six-month undercover assignment was extended a month and now in a matter of minutes it would all come tumbling down. Once he gave the signal, FBI SWAT would swarm the warehouse and multiple arrests would be executed. A smile crossed his face as he watched lightning spider the horizon and heard thunder crack in the distance. As one of his tactical instructors schooled the class at the Bureau's academy in Quantico, Virginia, "good agents *never* get wet" and the Dallas SWAT team was about to get soaked. At least for today, Jake was glad he had the indoor assignment.

Both satisfaction and a sense of sadness washed over him. The satisfaction would come with the completion of another successful UC assignment, more filth off the streets, but the arrests meant no more adrenaline rushes, at least in the short term. Without Katie in his life, he only lived for those surges of excitement racing through his veins like an RPG streaking toward its target. If it were up to him, he would never surface, remaining in a constant state of dual identities, taking on a continual run of UC missions.

Prior to coming to Dallas, he spent time outside Indianapolis targeting members of a white supremacy group living off the grid and spewing hatred in every conversation. At least in Big D, he could shower daily. The assignments kept coming and though he was looking forward to returning to Los Angeles, he had no desire to return to office politics and "blue-flame" bureaucrats more concerned with the brass ring than justice. He hadn't stepped foot inside FBI office space for thirteen months, a personal record, but once he got back to L.A., he would at least need to report to management, requiring his presence at the Wilshire Boulevard federal building in Westwood.

Back-to-back UC assignments could be taxing but changing roles, back stories, and targeted violations kept it fresh. In Dallas, it was an international smuggling ring, but not the usual fentanyl and other drugs so often associated with whatever surged across the porous Southwest border. In fact, because this group specifically steered clear of drugs, the cargo containers crossing at El Paso, McAllen, and Brownsville never triggered a dog-alert. For the most part, the trucks were hauling anything manufactured south of the border that had worth to the *Norte Americanos*. In the past seven months, everything from refrigerators, toilet bowls, tires, guitars, even crayons passed through the undercover warehouse.

Maybe Jake's most important contribution was a forty-foot container of medical supplies manufactured in China and shipped through Mexico. Knowing the contents, when the driver of the rig made a last-minute restroom stop in the warehouse before heading north, Jake disabled the brake lights on the trailer. After the driver and his cargo left, Jake alerted his case agent who arranged for the Texas Highway Patrol out of Coleman to stop the rig for a faulty brake lights violation. The medical equipment was seized and quickly distributed to area hospitals treating the latest COVID variant. Jake was only too happy to quash the entrepreneurial spirit of the driver and his boss. Both lost out on a major payday as the pilfered equipment was in short supply.

As with every container, the smugglers' costs were next to nothing since everything was stolen directly from a Chinese manufacturer shipping the material through Mexico or from hijacked semi-tractor trailers en route to the United States. If customs or law enforcement cared to check the contents of the containers, even the bills of lading were accurate. Rightful ownership was the only issue and easily concealed with creative paperwork.

Jake's wardrobe throughout the investigation was denim and cowboy boots, no frills and no iron; just the way he liked it. He looked blue collar and played it well. A primary rule of any cover: sell it. And Jake sold it.

The main target, William James Dotson, a.k.a. Fat Willie, had a criminal record dating back to his juvenile days but only one conviction, a Tennessee truck hijacking resulting in a five-year sentence. The singular lesson Willie learned while incarcerated was to let others take most of the risks; never drive the trucks or handle the merchandise. He learned to use "sub-contractors" for this kind of work. He would always show up when the containers arrived at the UC offsite but left most of the heavy lifting to those in the distribution chain. On the plus side, though a criminal, he was polite and personable. He and Jake shared many a beer while discussing guns and country music legends. And Fat Willie was almost always on time. His drivers operated on a schedule; no "dope dealer" time for these long haulers. If Willie said he and his men would arrive at a certain hour, you could start the Keurig and have hot coffee waiting when they pulled into the yard.

Jake's role in this assignment was limited to the Dallas warehouse and those who came and went from the undercover offsite. He never traveled to the ultimate destination of the poached goods, leaving that aspect of the operation to multi-agency surveillance teams.

Earlier in the week, Jake learned a federal grand jury returned seventeen indictments, to include the receivers of stolen goods in Kansas City, Cincinnati, and Chicago. Agents in the respective field offices were sitting on those targets and once Fat Willie and his partner, Charlie Hendrix, arrived at the warehouse, the hammer would drop with simultaneous arrests occurring across Middle America.

Though Fat Willie was circumspect during his latest call to Jake, he did say they would be arriving within the hour. Willie didn't identify the contents of the container but told Jake to expect two men to be arriving shortly who would take the product away once it was offloaded.

Jake notified the case agent that a couple more players would be showing up for the big game, but with overwhelming SWAT support, a few additional bodies would only make for a juicier six o'clock news story.

A U-Haul box truck and a rusted silver panel van with Texas-size dents pulled into two parking slots in front of the warehouse office. Jake watched two Latin males, each about 5'6" or 5'7", both in their mid-twenties, exit the vehicle and stride toward the office. Jake waited for them to jerk unsuccessfully on the locked front door and then buzz before he moved his size twelve boots off the desk and headed for the entrance.

Unlocking the double-cylinder deadbolt and opening the door, Jake said without offering a smile, "Yeah, can I help you?" as his words blew across the parking lot with a strong gust of wind.

The driver of the panel van smelled like a truck stop strip joint: beer, cigarettes, and cheap cologne. He replied in heavily accented English, "We are here to see Guillermo." With his left hand, the driver reached for the front pocket of his burgundy Wrangler, cowboy cut, long-sleeve shirt and pulled out a pack of Camels. Tapping the pack on his right wrist, a cigarette slipped out of the pack, and he grabbed it with his lips. After replacing the pack, he reached deep into his left front pants pocket, eventually removing a Bic lighter. Cupping his right hand to prevent the wind from extinguishing the flame, he was successful after two or three tries. So much effort for so little immediate satisfaction. Since all form of tobacco was banned in federal prisons, Jake decided to let the newest co-conspirator in the UC operation finish what might be his last smoke for at least a decade.

More because he loved screwing with people, than maintaining his bad boy image, Jake said, "You got the wrong taco stand, guys. There's no Guillermo here."

With only a slight accent and apparently sober, the box truck driver interrupted, "He means Fat Willie. We're here for Fatso. He's got some product we paid for, and it was due yesterday." There was a cultivated hatred in his reptilian glare, glistening like shards of obsidian with a commanding presence wreaking of institutional leadership.

Prison tattoos, seeping out from beneath the collar of his long-sleeve shirt and splayed across his knuckles, screamed "outlaw."

Jake nodded as if the cloud of confusion dissipated with this terse but clarifying explanation. Pointing toward a blacktop road at the end of the building, Jake said, "He isn't here yet. He's still a few out. If you guys want to pull your trucks around to the alley, I'll open the back entrance and you can park inside. Once Willie gets here, you can load up and be on your way."

With a veneer of politeness and sounding accommodating, Jake's hospitality was designed to incapacitate the trucks by locking them in the building and minimizing potential escape vehicles.

Answering with only a grunt, both men returned to their trucks.

This time, Jake purposely left the front door unlocked and made his way toward the hallway, past the small reception area and into a cavernous warehouse large enough to handle several trucks and the contents of multiple cargo containers.

The Dallas FBI tech agents did it up right. Every cubic foot of the interior of the building had video and audio coverage. Tiny recorders sensitive enough to pick up rat farts ensured the FBI captured each conversation taking place within the off-site. The technical surveillance was excellent, and the recordings guaranteed convictions for the multiple defendants who would be receiving some well-deserved R&R courtesy of the U.S. government's penal system. The taco twins were late hires but could be quickly added to the post-season roster.

As with any arrest, it was always hard to tell how much of an impact the operation would have on the community—usually none. Once Fat Willie and his crew were off the streets, some other group would sidle in and continue wheeling and dealing with its own distribution network. But that was the nature of crime. The violence hadn't stopped with Cain and Abel, and the thieving wouldn't be abruptly halted when this criminal clique hit a medium security federal facility.

Jake punched a button and the large metal door at the back entrance to the warehouse began to slowly lift. The main entrance, off the frontage road, was at the other end of the building. Deep enough to handle a sixty-five-foot-long cab and trailer, the semis could back into either of the two loading docks. A forklift was available to quickly off-load any contents. It was a procedure replicated time and time again as each delivery and subsequent pickup was caught on digital recorders.

As the two vehicles entered, Jake directed the drivers to the far side of the building. He lowered the door just as the clouds opened and the rain began its assault, fulfilling the morning weather reporter's prediction. Typically, the sky lights in the ceiling provided sufficient illumination for the storeroom's interior, but now the storm clouds hid the sun, darkening the warehouse. Maybe he was slipping. Maybe he was too complacent. Maybe his smile at the launch of the afternoon downpour had a hint of malice, but it was evident even in the increasing shadows.

"What are you smiling at?" demanded the smaller of the two men, the sober co-conspirator.

"I just love a good thunderstorm."

Though he slurred his words, the other said, "You one crazy *weddo*. Nobody likes *la lluvia*."

Jake's smile got a little bigger. "You guys got names? I'm Jake," said the undercover agent extending his hand.

Neither answered nor returned the civilized gesture.

"We won't be here long enough to require introductions," said sobriety.

"That's fine with me. I'm not looking to make fast friends, but just for clarity's sake, I'm calling you Poncho and your less-than-sober companion, Lefty."

"If that's your game, that's fine with us," said Poncho.

"You guys want a beer?" asked Jake as he headed toward a heavily scratched white refrigerator along the near wall next to some metal storage shelves crowded with dust-covered boxes.

Lefty didn't hesitate, "Yeah!"

"Dos Equis, Coors, or Shiner?" asked Jake.

"Yeah," said Lefty.

"That was an 'either or' not all three," hollered Jake over his shoulder, grabbing three bottles of Shiner Golden Ale out of the old cumbersome Maytag whose only value was keeping beer and sack lunches cold. The bottom freezer unit never worked properly in the seven months Jake was at the offsite.

The limited conversation ceased as both Poncho and Lefty began guzzling the beer once the bottles were in their hands.

Jake paused long enough to let them take a few gulps before casually asking, "So, what are you guys picking up today? Willie's been bringing in all kinds of swag from down south. What's today's bounty?"

"*Chicas,*" said Lefty.

"*Quieto, tarado,*" responded Poncho with a hard shove, knocking Lefty into the U-Haul.

"*Chicas?*" asked Jake, confused by Lefty's immediate, uncensored response.

Before the conversation could continue, Johnny Cash's "Folsom Prison Blues" ringtone erupted from Jake's back pocket. Pulling the iPhone from his jeans, Jake saw Fat Willie was calling.

Answering, Jake said, "Hey, you're running late, big guy. What happened? Did you have a date with a doughnut?"

"We're just down the street. Open the doors to both loading docks. It's pouring and I don't want to get wet. Charlie can take dock one and I'll pull into number two," said Willie, barking orders like a drill instructor.

"Your two playmates showed up and are waiting for you."

"Good. Don't break out the beer. The one guy thinks alcohol is our national currency and I don't trust either of them sober, let alone drunk."

"You should've issued those orders on your earlier phone call," responded Jake, shaking his head.

"Okay. In that case, cut 'em off and open the door."

CHAPTER TWO
Dallas, Texas

Jake hustled toward the loading docks. On the wall, to the left of the truck-size openings, he pushed the top button on the individual control panels and the two gun-metal gray doors began to slowly retreat on the track toward the ceiling.

As if angry clouds suddenly unleashed more of their pent-up rage, thunder roared, and a new round of torrential rains emptied onto the Dallas streets.

Fat Willie pulled in headfirst as Charlie Hendrix prepared to back the semi up to the loading dock. More thunder clapped, as Willie slowly poured from the driver's side of his 2017 Ford F-350 Super Duty and lumbered toward the undercover agent.

"Glad I didn't wash my truck yesterday," said Willie as he extended his oversized, fleshy hand toward Jake.

"Somebody's getting wet out there," said Jake with a laugh, knowing everything he said was being heard by the SWAT leader.

With the alley garage doors closed and locked, the only exit from the windowless warehouse was through the office or the now opened warehouse doors at the front of the building.

The plan called for a couple of SWAT team members to seal off the office escape route and once Charlie had the semi backed in and the rear doors to the twenty-foot cargo container opened, Jake would give the verbal signal. A tiny microphone concealed in Jake's belt buckle was broadcasting his conversations and when the magic words were said, the drenched SWAT agents would "wash in" through the frontage road warehouse entrance.

After skillfully backing the big rig up to the loading dock, Charlie Hendrix, who may have been a jockey in a previous life, exited the cab of the aging Peterbilt. Charlie always looked like he'd been "ridden hard and put away wet." His sunbaked face had wrinkles betraying his true age, but maybe two multi-year prison stints had something to do with his seasoned appearance. At only 5'5" and about 130 pounds, Jake wondered how the balding, forty-year-old Teamster reached the pedals. With tattoos of naked women gracing both his pencil-thin, white-trash arms, Charlie made it clear on numerous occasions he had no desire to return to Huntsville where he twice served time. Swearing like a drunken sailor on liberty, the air turned blue as his feet hit the warehouse floor and he offered his opinion on everything from the weather to the current administration.

"Charlie, so glad to see you again. Your bright, cheery disposition makes my day and I always appreciate your take on current affairs," said Jake awaiting a colorful response.

With Fat Willie contributing a huge belly laugh, Charlie didn't disappoint, responding with machine-gun-fire obscenities. Stabbing out a cigarette on the wall of the warehouse, Charlie moved to the rear of the tractor-trailer, preparing to open the steel doors of the cargo container.

Willie began conferencing with Poncho and Lefty near the U-Haul. No handshakes or smiles were evident as Poncho tried to get up into Willie's face. But at a slim 5'7" there was no way Poncho could overcome Willie's height and tremendous girth for a face-to-face confrontation. Jake decided not to intercede, allowing the felons to resolve their own playground issues.

Charlie fooled with the key for several seconds before finally yanking hard on the stainless-steel Master padlock securing the cargo doors. The distinctive click of the latch signaled the container's contents were about to be revealed.

With that, Jake recited the verbal sign to the SWAT team, now stacked along the side of the building. In a voice, just a little louder than normal to ensure the team leader heard him, Jake said, "Open those doors, Big Charlie, and show Papa Bear what you brought me today."

As the doors popped open and the FBI SWAT team made its dynamic entry, a dozen worn and exhausted Asian females in their teens and early twenties stumbled from the cargo container.

"FBI, freeze! Nobody move!" shouted the SWAT team leader in a booming voice as the team, saturated from the afternoon storm, raced into the building.

But the baritone command was masked by the women exiting the container as their high-pitched screams of "*Yimin!*" the Chinese word for "immigration" echoed off the warehouse walls.

Any combat veteran will tell you, most battle plans, no matter how well conceived, don't survive first contact with the enemy. The SWAT team's textbook entry into the warehouse fell apart within seconds.

The dozen women ran to the only visible exits which were the open garage doors through which the FBI agents, clad in black tactical gear with the letters F-B-I stenciled in bold, fluorescent yellow, visible on the front and back, entered. The FBI agents were momentarily distracted as the women raced toward the exit. Discipline on both sides collapsed as the agents weren't sure whether to let the females run or if they were part of the arrest scenario. Agents began grabbing the women and herding them at gunpoint toward the nearest wall. Screams, shrieks, and cries flooded the warehouse as chaos temporarily reigned.

Simultaneously, the real targets of the investigation, Fat Willie, Charlie, Poncho, and Lefty recognized their avenues of retreat were limited. All four men were carrying. After all, it was Texas, where even housewives were typically packing outside Walmart while selling Girl Scout cookies. Every arrest situation in the Lone Star State assumed a possible armed encounter. With Charlie previously announcing his decision to never return to prison, his immediate response was explosive.

Jake, who took cover behind a stack of wooden pallets, saw Charlie draw a small semi-automatic from his waistband and was gaining a clear sight picture, focusing on the SWAT team's point man who led the charge into the warehouse.

The agent, whose eyes were still adjusting to the darkened warehouse, was looking to his left where Willie, Poncho, and Lefty were retreating. He didn't see Charlie to his right, concealed by the shadows.

Jake's decisive violence came with an on/off switch. It immediately snapped "on." No time for proportional aggression, Jake was ready to exercise disproportionate force. Without hollering instructions for the unsuspecting semi-truck driver to drop his weapon, a single round barked from Jake's semi-automatic. The bullet, with Charlie Hendrix's name on it, hit center mass and the ex-con slumped to the cold concrete floor.

Jake's thunderous blast added to the anarchy as everyone focused momentarily on Charlie's body lying in a quickly enlarging pool of his own blood.

On the far side of the warehouse, Willie reached beneath several layers of fat and pulled a large caliber semi-automatic from his waistband. For a fat man, he moved quickly. Joined by Poncho and Lefty, who also drew concealed weapons, the three raced to the back of the U-Haul box truck, rapidly firing as they moved. Poncho's actions were more precise as he fired with purpose toward the agents. The inebriated Lefty fired over his shoulder, gangster-style, with his rounds spraying off the walls; the sustained blister of gunfire echoing throughout the building.

Though all three were quickly hit, they continued firing in the short-lived shootout. The trio managed to strike two SWAT members, but the fourteen Dallas agents returned fire with dozens of rounds from their M4s. Struck multiple times by numerous agents, Willie, Poncho, and Lefty committed their last felony.

Amazingly, not one of the dozen human trafficking victims was harmed, though most were frightened to the point of continued screams and tears.

When the firing ceased, Jake made his way to Willie whose life would be over in minutes, if not seconds. As Jake knelt next to him, Willie asked in a weak nonconfrontational tone, "So you're FBI?"

Jake struggled to hear, the sounds of gunfire still ringing in his ears. "Yeah, I am."

"You were good. I never suspected. I should've caught on with the 'Folsom Prison Blues' ring tone."

Jake offered a soft smile.

"I'm glad it wasn't you who shot me. I always liked you, Jake."

Jake said nothing as Willie coughed up blood trying to catch a breath that wasn't easily coming.

"I guess I should have stuck with refrigerators and crayons, but the money was just too good to bring these girls across. I couldn't pass it up. Was it the girls that brought me down?"

"No, Willie, you were going down anyway. I was as surprised by the women as you were by the FBI."

"Oh, I guess it doesn't matter." Willie coughed up more blood and his voice weakened. "What day is it?"

"It's Tuesday, Willie."

"That's what I thought."

A thin smile crossed Jake's face. Arrests were usually set for early in the week so the mounds of paperwork would be done by Friday and weekends could remain unencumbered by bureaucratic mandates and deadlines.

"Tomorrow's my birthday. I guess I won't see it now," said Willie trying to smile.

"Sorry, Willie, but I don't think you will."

As he weakened, knowing death was near, Willie asked, "Do you believe in heaven, Jake?"

"Yeah, I do, Willie."

"You think I've got a chance at making it?"

"My Bible says if you believe in your heart and confess with your mouth that Jesus Christ is Lord, you will be saved."

Through bloodstained teeth, Willie attempted to smile, "Do you believe that Jake?"

"Yeah, Willie, I do."

The smile grew a little bigger, "I guess I better hurry then."

Willie's eyes grew heavy and gently closed as the strength began to leave his body. Jake watched as the fat man's lips moved making a silent plea—maybe he got to God in time.

The SWAT team leader who was attending to his wounded men and managing the dozen young women now in temporary custody, made his way toward Jake, "Are you okay?"

Still kneeling next to Willie, Jake nodded.

"You saved my first man through the door. Thanks," said the leader.

"Are the rest of your guys okay?"

"Yeah, two took rounds, but they'll make it. They were flesh wounds, but I'm sure within a month or two, they'll claim they were life-threatening and will be seeking hero-status."

Jake smiled, "What about the Chinese girls?"

"They're all okay. Not a scratch. At least that saves us some paperwork," said the SWAT leader. "How'd you know they were Chinese?"

"They were hollering '*Yimin*'—I figured they were all from China."

Jake looked down at Willie, then over toward the females huddled along the wall. "That's why Willie said the money was so good. Last I heard, they were paying about $40,000 a person to get here. Might have made an interesting trial."

Surveying the blood-soaked warehouse floor, strewn with four dead bodies and several hundred expended casings from various caliber weapons, the SWAT team leader said, "Doesn't look like there's anyone here left to prosecute."

Knowing each spent cartridge would need to be married up to its respective weapon, Jake nodded. "Nobody here gets prosecuted, but somebody's going to have to write a multivolume shooting report. Glad I'm not getting that ticket."

"Yeah, me too. OPR's gonna love this one," said the SWAT leader. He was referring to the FBI's Office of Professional Responsibility, the Bureau's answer to Internal Affairs which handled all shooting inquiries after the field office did its initial investigation.

Jake nodded as he rose to his feet, stumbling with a quick step as he caught his balance, now realizing the shooting took more out of him than he was willing to concede. Offering an anemic smile, he said, "Time for me to head back to L.A. before the suits from the D.C. Puzzle Palace arrive."

CHAPTER THREE

THURSDAY, APRIL 7
Agoura Hills, Los Angeles

The hour was late, and Jake quietly knocked on the door. He was hoping he wouldn't wake the baby but was looking forward to spending a little time with Joey's mom. It had been a roller coaster of emotions these past several years. He and Natasha lost the loves of their lives; the person with whom they promised before God and man to love "until death do us part." But death did happen, long before anyone wanted.

He wasn't sure how Natasha felt. Neither verbalized feelings toward the other, but Jake knew something was stirring, his heart was changing. For him, it was more than merely a friendship; a passion was developing. This new emotion wasn't the result of pity or sympathy or even kindness. It was love.

He wondered if Natasha was experiencing the same excitement, but he was afraid to initiate the conversation. Without flinching, he faced down terrorists trying to end his life. He went toe-to-toe with some of society's most evil men. He walked into situations wondering whether he would come out alive, but on this truly personal issue, he was having trouble summoning up the courage to express himself. He was afraid to convey the feelings welling up inside.

There was the quiet guilt of whether he was betraying Katie. She'd been dead almost four years but was still so much a part of his life. Thoughts of her happened even in the middle of an undercover operation when he would think, *I can't wait to call Katie and tell her about this latest twist.* But just as quickly he'd realize she was no longer there to listen and respond and comfort. She had been his tether to reality in a world of evil and uncertainty.

He violated more than one FBI directive by sharing with her some of the most intimate details of his investigations. Maybe not names, maybe not locations but enough for her to understand what life was like in the shadow world where he lived. He put up a great front. The psychologists he saw every six months to clear him for continued undercover work thought of him as a loner who needed no friends.

They were wrong. He didn't need anyone back then because God gave him Katie. Why hang with the guys when you could spend all your free time with your best friend? Now his best friend was in heaven as he deflected all the world threw at him.

He hadn't dated anyone since her death. No one held his interest, and he certainly wasn't looking. He immersed himself in his various undercover assignments and each of those projects became his mistress.

He spurned any effort by those at church who tried to fix him up with that "really sharp friend" who had "a great personality." The ladies were respectful at first, but as time passed, the mothers with single daughters still at home waxed bolder with their overtures—invitations to Sunday dinners, holidays, and special celebrations.

Had he milked the system, he probably could have had a home-cooked meal every evening. He was running out of excuses and seriously considered changing churches just to avoid the barrage of looks, inquiries, and offers. Thirteen months out of town may have cooled the overbearing hens shopping their chicks, especially when none received a post card or phone call. With the collective mommies' persistence, maybe all were married off and Jake could focus on the sermon.

Due to their previous relationship and their current bond, the situation with Natasha was different. She was Katie's closest friend and her husband, Joe, was Jake's best man when he and Katie married at her family church in Santa Barbara. Katie's dad was a pastor and married them on a perfect June day shortly after they met. Her parents were also in the hospital room when she died, Jake holding her hand as they watched her take her final breath. Tom was a rock and losing his youngest daughter only strengthened his faith. For Jake, it wasn't as easy. He and God were still wrestling over the loss.

Joe's death was so much different for Natasha. She wasn't there and didn't even know about it until late the next day. He was in Afghanistan. She was at Camp Pendleton just north of San Diego. She didn't know the town or village where Joe was assigned or even what he was doing. She only knew it was dangerous as were all combat deployments.

The sun was down and she was quietly sitting in her living room reading the latest motherhood guidebook when there was a knock at the door. Natasha and Joe lived in quarters on base, so she knew it wasn't a solicitor, maybe a neighbor hoping to borrow a cup of sugar. When she turned on the porch light and peered out the window she knew instantly. Her heart sank and she began to shake. Fear washed over her as she fought to control her reactions, thinking of their baby growing inside.

It wasn't a neighbor. It was a CACO—a Casualty Assistance Calls Officer—a notification team the Corps provides to inform the next of kin of something they never want to hear. It's the absolute worst duty, but it has to be done. In this case it was a U.S. Marine lieutenant colonel, a Navy chaplain, and two corpsmen. The Marine Corps knew she was six months pregnant, and the corpsmen were there as a precaution. She opened the door, but the words didn't come. The tears flooding her face said all that needed to be said.

Joe stepped on an IED, an improvised explosive device, while working on a village stabilization project in Afghanistan's Helmand Province. He was an operator as a member of the elite Marine Corps Forces Special Operations Command. Originally MARSOC, the Marines changed the name to Raiders in 2014. They were the Marine Corps' answer to the Navy SEALS, the Army's Delta Force, and the USAF Special Ops Command. Joe was a warrior and a patriot. On that day, in the shadows of a war the nation wanted to forget, he became a statistic and made Natasha a Gold Star wife, a designation no one sought.

Jake and Joe met in Quantico, Virginia, at the Marine Corps Platoon Leaders Class, an officer selection program in which "candidates" as they are called, attended two six-week sessions during their college summers. After obtaining their bachelor's degrees, both candidates were commissioned second lieutenants. From there the J-Warriors, as they called themselves, Jake and Joe, went through the six-month officer basic school, known as TBS, and then the Infantry Officer Course, IOC.

Both were assigned to the 3rd Marine Regiment, RCT-3, and were part of the invasion of Iraq in 2003. On the way to Baghdad and later in the Anbar Province, Jake watched too many of his men die and others suffer catastrophic wounds. It was something he would never forget. Still today he thinks about his men, those who fought and those who died.

Combat changed Jake, as it does everyone who experiences it. He grew up quickly in the "sand box." He was wounded in Fallujah, shrapnel from a rocket-propelled grenade, an RPG. The cumulative effect of the war and the losses he incurred made him rethink his career plans. As he was being treated, first in a field hospital, then at Balad, the triage hospital at Landstuhl, Germany, and finally at U.S. Naval Hospital, Bethesda, Maryland, Jake thought about the FBI.

Ever since his Marine training in Quantico where the FBI has its academy, he entertained the idea of becoming a G-Man, if he didn't stay in the Corps. With all he experienced in Iraq, serious deliberation took place. The FBI seemed like a better fit. He would still be a warrior, but the battlefield changed as would his responsibilities. He would no longer be commanding men and maneuvering fire teams, squads, and platoons down range in the line of fire. In the Bureau, he would be accountable for one man—himself.

For Joe, however, the Marine Corps was his life. He had no intention of donning "civies." He was staying in the uniform for the long haul. He loved the Marines and all it stood for. He believed in the mission, and he personified honor, courage, and commitment. When MARSOC was officially activated in February 2006, he was one of the first officers to complete the training. He was awarded a Silver Star for heroism during his first MARSOC deployment to Afghanistan in 2009, but his second deployment to Helmand Province, his fourth combat deployment overall, proved to be his last. Joe came home a hero to rest in Arlington National Cemetery with some of the nation's greatest warriors.

With the withdrawal from Afghanistan a year earlier, Natasha, like many of the Gold Star families and those wounded in action with scars seen and unseen, questioned whether the sacrifices had been worth it. Jake questioned too, but assured her that for twenty years, the military kept terrorism from our shores. Joe's death was not in vain. It may have seemed like a long road to nowhere, but Joe served honorably when his country needed him most. He was part of a generation of warriors who would be remembered for putting nation above self.

Natasha moved back in with her parents after Joe's death. Her mom was a lifeline as the recently widowed new mother struggled to keep life balanced. Two months ago, Natasha purchased a three-bedroom townhouse-style condominium near the western edge of Los Angeles County in Agoura Hills just off the 101 Freeway. It was a few miles from her parents but afforded enough independence to begin a new journey.

When the porch light of the townhouse came on, Jake saw the security peephole darken and heard the distinctive click of the deadbolt being unlocked. Though he called and texted during his undercover assignments, this was the first time to see her in more than a year. The butterflies erupted in his stomach as a chemical cocktail of dopamine and adrenaline raced through his body.

Natasha opened the door and offered a welcoming, if not playful, smile. Her complexion was nearly perfect and her soft dark hair spilled over onto her shoulders. Her warm brown eyes sparkled and even in one of Joe's old Marine Corps sweatshirts she looked elegant; she made baggy and olive-drab a fashion statement. He fought the urge as his lips wanted to reach for hers. Maybe someday. For now, the intimacy was limited to an extended hug.

CHAPTER FOUR

TUESDAY, APRIL 12
Westwood, Los Angeles

The sun would be up in less than an hour. On the first level of the FBI garage, just off Sepulveda Boulevard, Tonya Rodriguez was about to brief L.A.'s ICAC team.

On February 2, 2021, FBI Special Agents Laura Schwartzenberger and Daniel Alfin, of the Miami Field Office, were killed at a Sunrise, Florida apartment complex while executing a federal search warrant. Three other agents were wounded. Alfin, married with a child, was recognized in federal court as an expert in computer forensics. Schwartzenberger, a fifteen-year veteran of the FBI, was a married mother of two. Though well in excess of 30,000 federal search warrants were issued each year, this one would be remembered as one of the darkest days in FBI history.

Since circumstances can change in an instant, no law enforcement effort should be considered mundane, but there was nothing to suggest the February 2 operation would be anything but routine. The agents were merely serving a search warrant on fifty-five-year-old David Huber, a licensed pilot who previously owned a computer consulting business. The agents had no immediate plans to arrest him. They just wanted to seize his computer to determine if it contained child pornography. Huber's only brushes with the law were minor traffic violations, but the divorced father of two got caught up in "Playpen."

Authorities described Playpen as a "highly sophisticated global enterprise dedicated to the sexual exploitation of children, organized via a members-only website operating on the dark web." The FBI estimated Playpen, the world's largest known child pornography website, had 150,000 subscribers who viewed tens of thousands of graphic images of children. Created by Stephen Chase, it operated on Tor, open-source software allowing users to communicate anonymously.

After Chase was arrested in 2015, the FBI kept the website open for two weeks, identifying other users. By embedding malware in the images, the Bureau discovered the users' IP addresses. Through this investigative effort, thousands of leads worldwide were developed. The investigation resulted in the arrest of 350 people based in the United States, the prosecution of twenty-five producers of child pornography, and the arrest of fifty-one "hands-on abusers." Overseas, the investigation yielded 548 arrests. There were few incidents in any of those arrests. David Huber changed that.

The tragedy brought a new awareness to agents working on the Internet Crimes Against Children task forces, known as ICAC throughout the law enforcement community. Suspects, often thought to be weak because of their gravitation toward pornographic pictures of children, were now taken as seriously as a Top 10 Fugitive.

Special Agent Tonya Rodriguez spent part of the previous day sitting in a nondescript white, 2014 Ford Econoline E-150 van outside the residence of Preston Brookside. Attempting to discern anything of importance for the next phase of the operation, she was looking for occupants at the house other than the two already identified. Maybe she could find an anomaly like vicious dogs in the backyard or contractors working at the house who might provide a convenient "reasonable doubt" dodge for the images she hoped to find. Defense lawyers were known to blame anyone but their client for downloading the criminal images.

From the backseat, through tinted windows and using a high-powered monocular scope, she attempted to determine whether Brookside had a Ring security system or any other obvious external surveillance cameras. In Sunrise, Florida, it was believed a simple doorbell security camera may have alerted the suspect to the approaching agents and ultimately the deaths of Schwartzenberger and Alfin. Rodriguez saw no overt security system at the older, one-story, West Los Angeles residence.

Brookside accessed a less popular website but similar to Playpen, and now federal agents were picking off the low-hanging fruit. Rodriguez's affidavit demonstrated probable cause to believe Brookside had child pornography on his computer. At this point, Rodriguez had no intention of arresting Brookside. Between the back up at the FBI's Los Angeles CART, the Computer Analysis Response Team, and the U.S. Attorney office's legal meandering, it might be six to eight months before a federal arrest warrant would be issued. Seizing the computer was only another step in the investigative journey.

The delays were always frustrating to Tonya, who viewed her job targeting those who exploited children as some of the most important work in the Bureau. She did her due diligence on Brookside, a Los Angeles native and graduate of UCLA's Anderson School of Management. Grossly ordinary in every way, he was a fifty-seven-year-old, white, male, married with two adult children. Overweight and bald, the successful entrepreneur owned an office supply business catering to a boutique clientele in Beverly Hills and Los Angeles's coveted Westside.

The company employed two dozen sales, front-office, and delivery personnel. Though his business was hit by the pandemic since many of his customers cut corners wherever they could, gross revenue was now almost back to pre-COVID levels. His wife, an elementary school principal, was recently honored in the school district for her implementation of innovative administrative protocols resulting in increased federal funding. There was nothing in his background to hint at an addiction to pornographic images of prepubescent girls. He seemed to be respected in the business community and active in several philanthropic organizations. Tonya was confident every neighbor would sing his praises if TV news vans rolled up on the scene during the execution of the search warrant.

She had been at this long enough to recognize there was no check-list to identify those whose perversions made them viable targets in the prison system. Those she arrested ran the socio-economic gamut. Race, age, and sexual preference were no indicators. She did know men who exploited children were viewed as the lowest of the low in any criminal institution. Few endured confinement without being physically and sexually assaulted. They were "easy pickin's" for hostile inmates who enjoyed meting out reformatory righteousness without the need for due process. Those preying on the predators almost made sense out of the violence. In most cases, Tonya wasn't ready to jump to the sexual deviants' defense believing the advertised threat of "prison justice" should be a recognizable deterrent for anyone seeking to harm a child.

Tonya always carried the passion for protecting the most vulner-able. As the oldest of four girls, she was the big sister willing to take on the neighborhood bully. Though never big for her age, she knew the rules of the street meant there were no rules in a fight. Many boys learned the hard way that Tonya could back up her play.

When she graduated from San Diego State with a bachelor's degree in psychology, there were few opportunities for the 5'7", 140-pound former high school point guard unless she continued her education obtaining a master's degree. Prior to starting at State, she worked two years at a daycare facility to save money toward college. Qualifying for some financial aid, she continued to work part-time at a Head Start facility during the four and a half years it took her to complete her degree. The bank account was depleted, and student loans loomed. Fluent in Spanish, she happened to check out a table being staffed by an FBI agent at one of the school's career day events.

The recruiter opened her eyes to the opportunities in the FBI available to a female, Spanish speaker with a college degree. Having been a devoted fan of *Criminal Minds*, maybe the thought of being a profiler heightened her enthusiasm. But when at least a third of the people at any family gathering were in the country illegally, a career in law enforcement was never viewed favorably by most of her relatives.

She and her three sisters were second-generation Americans. Both her dad and mom were born in East Los Angeles. Many relatives, however, on both sides of the family, took the less than legal route to the United States. Several cousins were deported numerous times, always managing to slip back into the country undetected by the Border Patrol. It became a running joke as her mother attempted to determine how many extended family members might show up at a holiday gathering. The head count typically depended upon whatever highly publicized border initiative had been implemented earlier in the week.

She still recalls the evening she and her parents sat at the tiny kitchen table in their three-bedroom Boyle Heights home and discussed her desire to join the FBI. She was surprised her father took such a positive view toward her career goal. He loved America and the opportunities it gave him to raise a family. He enlisted in the Marine Corps right out of high school and the patriotism instilled in him at boot camp remained. She had her answer.

Negotiating her way through the laborious application process, she eventually received an appointment to the FBI Academy at Quantico, Virginia. While there, she interacted with members of the FBI's elite Behavioral Analysis Unit. Now married, the mother of two, and working part-time toward a master's degree in psychology, she sublimated her desire to return to Quantico. Instead, she focused her efforts on those in Los Angeles who exploited children. Maybe someday she would head back to the BAU but uprooting her family now just to fulfill her career dreams didn't seem fair.

CHAPTER FIVE

Westwood, Los Angeles

"Everybody, let's get started with the briefing. I want to hit this guy before he wakes up," said Rodriguez as she began distributing the two-page operations order.

At this hour, about the only FBI agents the team would encounter in the garage would be those agents who hoped to beat the morning rush hour traffic, and hit a fully equipped gym at the far end of the three-story parking structure.

Eight agents, casually dressed, looked like a politically and culturally correct TV crime drama—white, black, brown, Asian, male, and female. The days of J. Edgar Hoover's all-white male Bureau was long gone. Button-down collared dress shirts also took a sabbatical for most agents not working white-collar crimes. Steam rose from coffee cups as agents gathered around Tonya's car. Mindful of the Miami tragedy, caution was paramount.

The team would be ready to hit the house at sunrise. For the most part, it made sense to execute residential search warrants first thing in the morning. Usually, the occupants of the house were present but groggy during a daybreak intrusion. Resistance was typically minimal as the targets of the investigation sought to come to grips with an overwhelming number of federal agents entering the house before breakfast.

Before pulling her shoulder-length raven hair into a ponytail, Tonya passed around a copy of the search warrant signed by a federal magistrate late the day before. Each member of the team initialed the copy, a procedural step to ensure for the court the agents were cognizant of what site was to be searched and what was to be seized.

Their primary focus would be any computers and the images believed to be contained on the hard drives. However, the warrant also allowed the agents to search the residence seeking any instrumentality of child pornography, to include photographs, thumb drives, magazines, calendars, day planners, and financial records demonstrating the purchase of pornography or fees granting access to criminal websites.

Except for a nervous probationary agent from an FCI (Foreign Counterintelligence) squad who needed to mark her new agent's checklist to include participating in a search, all the ICAC agents had been through this drill many times. Tonya's briefing, clear and concise, generated no questions. Complacency used to be a problem and may become a problem as the memories of the Miami shootout fade, but all were alert and anxious to "kit up."

After putting on their Kevlar ballistic vests, the agents teamed up in twos and prepared to move out in four Bureau vehicles toward the West Los Angeles address. Less than three miles from the FBI office, the trip should have taken only minutes, but the traffic on Sepulveda Boulevard was unusually heavy. A quick glance of the freeway revealed a parking lot on the 405. It only took one fender bender pulled to either side of the eight-lane interstate to bring the morning commute to a near standstill. Motorists trying to cheat the delay dropped down to surface streets.

The Angelenos even had a name of such traffic jams: Sig alert. Named after Loyd Sigmon, vice president of Golden West Broadcasters, the former Army Signal Corps soldier designed a machine which allowed local radio stations to learn of traffic alerts posted by the Los Angeles Police Department. In 1955, the messages were referred to as a "Sigmon traffic alert" which was quickly shortened to "Sig alert." Defined as any unplanned event closing a lane of freeway traffic for more than thirty minutes, this morning's 405 commute was experiencing a prime example.

The American-made sedans would fool few as they traveled south on Sepulveda paralleling the freeway. In the land of BMWs, Mercedes, and high-end Japanese cars, a Chevy Malibu or Ford Fusion stood out like cowboy boots at a black-tie affair, but this morning, stealth wasn't the issue.

Los Angeles real estate was off the charts. Though Brookside owned a 3,500 square-foot log home in Big Bear Zillow valued at $1,499,000, his primary L.A. residence, a three-bedroom, two bath 2,300 square-foot home, was valued at $2.1 million. In the Midwest, the one-story ranch house might garner a couple hundred thousand. Two million could buy a city block in most small towns across America, but as the land barons say "location, location, location." Despite politics and taxes, many were still willing to pay the California "sunshine tax," and property values continued to soar.

Within thirty minutes, the agents arrived at Brookside's home just a few blocks east of the 405. The agents quietly exited their cars and took their assigned positions. Two agents headed to the back, positioning themselves at each of the home's rear corners. Two other agents covered the front corners, carefully noting the location of the agents to the rear to avoid a crossfire situation should things head south in a hurry. The remaining agents stacked just off to the left of the front door avoiding the large picture window facing the street.

This would not be a dynamic entry. It wasn't a no-knock situation which the courts disliked. Unlike drugs, which might be flushed down the toilet if the entering agents gave notice, computers weren't easily destroyed in a few seconds.

In fact, if Brookside didn't come to the door, Rodriguez planned to make a subterfuge phone call to the residence hoping to talk either Preston or his wife into opening the front door. If that didn't work, the agents were authorized to use a handheld battering ram to make entry. From a practical standpoint, the only problem with the ram was increased paperwork justifying the damage. Since no case agent wanted intensified bureaucratic oversight, Rodriguez hoped the entry could be handled with minimal force.

Knowing full well few front doors could stop a bullet, Tonya stepped off to the side of the door as she knocked hard several times. When that didn't work, she repeatedly rang the doorbell.

Within a minute, a raspy male voice came from behind the door, "Yes. Who is it?"

Tonya Rodriguez answered in a calm yet authoritative voice, "Mr. Brookside?"

"Yes."

"Mr. Brookside, my name is Special Agent Rodriguez. I'm with the FBI, and I need to speak to you right away."

Still rattled by the early morning wake-up call, Brookside opened the door with the safety latch still attached.

"Yes, what's this all about?"

Holding up her credentials, Rodriguez said, "Mr. Brookside, I need to come in and speak to you. It's important."

Brookside instantly understood. In the back of his mind, he feared this day would come. Had he believed in God, maybe he would have offered a prayer making promises he would never keep. With his voice quivering, he said, "Is this about my computer?"

Tonya Rodriguez, unwilling to give it up yet, responded, "I'd rather talk about this inside."

The other agents remained concealed by the shrubbery in the front of the residence, as Brookside closed the door. Though it usually took just a second or two, every agent questioned that moment when the door closed awaiting the person on the other side to release the security latch. Would the target surrender or would it take the ram?

Tonya's stomach knotted as she signaled the breacher to prepare for a dynamic entry. If Brookside didn't move quickly, the next sound would be the shattering of an exterior wood door.

Then the distinct sound could be heard of the metal chain being removed from the security latch. As Preston Brookside, wearing a white terry cloth robe, opened the door, Tonya Rodriguez walked in followed by the FBI entry team. Their Kevlar vests with large bold yellow letters F-B-I emblazoned across the front and back demonstrated governmental authority and an intrusion Brookside hoped might never materialize. He was wrong. Because of his computer actions several months earlier, his world was about to implode.

Tonya quickly took charge asking, "Is there anyone else in the house?"

"Yes, but please don't say anything to my wife. She's in the back bedroom. Let me go back and get her."

"I can't let you do that by yourself. I'll have to go with you," said Tonya.

The other agents quickly cleared the rest of the house, ensuring no one else was present, positioning themselves to make entry into the master bedroom.

"Do you have any weapons on you or in the house?"

"Of course not. I would never own a gun."

"For everyone's safety, we're going to pat you down. Do you have anything sharp in your pockets? Knives? Needles?" asked Tonya.

"No. Please, I'm not a violent person. I made a mistake downloading pornography, but I've never hurt anyone."

Tonya's stoicism gave way to a brief smile. He was giving it up quickly. This was shaping up to be a slam dunk. She nodded toward a male agent who did a quick pat down of Brookside.

"I know what this is all about. I deleted all the pictures. I swear I did. Please, let me just give you the computer. I don't want my wife to know. She will kill me if she finds out what I had been doing."

"Maybe you should've thought about that before you started downloading images."

"But I deleted them. I swear. Please, I'll cooperate. Just let me break it to her when the time is right."

As Tonya peered into the master bedroom, she saw Brookside's wife asleep in a king size bed, a CPAP mask covering her nose and mouth, a gentle white noise hiding the FBI agents' entry.

"My wife suffers from sleep apnea. The machine gives her a restful night's sleep. Please, let me gently wake her."

Tonya saw no need to go Dirty Harry on the fifty-seven-year-old in his bedroom, allowing the defeated man to maintain his dignity and wake his wife.

As Evelyn Brookside rolled over, she saw two FBI agents, male and female, dressed in tactical gear, standing at the foot of her bed.

Startled, Evelyn shouted, "Preston, what's going on? Why are these agents in our bedroom? Is it our boys?"

Before Brookside could explain to his wife, Tonya spoke up. "Mrs. Brookside, my name is Special Agent Rodriguez. I need you and your husband to come out to the living room. We are just executing a search warrant and the faster we can get the items we need, the quicker we can leave your home."

"Search warrant?" she bellowed. "Why are you executing a search warrant in my house? Preston, what have you done?"

The other agent grabbed Evelyn's robe from the chair on the other side of the bedroom, searched the pockets, and handed it to Tonya to give to Mrs. Brookside.

"Here, Mrs. Brookside, please put this on. We'll all go out to the living room, and I'll explain to you why we are here."

Shocked and angered, Evelyn Brookside poured out of the bed, and slowly stood. She outweighed her overweight husband and was at least four inches taller. She put on the red silk robe and reluctantly accompanied her husband to the immaculately decorated living room where they both took a seat on a Perigold Moss Studio sofa centered beneath expensive wall hangings.

"Now, can someone please tell me what's going on?" demanded Evelyn.

Before Tonya could say anything, Preston intervened. "Honey, they just need to look at my computer. This has to do with a business arrangement I had with one of our vendors. I think I mentioned it to you. I'm sure it can all be straightened out once I explain it to Special Agent Rodriguez."

"Vendor? What vendor? Was it that guy we had dinner with last month? I told you he was no good. I didn't trust him then. I warned you not to do business with him. I don't appreciate these storm troopers breaking into my house, waking me at this ungodly hour." The anger blew from her lips like a violent Midwest thunderstorm.

Off to the side, Tonya could see two of the agents beginning to smile. She threw them a look. *Keep it professional. Keep it taut. Don't break the tension.*

Cowering, Preston Brookside responded, "Honey, please. It wasn't William. It was someone else. I'll be able to straighten it out. I promise."

As Mrs. Brookside looked to Rodriguez for answers, Tonya took this opportunity to corner the target of their investigation. "Mr. Brookside, we're going to let you get dressed. Then we'll go back to the federal building in Westwood and give you an opportunity to explain everything. But we will be taking your desktop computer tower and your laptop as per the search warrant."

"Preston, you better straighten this out. I don't know what I'll tell the neighbors. Do you want me to call Philip?

"Who's Philip?" asked Rodriguez.

Almost indignantly she responded, "He's my brother, and he's *our* attorney."

Preston Brookside swallowed hard knowing if his brother-in-law got involved, his wife would learn the whole story. With Philip, the attorney-client relationship didn't extend to his sister's husband. He learned that the hard way several years earlier.

"That won't be necessary. I'm sure the agent and I can clear this up quickly once I explain the business relationship with the vendor."

Tonya gave the guy credit. First thing in the morning, with FBI agents pounding on his door, startling him out of a sound sleep, and about to confront him with life-changing criminal charges, Brookside adroitly held off his wife—at least for the short term.

CHAPTER SIX

Westwood, Los Angeles

Tonya was experienced enough to know fruitful interrogations didn't require another agent to be in the room. In fact, sometimes one-on-one was the best way to conduct the questioning. It wasn't about power; it was about conciliation. Since the recording devices were activated, she wouldn't need a witness if this came down to a "he said, she said" argument. The digital recording would provide all the corroboration she would need in court if issues arose.

To make Brookside feel more comfortable before entering the soundproof interrogation room, she provided black coffee for both of them and gave him the opportunity to use the restroom. After directing him to a rather uncomfortable metal government chair with minimum cushioning in the seat, she moved her chair off to the side of the desk. No interrogation table separated them. She used this ploy before and each time she found success. She tried to convince her superiors a room with a comfortable couch and chairs could be even more effective in eliciting cooperation. Though some in the chain of command agreed, such a room was never established. If she ever chose to ascend the administrative ladder, she vowed to make one of her first priorities a comfortable interrogation room for appropriate situations.

Frequently, interrogating pedophiles was somewhat easy. For the most part, they knew they were caught and expected to be subjected to harsh interrogation techniques like those commonly displayed on primetime television. In reality, the "good guy-bad guy" questioning only works in Hollywood. Even the most inexperienced criminal knows if he asks for an attorney, all questioning ceases. Verbal waterboarding seldom works. As the lead interrogator of Saddam Hussein, FBI agent George Piro proved relationship-building can often be the most effective technique in winning cooperation and a confession.

At the U.S. Attorney's office, Tonya Rodriguez was referred to as "Paste." It was short for toothpaste and not because of her bright smile. Unbelievably, a high-priced defense attorney, in court and on the record, complained to the judge about Tonya's interrogation techniques. He stated her unassuming and relationship-building style lulled his defendant into believing she was a friend to whom he could confess without consequences. Though the defendant was advised of his Miranda rights and signed the waiver, the Ivy League-trained lawyer claimed the rights were given after the relationship was built and "the toothpaste was out of the tube." The federal district court judge, not known for his sense of humor, actually laughed out loud at the accusation and shamed the attorney into taking his seat.

Tonya handled herself professionally at Brookside's home. The relationship was solidified when she played along with his lie about the nonexistent vendor. She would continue with the proven approach of empathizing with her subject. Because of guilt and shame, most were willing to view the FBI agent taking this tact as a father confessor. She hoped Brookside would willingly empty his soul and the case could be resolved quickly.

"Mr. Brookside . . ."

As he adjusted his glasses, he said, "Please, call me Preston."

Promising.

With her hair no longer in a ponytail, but laying softly on her shoulders, she leaned forward. "Okay, Preston. I'm really interested in hearing your side of the story. You seem like a nice guy who maybe got caught up in something that just got away from him."

He looked at her, believing he may have found an ally. "I did. I really did."

"I thought so," came the reply in a calm, reassuring voice.

He maintained eye contact, sincerely hoping to gain her support. "Thanks for being so understanding and thanks for not telling my wife."

Tonya offered a warm smile. "You're welcome. We've all stumbled. We've made mistakes. I believe in forgiveness. I believe in redemption. I believe in second chances."

For the first time since Brookside opened his front door this morning, he smiled. "Thank you for understanding."

With continued kindness in her voice and a sympathetic smile, Tonya said, "Even the best cars can get a flat tire. Let's see if we can't fix your flat."

His eyes roamed her features, seeking sincerity.

She let the moment linger knowing he needed hope, then quietly said, "I just want to get some preliminaries out of the way. You understand you are not under arrest. You are free to go at any time, but I am still going to read you your rights under Miranda."

Relieved he was not taken from his home in handcuffs and wasn't restrained now in the interrogation room, he softly responded, "That won't be necessary. I understand my rights."

Tonya was cautious. Though the circumstances may not have amounted to a "custodial interrogation," the threshold for Mirandizing a subject, she wanted to ensure there would not be an issue in court should his attorney contest the interview.

Continuing with a warm, accepting smile, and a slight laugh, she said, "Yep, we all watch TV. Every crime drama, even the comedies, recite Miranda, but let me just read them to you anyway. It will only take a minute. I don't want there to be any misunderstandings between us. This way we can both be on the same page. It keeps it all clean and avoids any issues later, especially, if your brother-in-law Philip gets involved."

Brookside winced at the mention of Philip. "Believe me, if I need an attorney, it will not be Philip."

She chuckled, continuing to build rapport. Taking a long sip of coffee, she wanted Brookside to feel relaxed and not sense the seriousness with which the FBI and the U.S. Attorney's office took for those who subjected children to vile and cruel sexual acts.

Though Tonya knew the Miranda rights by heart, she shuffled through some forms as if they weren't really that important before coming to what was known in the FBI as an FD-395. "Here it is. I knew I had one in here somewhere. Just let me read you your rights."

When she was done reading from the form, she asked Brookside if he understood.

He nodded.

She laughed, "No, Preston, I need a verbal response. Nodding your head isn't enough. This is like sitting in the emergency row on a 747. Think of me as your flight attendant. Do you understand your rights as I explained them to you?"

Managing a weak grin, he said, "Yes, I understand. I'm even buckling my seatbelt."

With a warm laugh, she said, "Good. Then I need you to sign this form, waiving your rights."

She slid the FD-395 across the table and gave Brookside a minute to read over the form before he signed it. She countered with her signature acknowledging she witnessed him waiving his rights. Of course, all this was captured on video, so if the voluntariness of what she hoped to be a confession was challenged in court, there would be little the defense could argue.

Softly, she asked, "So, what are we going to find on those computers?"

"You won't find any images. I deleted all of."

"So, you are admitting you downloaded images of child pornography."

For the first time during the interview, he diverted his eyes from hers. He was staring at the floor. Ashamed and embarrassed he had been caught, tears welled as he half-swallowed, choking out, "Yes, I downloaded images of naked children."

She had the confession. She was confident the images would be found on the hard drives of the desktop computer and laptop. From a computer forensic standpoint, "delete" does not mean delete. The evidence remains. To date, Tonya never lost a case because a defendant attempted to delete the images. Whether it be in the defendant's "cloud" or buried deep in the bowels of the computer, the FBI's forensic experts could recover the images.

Her façade of caring remained as she dug a little deeper. "Preston, we know it was more than just pictures of naked children. We know what websites you accessed. The photos you purchased showed men engaging in sexual intercourse with girls as young as six years old."

Now the tears were flowing. In a weak voice, he said, "But I deleted all of those images."

"Preston, I know, and I hear you. You say you deleted those images, but our computer experts will be able to pull up those images from your computer and your laptop. Deleting them isn't really a defense. In fact, saying you deleted the photos is evidence you downloaded the photos and you viewed the photos. A jury isn't going to care if you deleted them."

He mumbled a question. "Isn't there something I can do that can make this all go away?"

Though Brookside's eyes remained focused on the ground rather than on the agent sitting across from him, Tonya shook her head. "Preston, there is very little you can do. The exploitation of children is a very serious offense. This isn't like some crimes when we're willing to turn a blind's eye if you're able to provide information of other criminal activity. We call it 'working off your beef' and there just aren't very many opportunities for someone to do that when they have been involved in this violation."

Brookside sat there for an extended moment with his head bowed, then he looked up. With a flicker of hope in his voice, he said, "Maybe there's something I can do. Maybe I have something which might interest you."

"Does it involve the exploitation of children?"

"Yes and no."

"Well, if it's 'yes' and involves children, I might have an interest. If it has nothing to do with sexually exploiting children, I probably don't care."

CHAPTER SEVEN

MONDAY, APRIL 18
Westwood, Los Angeles

The near-perfect year-round weather in Southern California makes it difficult to judge the age of any structure. Without the snow, torrential rains, and hurricane-gust winds prevalent in other areas of the country, it was only the sun's warmth that lightly impacted the buildings' exteriors, easily concealing age like a layer of Mary Kay on a middle-aged model.

The federal building at 11000 Wilshire Boulevard on Los Angeles's tony Westside was one such edifice. Completed in 1969, the white concrete façade, seventeen-story building still looked new on the outside. Sitting in the middle of a twenty-eight-acre former golf course and described as "Late Modernism," the precast concrete fins shading the windows in daylight gave the building an ominous stealth appearance in the evening. The lit windows at night in any of the occupied offices looked blurred to those traveling the 405 freeway, almost as if concealing what went on. Sharing office space with other federal agencies, the FBI's Los Angeles field office occupied the top nine floors.

A three-level garage to the southwest of the building housed the FBI's parking, technical facilities, and auto maintenance department. Secured by a key-card-operated security gate, Jake's access card was deactivated more than a year earlier when he took the UC assignment in Indianapolis. That meant for today, he would park for free with the masses in the too-few spaces made available to the public. For whatever reason, the lot was crowded this morning, requiring two trips up and down the lanes before he spotted a family of four, passports in hand and all smiles, enter a new Range Rover with paper license plates.

Jake waited patiently as the mother, who was driving, fixed her makeup and marveled at her reflection in the rearview mirror. She seemed oblivious to those in the lot lined up to take her spot. Once the passengers were buckled up and she was satisfied with her greasepaint, she put the Range Rover in reverse and slowly backed out, moving with the speed of an overnight laxative.

Only the fact Jake had little desire to rush into his meeting with the Assistant Director in Charge, the ADIC, prevented him from laying on the horn.

As the space opened, another driver raced down the lane hoping to grab the spot, before spying Jake waiting patiently to pull in. Jake offered his practiced death glare to the college-age driver who threw up his hands in mock surrender.

Once the delayed parking ritual was complete, Jake exited his Jeep Wrangler and immediately heard the indistinguishable chants of pro-testers standing on the sidewalk paralleling Wilshire Boulevard. Now the crowded parking lot made sense. The Wilshire Boulevard corridor was one of the most heavily trafficked streets in Los Angeles. The federal building was a convenient target for protesters who could spew their complaints at passing motorists. While parking on L.A.'s coveted Westside could easily cost $20 an hour, the free parking at the federal building provided another incentive for protesters to target the corner of Wilshire and Veteran Avenue. If the feds charged for parking, it might limit the annoying exercise of free speech.

Jake made his way toward the federal building, dodging the con-crete barriers designed to prevent "vehicle borne improvised explosive devices" (VBIEDs in counter-terrorism vernacular) from getting close enough to the federal building to replicate the February 1993 attack on the World Trade Center.

The main office facility was flanked by two one-story structures known as the East and West annexes. The West annex, which years ago housed the post office, was in a continual state of remodel and repair for years. Now, it served as the processing facility for anyone hoping to enter FBI space.

After climbing the steps leading to the entrance of the seventeen-story structure, Jake heard a familiar voice coming from his left. "Hey, devil dog."

Jake turned to see Tyrone Greer, cigarette pack in hand, offering a huge smile as he was coming from the "smoke pit" on the westside of the building.

"Rangers Lead the Way," said Jake.

Greer was a short, compact former Army Ranger who did multiple tours in Afghanistan before joining the FBI. One of the strongest men Jake ever encountered, "Rone" could throw around some serious weight in the FBI gym housed in the parking garage. Newcomers to the gym marveled at Greer as he loaded plate upon plate on the Olympic bar. His disarming smile fooled many who failed to take the former snake-eater seriously, a mistake that on two occasions in Los Angeles proved fatal.

"Man, look at you, a suit and tie. Don't tell me you're going management," said Jake as the two shook hands and gave each other a half-hearted manly hug.

"When did you get back into town?" asked Rone with an enormous grin that should be featured in a toothpaste print ad.

"Two weeks ago. This is my first day back but don't change the subject. What's up with the Joseph A. Banks Halloween costume?"

"You haven't met the new ADIC. She came here after a two-year stint at EEO and is about as PC as they come."

"What's that have to do with you?" asked a confused Jake.

"In case you haven't noticed, I'm 'African American,' her words not mine. I told her I was black, adopted, and don't know who my biological parents are. I might not be African or American. Until the FBI is willing to pay for ancestry.com DNA testing, I have no idea what I am and prefer to just stay an American. Turns out putting a black man on a fugitive task force was, according to her, 'racial profiling,' and could adversely impact my career. I think she really meant her career. So, she transferred me to one of the bank fraud squads to represent the 'diversity of the cosmopolitan arena we are investigating.' Her words not mine. She also put me in the relief supervisor program, grooming me for an opening at Headquarters. Despite my protestations, I'm investigating bank fraud and wearing a tie every day."

"Sounds like masser has all her chillens' lives planned out."

"Yep, I'm still a token. If I were white, I could be another lazy, unambitious agent like you. You have no idea the impact white privilege has had on your life."

"What about the pseudo folliculitis card? Didn't you play that? That could at least get you out of wearing a tie," said Jake with an ear-to-ear grin.

"Man, I didn't even think of razor bumps. I wonder if it's too late to bring it up now?"

"Didn't you tell her you were adopted by two Caucasians in Boise who vote Republican?"

"Didn't do any good."

"Is that why you took up smoking again?" said Jake shaking his head.

"It took me so long to kick the habit once I returned from Afghanistan, but I needed an excuse to get out of the office. I spend my entire day poring over ledgers and financial spreadsheets."

"That's what you get for being an accountant."

Shaking his head, he said, "That's what I get for being a black accountant."

"No, an African-American accountant," said Jake with mock indignation.

With a slight smile creeping across his face, Rone asked, "So, what's up with you? Are you back in the office?"

"I'm not sure what I'm up to," said Jake looking over Rone's shoulder.

"But I hope you're back in L.A. for a while. I need somebody to bounce around on the wrestling mat during defensive tactics training. The last half-dozen boots we've gotten out of Quantico have been PhD misfits with degrees in chemistry and computer science. Not an MMA retread in the bunch."

"Oh yeah. I can't wait. I've always so NOT enjoyed being your practice dummy as you demonstrate the double-reverse figure four leg lock to the administrative bean counters and feather merchants," said Jake as he began focusing his attention on a too-thin white man in his early twenties.

Tinkerbell flittered about, approaching everyone as they exited the federal building. Jake watched as one man reached into his pocket, gathered some loose change, and gave it to the unauthorized solicitor. Without even saying thanks, the kid moved on to a couple as they exited the building. They ignored him and continued walking. He was undeterred and waited for the next visitor to the Wilshire federal office complex to exit through the automatic electronic doors.

Within seconds, an elderly black woman, wearing a flower-print sundress tottered through the exit and was confronted by the beggar. His aggressive tactics forced her to sidestep him to avoid a direct confrontation. Apparently, the panhandler saw the grandmother-type as an easy mark and continued to follow her as she made her way toward the parking lot.

"I thought the federal police patrolled this area," said Jake.

"They do," responded Rone. "But usually, they are inside manning the security booth and metal detector. What's up?"

"We better help that lady to her car," said Jake.

Just as Rone turned to see what Jake was referencing, the lady let out a scream as the panhandler grabbed her purse and began running south down the steps.

"Damn. Let's go get 'em Tonto," said Jake.

The two federal agents gave chase. Maybe it was the street shoes both agents were wearing or the chemical cocktail consisting of some percentage of methamphetamine the kid consumed, but the purse snatcher took an early lead in the foot pursuit. It wasn't until the runner reached a busy Veteran Avenue that he was forced to slow, giving Jake and Rone an opportunity to gain valuable ground. As the runner attempted to cross Veteran, dodging cars that were racing to make an extended green light at Wilshire, he was clipped by a silver Mercedes SUV and stumbled across the street.

By now the cars were braking and—as if a parting of the Red Sea—Jake and Rone were able to safely and quickly cross Veteran before the runner regained his balance and renewed his now less-than-full-speed escape. Jake was within a few feet of pouncing. Rone fell behind but wasn't going to allow a former jarhead make a solo arrest.

Jake's afterburners kicked in and when only a step or two behind, did a semi-flying tackle carrying both himself and the panhandler into a row of oleanders. But the landscaping was in the middle of an artificial drenching from a sprinkler system working overtime. Now soaked, Jake grabbed the equally wet runner by the dirty long-sleeve Nike jacket, throwing him hard to the sidewalk. Jake quickly flipped over his captive, pinning the robber's hands behind his back, and planting a left knee firmly on the back of the runner.

Both captor and captive were breathing hard and as the purse snatcher attempted to scream obscenities, Jake buried the felon's face into the sidewalk, muffling the spewed urban vitriol.

Rone caught up to the subdued melee.

"I don't have any cuffs. Let me borrow yours," said Jake fuming over getting wet. Then the anger intensified when he spotted mud all over his pants, "Damn, I just had these dry cleaned."

Rone reached to the small of his back and pulled out a set of handcuffs. Handing them to Jake, he said, "My cuffs. My collar."

"Just give me the cuffs! You can have the stat."

CHAPTER EIGHT

Westwood, Los Angeles

Most offices in the FBI were commanded by a Special Agent in Charge or SAC. Unlike other federal agencies who pronounced the term "sack," the FBI pronounced each letter. No one ever explained why.

This authority structure differed in New York, Washington D.C., and Los Angeles. These three offices were so large they were headed by an Assistant Director in Charge or ADIC, with several subservient SACs in the chain of command; the bureaucracy seemed to evolve as the mission expanded.

Valerie Carlisle was named L.A.'s ADIC six months earlier. Prior to landing her promotion to ADIC Los Angeles, she spent two years at the Bureau's Equal Employment Opportunity office, EEO in D.C. following her two-year assignment heading up the San Francisco field office.

Valerie's parents, both tenured professors at Columbia, were shocked when their only child, who had her undergraduate and law degree from Columbia, left a prestigious Wall Street law firm within two months of 9/11 to join the FBI. "Patriotism" was not a word discussed around the dining room table as their daughter was growing up. Believing they imposed their progressive values on Valerie, they never saw her tilt toward conservatism. In embarrassment-tinged voices, they told their friends about the daughter who joined the Bureau.

Mom and Dad had a ray of hope when the previous director and his inner circle went after President Trump, but all that waned when Valerie spelled out with lawyer-like closing argument passion why anyone regardless of party should be angered by the party in power going after its political enemies. Mom, Dad, and daughter eventually reconciled, but holiday gatherings were more comfortable when politics were left off the menu.

Immediately after 9/11, the FBI increased Headquarters and created new investigative and intelligence-gathering initiatives. These increased slots in D.C. created supervisory opportunities for those in the field. With a new program in place, agents with minimal time on the street were eligible for temporary eighteen-month assignments at the Hoover building. Following the U.S. invasion of Iraq and a burgeoning bureaucracy, Valerie took advantage of one of the newly created positions and was on the administrative fast track ever since.

With just under two years of investigative experience working bank fraud in Denver, she parlayed her intelligence, charisma, and quite frankly, her good looks, for a meteoric rise in the FBI management hierarchy. It wasn't a matter of sleeping her way to the top, she just had keen acumen for bureaucracy and a disarming charm that welcomed advancement opportunities of which she took full advantage. Adding to that was the fact she had several well-placed "rabbis" and scandal-free administrative assignments throughout the Bureau. Her platinum performance in every management position brought on fast and furious promotions.

Traditionally, the ADIC slot in L.A. was the last stop for an FBI executive who then found lucrative employment at a Hollywood studio or a top-level security job at a Fortune 500 company. But for two recent L.A. ADICs, a different pot of gold awaited. Olivia Knox and Valerie Carlisle were female and the Bureau's number two spot, the Deputy Director position, seemed to be within their grasp.

A growing chorus of liberal politicians were calling for the Director to name a female deputy. When he selected a well-qualified male administrator who had a proven track record in the field and in management, those on Capitol Hill who decried the FBI's perceived glass ceiling threatened behind closed doors to reduce the Bureau's funding until a female was appointed to the number two slot.

The Bureau was hit hard from both sides of the aisle during and immediately following the reign of James Comey who headed the organization as its seventh director from 2013 until his dismissal in May 2017. In many people's eyes, the Bureau was no longer the Golden Child, and the new Director heard all the whispers. He remained resolute and had as his top priority the nation's well-being. That wasn't to say a female was incapable of handling the responsibilities of the Deputy Director, but the man currently in the position was doing an outstanding job and had the support of Headquarters and the field.

The Bureau's two top females, Olivia Knox and Valerie Carlisle, would welcome the number two position, knowing in today's climate, it could mean the eventual appointment as the FBI's first female director. Though they made no secret of desiring the Deputy Director spot, they were also vying for any agency directorship. They knew John Pistole, Robert Mueller's deputy, went straight from that position to heading up TSA. Their names were bantered about for federal law enforcement leadership positions in various agencies as placements became available. Both hoped for the ultimate prize if they could grasp the gold ring.

Knox was the ADIC in an L.A. investigation dubbed by the FBI and CIA as "Operation Counterfeit Lies." What began as an undercover probe of a smuggling ring operating in Southern California quickly evolved into a contract killing capturing the attention of the CIA, the U.S. Secret Service, and officials at the highest level in Washington. Jake was the UC in that case and before he knew it, he was plunged into a deadly underworld of North Korean espionage and Hezbollah terror.

In a bizarre move, unlike anything Jake ever saw, no one was prosecuted for the espionage, murders, or other crimes committed during the investigation. The Department of Justice and the Director of National Intelligence declared all the activities and events that took place during the span of the operation to be a "foreign intelligence activity." The DNI classified all files, debriefs, and audiovisual surveillance records as Top Secret/Codeword—meaning everything about the case would remain classified well beyond standard thirty-five-year declassification limits.

The undercover recording devices and associated memory chips worn by Jake and CIA operative Gabe Chong, who was tortured and killed during the investigation, were placed in an FBI evidence container, transferred to the office of the Director of National Intelligence, and buried deep in government intelligence archives.

All government participants in the investigation were required to sign nondisclosure agreements pledging to never reveal what they knew of the UC operation.

For her part in the probe, Olivia Knox was promoted and assigned to head the National Counterterrorism Center. Formerly known as the Terrorist Threat Integration Center created by a 2003 executive order of President George W. Bush, the center was re-named and re-tasked by the 2004 Intelligence Reform and Terrorism Prevention Act. The nation's Counter-Terrorism Center henceforth would answer to the Director of National Intelligence. Based in Liberty Crossing near Tysons Corner in McLean, Virginia, the fusion intelligence center merged the efforts of the FBI, CIA, Department of Defense, and other federal agencies. Knox had been there for two years and by all appearances was doing an outstanding job.

Jake and Knox butted heads throughout her tenure in Los Angeles, but by the conclusion of Operation Counterfeit Lies, she was a strong supporter of the undercover agent. It was her leadership in overruling the misguided directives of Charles Hafner, a feckless Assistant Special Agent in Charge, that led to a successful conclusion of the case. Though no one can talk about the investigation, she credits Jake for the position she now holds.

CHAPTER NINE

Westwood, Los Angeles

Jake and Rone quickly turned over custody of the purse snatcher to the federal police who escorted the meth head to a holding cell in the basement of the federal building. It was unclear how they were going to proceed against the beleaguered thief.

Knowing Jake was late for a meeting with the ADIC and being completely bored with his bank fraud investigations, Rone agreed to do the paperwork and contact the U.S. Attorney's office. Though a felony committed on federal property technically fell within the jurisdiction of the FBI, the federal prosecutors did not welcome "common criminals." Rone was expecting a prosecutorial declination. If that happened, the former Army Ranger would arrange for transportation to the LAPD West Los Angeles substation on Butler Avenue and the filing of state charges.

Jake worked his way through the federal building's first floor security maze and caught an elevator to the eleventh floor. He wasn't sure what to expect of the ADIC in their initial meeting, but with wet and mud-stained khaki trousers, he obviously wasn't going to make a great first impression. Though he was late for the scheduled meeting, ADICs were notorious for keeping street agents waiting in the reception area long after the appointed time. Maybe his untimely arrest of a bottom-dwelling street cretin wouldn't actually delay his mandated meeting with L.A.'s top FBI executive.

When the elevator doors opened, and he walked out onto the eleventh floor, Jake observed not much had changed since he left the division more than a year earlier. As he headed toward the entrance to the office space bracketed by the U.S. flag and a banner of the FBI seal, he noted the large display of the FBI's Top Ten fugitives to the left and a wall filled with the photographs of agents killed in the line of duty on the right. The area was bright and welcoming and created a great initial impression to those coming to the FBI offices on official business.

Because Jake's identification badge allowing access to the building expired, he needed to be buzzed into the workplace. He depressed the call button and a pleasant "May I help you?" responded.

"Hi, this is Special Agent Jake Kruse. My access badge has expired. I've been out of the office for more than a year, and I have an appointment with the ADIC."

"Hey Jake, it's Melanie Rose. Glad to have you back." Then with a giggle, she said, "I'm sure management is thrilled."

Even the support staff knew of his checkered past with the organizational hierarchy.

There was a distinct buzz, followed by a loud click, unlocking the secured door. Jake grabbed the handle, opened the door, and entered L.A.'s secret federal law enforcement lair.

CHAPTER TEN

Westwood, Los Angeles

She began her employment with the FBI as a twenty-year-old graduate of Pierce Junior College where she concentrated on English and business office practices. Her husband of nineteen years, a general contractor, died of mesothelioma two decades earlier. They were childless and spent most of their vacation time traveling throughout the United States. No one could ever replace her husband Jeffrey, and now she was married to the Bureau.

At sixty-four, Barbara Nolan was the oldest support person in the FBI's Los Angeles Field Office. As the gatekeeper, she guarded the ADIC's door with the ferocity of a Rottweiler in heat. If there was one person in the office you did not want to cross, it was Barbara. She had been the secretary for the last four Assistant Directors in Charge and in FBI lore, at least on the West Coast, she was legendary. She would never reach the heights of Helen Gandy who served fifty-four years in the FBI, serving first as a typist for J. Edgar Hoover in 1918 and becoming his executive secretary when he was named Director in 1924. Everyone understood during that time, Miss Gandy exercised as much behind-the-scenes influence on Hoover and the workings of the Bureau as anyone in history. She officially retired the day Hoover died on May 2, 1972.

As the ADIC's secretary, Barbara knew where all the bodies were buried. Truth be told, she had more top-secret information floating around in her head than entire squads handling the nation's most sensitive investigations. But it wasn't just sensitive intel at her disposal, she was privy to most of the gossip frequenting the halls of 11000 Wilshire Boulevard.

FBI administrators came and went. ADICs typically were two years and out. SACs were known to stay merely months before moving on to another division. Assistant Special Agents in Charge rotated through like 3,000-mile oil changes on a Greyhound bus. The street agents referred to these administrators as "Christmas help" because their longevity lasted about one holiday season. The only constant on the eleventh floor of the federal building was Barbara Nolan. When administrative problems arose, if she liked you, she could get a problem resolved with a phone call back East. A holiday or birthday Chick-Fil-A gift card kept you on her good side and Jake was well-known to be a frequent purchaser of the plastic bribes.

For a law enforcement administration center, the outer room to the ADIC's office was warm and hospitable. Large lithographs of Los Angeles in the fifties hung on the walls. It was almost as if the photos represented a simpler time when the FBI was focused on bank robberies and car theft rings. As the city grew, so did crime problems. Terrorism, human trafficking, and cyber-crimes, issues that didn't plague the Bureau in the fifties and sixties, were now top priorities. In fact, many criminal problems took a backseat to these twenty-first-century concerns. Kidnappings and cartel drug trafficking organizations dominated the criminal side of the house.

As Jake crossed the threshold into the ADIC's warren, Barbara Nolan without looking up from her desk said, "You're late."

"So great to see you too, Barbara. I always look forward to your sweet smile and sour disposition. Each time I darken the door of management, I know you will be there to greet me and make me feel welcome."

"Screw you, Special Agent Kruse," said Barbara with a laugh as she looked up to see a wet and muddied FBI employee. "What in the world happened to you? Was this your morning to slop the hogs?"

"Would you believe I picked up an arrest stat on the way into the office this morning?"

"I would stick with the 'slopping hogs' story. In your case, that's more believable."

As Jake nodded toward the ADIC's office, he asked, "Has she been asking for me? Is it okay if I go in?"

Shaking her head, Barbara said, "You aren't even important enough for her to care. Besides, she's been on a conference call with Headquarters most of the morning. You would've just been waiting for her."

Jake walked over to one of the dark blue sofas lining two walls, but before he sat, Barbara said, "Don't you dare sit on my couch. I'm not interested in spending the rest of the morning with leather cleaner trying to correct your mess."

"Leather? This is federal furniture. There's no way this is *real* leather. I'm sure it cleans up with a Wet Wipe."

Barbara looked down at her phone and saw the extension light was out. "She's off the phone. You can go in."

As Jake headed toward the door, Barbara asked, "Seriously, how are you doing? I heard the arrest in Dallas didn't go as planned. Are you okay?"

"Yeah, Mom. I'm fine. Thanks for asking."

Barbara winked and whispered, "Jake, you are one of the Bureau's prodigal sons, but you're my favorite prodigal son."

Jake walked into the large office, about three times the size of any other administrator's office in the building. Because she was the face of the FBI in Los Angeles, Valerie Carlisle's office was professionally decorated with a panoramic view of the mountains and the Los Angeles National Cemetery where more than 85,000 veterans, including fourteen Medal of Honor recipients, were buried. Opposite the windows was the obligatory "I Love Me Wall" with plaques and photos documenting her career. Most impressive was the oversized iconic photograph of J. Edgar Hoover sitting on the edge of a glass-covered table in his office, the mirror image of the Bureau's first director and the FBI seal reflecting off the desk.

"Come in, Mr. Kruse," said the ADIC. "I would tell you to take a seat, but I usually have important visitors in this office, and I don't need to offer my guests water-stained chairs. Besides, this won't take long." She paused for a second before adding, "Did you piss your pants? Apparently, you got the memo ordering everyone who graces my office to arrive in mud-splattered clothing."

Carlisle said it without a hint of a smile and Jake couldn't tell if this were a halfhearted comedic moment or meant as intimidation.

"Yes, ma'am."

"You mean 'yes, ma'am, you got the memo' or 'yes, ma'am, you're wearing mud-splattered pants'"?

Jake decided to play along, "I've been off L.A.'s grid for months, so I didn't get any memos, but I acknowledge my attire looked a lot better when I arrived in the parking lot this morning. That was before I decided to do wind sprints through the neighbor's sprinkler system." He paused for a response, hoping for a laugh, maybe just the hint of a smile. When neither was forthcoming, he added, "Believe it or not, Tyrone Greer and I got into a foot pursuit downstairs as I was heading up to our meeting. We grabbed a purse snatcher and Tyrone is processing him now."

She seemed distracted, shuffling through papers on her desk. Without looking up she said, "I assume Greer was hanging out at the smoke pit when all this erupted. Tell him he isn't fooling me. I checked the surveillance cameras, and I realize he's not inhaling. He's just using any excuse to get away from his white-collar responsibilities."

"Rone is a great agent. I would trust him to have my six in any situation."

She grunted, "Don't go tactical on me."

Jake shifted his weight to his right leg trying to fend off a tightening muscle in his left thigh. He would like to sit just to ease the growing discomfort, but as was apparent with the ADIC's comment, neither was expecting to engage in extended witty and entertaining conversation.

"As you are well aware, I can assign you to any squad. You serve at the pleasure of the Director and in this division, at my pleasure. It is not my policy to seek an agent's input when making my decisions. However, I have three openings in the division and if you want to volunteer for one of them, I'll entertain your desires. That doesn't mean I'll accept your request, but I'll let you make a case, if you want to opine."

Opine, thought Jake. *Who uses "opine"? She must have learned that word in ADIC school.* Jake said nothing and focused his eyes on the ADIC who was still searching for a file on her desk.

When she found it, she paused, formulating her words, then said, "When I knew you were coming back to the office, I reviewed your personnel file. Though you have had a variety of undercover experiences, your investigative and administrative experiences have been limited. If I were you, I would seriously consider one of the first two choices I'm offering. Either would be the most career enhancing."

Jake laughed out loud.

"What?" the ADIC shot back, now glaring at the undercover agent.

"With all due respect, ma'am, I have no desire to be anything other than a street agent. I'm not looking to advance administratively, and I'm certainly not looking for the opportunity to fill a slot back at Headquarters. I'm good at undercover work." He paused but only for an extended second, "No, I take that back. I'm great at undercover work. I hope you recognized that from reviewing my file, and you will keep that in mind if any opportunities arise."

As if ignoring him, which she may have been doing, she said, "We have an opening on the bank fraud squad. That could mean working with Greer."

Pass!

"We have an opening on the applicant squad. With the upcoming midterm elections and assuming there may be a change in who controls the House and Senate, there will be numerous background checks that will need to be completed in a timely fashion as Headquarters sets short deadlines during this transition period. This will sharpen your writing skills which based upon some supervisory evaluations I have read would be just what you need."

A few expletives raced through Jake's mind but didn't leave his lips.

"And I have an undercover slot—"

"I'll take it!"

"Would you like to hear the details?"

"I'm willing to accept it sight unseen. The first two options you've given me aren't exactly sending Chris Matthews thrills up and down my leg."

"I know all about you, Special Agent Kruse. Your last ASAC and I went through new agents training together at Quantico and earlier this morning I spoke with Olivia Knox. The reviews on you are mixed. One thinks you are the greatest thing since Cialis; the other views your worth as the equivalent of a defective prophylactic."

"Well, ma'am, if you have spoken to both Knox and Hafner, I think I can guess who offered the respective opinions."

"Olivia speaks very highly of you, and she filled me in on some of your exploits before I assumed the ADIC responsibilities. Hafner isn't a fan. But if you can do for me what you did for Olivia, I'll take that chance."

"Just give me a chance."

Carlisle flipped through several pages in the file before she came to the document she was seeking. "Have you been 'safeguarded' since the shooting?"

Safeguard was a program administered by the FBI's undercover unit out of Headquarters. It was designed to periodically evaluate undercover agents to ensure they were handling the stress undercover work could throw at you from every direction. It consisted of a series of tests and a face-to-face interview discussing the results of the testing and any personal problems the agent might be experiencing. Though the tests served a purpose—and on occasion, an agent was yanked before he crossed over—the successful UCs knew how to play the game. They knew a wrong answer could end an undercover career as quickly as a bullet and were cautious in expressing any true feelings or concerns unless they wanted out of the program or a particular operation. Jake was evaluated every six months by a neuropsychologist and Headquarters administrator. He played the game well.

"No, I get evaluated on Thursday."

Carlisle looked up from the sheet of paper and with a tinge of sarcasm in her voice asked, "Will you pass?"

"I can fake sanity."

"Well, assuming you can pass, I have an assignment and I don't have a certified UC agent available. I'm not willing to wait a month or two to find someone who is interested in entering the undercover program and then take money out my travel budget to send that person back for the two-week certification process at Quantico. And I'm not paying per diem for an out-of-towner. It's on the FCI side of the house. I'm not at liberty to discuss it with you at this time. You pass on Thursday and the assignment is yours."

"We can get started this afternoon. I've got the verbiage memorized so why don't you sign off on the paperwork now. All you have to say is, 'the agent conducted himself in a professional manner and is not over adapted nor is he attached to his undercover persona. Neither is he detached from reality nor displaying an exaggerated sense of importance. He is adequately coping and not in need of withdrawal support.'"

The undercover game was for the brave and audacious. He wasn't in this for trophies or awards. He just wanted the next UC assignment, whatever that was.

Carlisle finally offered a brief smile. "Impressive. I guess you have been through a few of these evaluations."

"I know how to pass."

CHAPTER ELEVEN

West Los Angeles

A low-hanging fog blanketed the Los Angeles coast, stunting nighttime visibility. Adding to the darkness was Franklin Lee's actions the night before when he shot out the lone light illuminating the entrance to Shooter's Paradise, the Westside's largest indoor gun range. Lee backed the stolen 2017 Ford Transit Connect van to the front door. Hopping out, he approached the front of the business and glanced up and down the street, looking for any vehicles. Seeing none, preparations began to breach the door with a small ball of C-4.

Located in an urban industrial complex just off the 405 freeway, Shooter's Paradise was one of the few spots in the city where gun enthusiasts could exercise their Second Amendment rights. The hypocrisy was stunning. Hollywood's elite pushed for more restrictive gun laws, making California one of the most anti-gun states in the nation, yet starlets, hiding from the paparazzi, with a baseball cap pulled low on their heads and sans makeup, showed up at the Paradise with a boyfriend or armed bodyguard, buying a weapon for personal protection. At the next publicized and politicized shooting, those same stars appeared on TV or in a public service announcement calling for more gun control. Though most celebs readily provided an autographed picture to adorn the walls of the local drycleaner or health food store, few wanted their signed headshots anywhere near the ammo display.

Lee had little interest in Constitutional rights, except for maybe the Fifth Amendment which he invoked on numerous occasions. Though born in the United States, the thirty-one-year-old was first-generation. His parents came from Hong Kong in the mid-eighties, hoping their legal immigration into America would provide a future for themselves and their children. With two daughters now nurses and their oldest son a teacher, the migration seemed successful until Franklin Lee, their youngest child reached his teens. He was the dog who wouldn't stay on the porch. He dashed parental hopes by joining the Monterey Park-Side of the Wah Ching. For him, getting arrested as a juvenile was just part of puberty and his conviction more honorable than a high school diploma.

The Wah Ching, literally "Chinese Youth," had its origins in San Francisco's Chinatown in the late sixties. Founded by teenage Cantonese immigrants from China and Hong Kong, it began as a protective force against larger youth gangs. Within a few years, it evolved into a full-fledged criminal organization, gaining control of Chinatown's gambling and loansharking underground. Also known as the "Dub C," the gang never looked back and never backed down.

It came to national attention in 1977 during what the media called the Golden Dragon Massacre. There was a long-standing feud between the Wah Ching and a rival gang, the Joe Boys. The Wah Ching controlled Chinatown and the Joe Boys, the Sunset and Richmond districts of San Francisco. In an attempt to assassinate the Wah Ching leadership, three Joe Boys members opened fire inside the Golden Dragon Restaurant killing five people and wounding eleven others. Though ten Wah Ching members were sitting at a table near the back of the restaurant, not one was injured during the revenge assault which lasted less than a minute.

The public outcry from the attack only enhanced the gang's bulletproof reputation. Various factions, called Sides, expanded throughout the state of California. Under Tony Young's leadership, the Wah Ching organized in the greater Los Angeles area.

Now decades old, the gang was known for engaging in murder, extortion, drug trafficking, and gambling. Like every organized crime group in America, it settled its disputes in blood. For gang members, violence was the first and last step. Brutality was "practiced" daily to the point members "perfected" the art.

The Asian immigrant community, tight-lipped by tradition, thanks to decades of communist rule in their native land, seldom cooperated with American law enforcement. Many neighborhoods were ruled by gangs, and police efforts were futile in stemming the tide.

Unlike the urban Los Angeles street gangs, the Crips, adorned in blue, and the Bloods, wearing red, the Wah Ching wore no distinctive clothing. They blended into the community, making their detection by law enforcement more difficult. In fact, many police officials believed the gang no longer existed or were of minimal concern in the greater Los Angeles area. The authorities were wrong.

Earlier in the evening, Franklin Lee slapped magnetic signs on the side panels of the van, identifying the vehicle as an independent heating and air conditioning company. It provided the perfect cover should someone drive by the business. By law, gun ranges needed extensive ventilation systems to filter the lead, carbon, and toxic particles emitted by the expended ammunition. Even a cop driving past might not question seeing the van at the popular business.

Franklin dropped out of school in the ninth grade and only received his GED in prison because it cut short by a few months his first of two prison terms. However, he had a PhD in street sense and had the urban combat skills of a trained warrior.

As Franklin opened the rear doors of the van, his three criminal associates for the evening, jumped out. One of the men was his uncle's son, his cousin, Calvin Lee, their relationship as strained as an aging rubber band ready to snap.

"We only have a few minutes once I blow the front door," said Franklin. "I can't disable the alarm. Because of the guns, the system signals the police department directly, not a security company. Some rent-a-pig won't be notified first. It will be the real pigs. Once the alarm is activated, the cops will be here in minutes. Follow the plan as we discussed. Grab every rental weapon off the wall first. The semi-auto long guns are important. Then the handguns in the glass display case. Some are used and some are new but bring them all. There won't be much time and throw as much ammo as you can into the bags. Don't worry about the caliber. We'll sort that out later. Do you understand?"

Two of the gang members nodded. Franklin looked at Calvin, who arrived from Hong Kong six months earlier. "Understand, ass wipe?"

Calvin nodded with a smirk. The twenty-three-year-old did time in a Hong Kong prison and thought that should have elevated him to shot-caller status, not just a common soldier. His attitude was corrosive, and Franklin wasn't happy the younger cousin was assigned to tonight's mission. The *dai lo*—literally the "big brother" but in actuality, the local crime boss—wanted Calvin to gain more practical criminal experience in America.

To the two others, he said, "While you're grabbing the weapons, I'll blow the door to the back room. That's where they keep the new guns still in their boxes."

"Calvin, watch the street," ordered Franklin.

Though Franklin was never in the military, he knew how to breach a door. He also knew ways to minimize the explosive concussion that would normally reverberate throughout the neighborhood.

From a small bag slung over his shoulder, he removed the first of three balled concoctions of C-4. He carefully molded the plastic explosive around the lock, planted the detonator in the C-4, and ran a few inches of fuse from the detonator.

Before he could finish the job, a rent-a-cop night watchman, walked up on them. The four men froze for a second as a slender black man, wearing a uniform two sizes too big, seemed less than professional in approaching from behind the building.

"What you guys be up to? Cleanin' out the filter system, huh? Nobody told me you'd be working tonight, know what I'm sayin'."

Franklin didn't realize the complex had night security. The plan had to be immediately modified and this unexpected contact needed to be neutralized. Franklin causally turned toward the guard and slowly approached. As he appeared to be about to engage the guard in conversation, Franklin drew a Glock17 from his appendix-carry holster and began beating the guard across his face. Taking pleasure in the brutality and force, Franklin's nonstop assault was so quick, the guard had no time to scream before he fell to the pavement unconscious, his face mirroring raw meat.

Franklin wheeled toward Calvin, his finger now on the trigger. "You were supposed to be watching out!" he shouted.

"It is taken care of. I wanted to watch my famous cousin in action," said Calvin.

"Watch the damn street," seethed Franklin.

Franklin finished the preparation by spraying a noise-muffling foam around the C-4 ball and lock. Calvin and his two associates climbed into the van. Franklin lit the fuse and hopped into the van, closing the rear doors.

Within seconds, a muted pop could be heard, and the front door sprang open. Franklin repeated the process on the lock to the wrought iron gate extending across the front of the store from the inside. After a second muted explosion, the men were in.

Franklin raced to the back room as the men began ripping the rental weapons off the wall. Using the third charge, Franklin blew the door off the hinges. Once inside the office, he hit pay dirt. At least two dozen new weapons, still boxed, lay on the floor. Before grabbing the boxes of new Smith & Wesson AR-15 M&P Sport II rifles piled in the corner, Franklin ripped out the video feed security system, ensuring the crime wasn't being recorded. He then grabbed six boxes and headed to the van.

The men had removed two dozen weapons from the wall, everything from carbines to shotguns. They were now throwing the handguns from the glass display case into two large canvas bags.

Franklin returned for a second trip to the office grabbing the remaining AR-15s. As he hurried out of the office, he spotted Calvin in the store sizing up the 5.11 shirts and jackets.

"I told you to watch the street. Not the damn clothes," screamed Franklin.

"You took care of the guard. How many night watchmen do you think they have?" protested the cousin.

Franklin dropped off the rifles and returned to the store where he caught Calvin piling clothes into his arms. Franklin reached his capacity, his volcanic temper about to erupt. Anything worth shooting was worth shooting twice. From less than six feet away, he pulled for the second time that evening the semi-auto from his waistband, this time firing two rounds into his cousin. Calvin collapsed in a lake of his own blood; his eyes wide in death.

"No one questions my orders!" said Franklin, who immediately searched for oversized tactical jackets and spread them on the floor. "Wrap his body in the jackets. Then throw him in the back of the van. We will toss him out on a street corner and make it look like a drive-by shooting."

The men did as they were told without question, terror having a multiplying effect.

Time was running out. By now, the alarm system would have notified the police. Knowing they only had seconds to flee, they piled as much ammo as they could into a large equipment bag and headed for the door. Just as Franklin passed the cash register, he grabbed a handful of Barrett ink pens made from .50-caliber cartridges—the perfect gift for his homies.

Within seconds, the men were gone.

Sirens wailed in the background as the van escaped southbound on the freeway.

CHAPTER TWELVE

THURSDAY, APRIL 21
Mexico City, Mexico

Named after the nineteenth-century Mexican statesman, Benito Juarez International Airport in Mexico City was that nation's largest international air transportation facility. With direct flights to more than three hundred destinations throughout the world, the complex served more than thirty million passengers each year. It was easy for the two to melt into the crowd of passengers exiting the Boeing 787-9.

They traveled almost eighteen hours, beginning in Beijing with a three-hour flight to Tokyo, then the fourteen-hour flight to Mexico City. It was uneventful. Thanks to doubling up on Ambien, both men slept most of the way across the Pacific.

The plane landed at Terminal One of MEX, the international designation for the Mexico City airport. They completed the FMM (*Forma Migratoria Multiple*) cards and the customs forms on the flight. Fraudulent visas as well as passports were provided by their handlers in Beijing.

As the men exited the plane, they were corralled toward one of two immigration areas. One served arrivals from Europe, North America, the Middle East, and Asia. A separate area was designated for passengers arriving from the Caribbean and Latin America. Like steers in a slow-moving Western cattle drive, the men maintained their places in the flow of traffic, refusing to jump the line and draw attention to themselves. The separate areas were clearly designated by the overhead signs but some passengers, especially those with small children, seemed lost as they tried to navigate the route toward immigration and customs.

It was a cacophony of noises in Tower of Babel-like languages: tired passengers complaining in multiple tongues, exhausted kids screaming in universal cries, and overbearing loudspeaker announcements in Spanish and English being ignored by those who just wanted to keep moving.

The two men patiently waited in line as they approached the immigration official; Song, the smaller and older of the two, in front, followed by Chen.

Song led the two-man team on this leg of the journey because he spoke Spanish, not Latin American Spanish but the more proper Castilian. In 2013, Spain's minister of foreign affairs announced his country's efforts in focusing on Asian markets. China saw this as an opportunity to expand its stranglehold on businesses worldwide. The Chinese Communist Party, the CCP, wasted no time in the call for Spanish speakers. Song was part of the first wave of students studying the language. His success in the classroom brought him to the attention of the Party leadership who arranged for his one-year study abroad in Madrid. Since his return from overseas, Song taught Spanish in Beijing. Though Chen spoke Mandarin, Cantonese, and English, his Spanish skills were minimal. His handlers in China feared he would be unable to negotiate the trip from Mexico City to the U.S. border without drawing undue attention.

As Song stepped forward, he handed his passport and FMM card to a lady sitting behind an elevated desk. Without offering a smile or a comment, she took the paperwork. Like most tired bureaucrats around the world, she seemed bored as she went through the motions of the ritualistic chore. A large woman, she sat uncomfortably in the adjustable chair, shifting as if stretching her lower back. Her long black hair was pulled back and her dark brown eyes seemed to penetrate each visitor as she compared the photo on the passport with the traveler's face. She silently read through the form, insuring all the information was completed without confirming the validity of the hand-printed data. After scanning the passport under an ultraviolet light and waiting a few seconds, she determined everything to be in order. She stamped the passport and returned a portion of the FMM card to Song, reminding him he would need to present that section of the form upon leaving Mexico.

She repeated the procedure with Chen who offered a practiced *gracias* as she returned the passport and FMM card.

Once the men arrived in the United States, they would be given new identification papers at the PRC consulate in Los Angeles, so neither was concerned about returning any paperwork to Mexican officials. In fact, they had no intent of revisiting Mexico once they crossed the border.

CHAPTER THIRTEEN

Mexico City, Mexico

Chen Ma Ho and Song Bing jockeyed their way past the passengers crowding around the carousel. They grabbed their luggage and headed toward the next round of Mexican government employees.

Handing over the customs forms to an official manning the X-ray machine, they placed their bags on the conveyor. To the relief of both men, the green light glowed on the computer's screen in the eyeglasses of the customs and immigration officer's and they were allowed to proceed to the arrival hall. A red light would have meant "secondary" and a visual inspection of the luggage. Neither was carrying anything illegal, but the less bureaucratic interference with the mission the better. They had no interest in drawing attention to themselves and appreciated the uneventful passage through immigration and customs.

The officials at MEX had bigger worries than Asian travelers. Cartel members plagued Mexico. Colombian tourists were cause for greater scrutiny, not Chinese citizens.

After clearing the bureaucratic hurdles for landing in a foreign country, the men followed the signs to "Ground Transportation" written in Spanish and English. They were warned to only take authorized cabs and avoided the gypsy drivers plaguing most major cities.

Song pretended not to understand when three different drivers approached and asked in Spanish and English if he needed a ride. His lengthy and obscene response in Mandarin to the third man drew a brief smile from Chen and a confusing look from the driver.

There was no line at the transportation kiosk. The older dark-skinned man behind the booth tried to sell Song the more expensive ride, a larger comfort van, but the traveler insisted on "*el sedan.*" He wasn't going to be played just because he was a first-time *turista*. Song pre-paid the cab fare, two hundred pesos, for a taxi to take them on the next leg of their voyage, a downtown hotel. Once he had a coupon in hand, he and Chen headed toward the departure area and found *Yellow Cab Aeropuerto*.

CHAPTER FOURTEEN

Santa Monica, California

The weather was perfect. The skies were clear, and the waves of the Pacific Ocean crashed ashore as the sunlight danced across the water. Jake had plenty of time to view the picturesque setting because the Pacific Coast Highway was moving along at near turtle speed. He gave himself a few extra minutes because for once he was actually looking forward to his meeting with the psychologist from the FBI's Safeguard Unit. Because of the Dallas shooting, he knew the meeting might take longer than normal, but this wasn't his first goat rope. He had been through this before and knew how to play the game. If he wanted to stay out of the office, he needed to put on his game face—his stable, lucid, rational game face.

It was a restless night because he understood the importance of this morning's meeting. If unable to convince the psychologist of his mental stability, he might be spending most of his investigative time either knocking on doors and asking inane questions while conducting background investigations or tethered to a desk analyzing ledger sheets.

He knew he had his head on straight and formulated the answers to the questions he thought the psychologist would ask, but if any curveballs were thrown, this might be his ultimate improv test. It always amazed him how criminals played such a small role in crime-fighting. Bureaucrats, lawyers, rules, and regulations far beyond the criminal code had a much greater impact on Jake's job than the illegal acts of those he was targeting. And then it was those same administrators and prosecutors who took credit for the successes of the risktakers in the field. He inhaled sharp and hard. Now was not the time for internal ranting about the judicial overseers. He blew out a cleansing breath. *Keep it together for a couple of hours.*

Though the drive seemed longer than it was, Jake finally made it to Santa Monica's Ocean Avenue and arrived at the Lowe's Santa Monica Beach Hotel. With valet parking at $50 a night, Jake decided parking was one expense he wasn't going to eat and wasn't interested in filing the massive paperwork to get reimbursed. He headed east a couple of blocks and found a public parking garage where the first ninety minutes were free and the next hour only a buck twenty-five. He knew the interview might take a little longer but was confident he would be through in two and a half hours.

The Lowe's was gorgeous inside and out, a perfect spot for those seeking an ocean view and all the amenities a Southern California hotel could offer. He knew the rates exceeded the government per diem but also knew the Safeguard Unit's budget was outside normal spending limits. It was reasoned the undercover agents needed a safe and comfortable setting in which to be evaluated and a place not offering prison-made government contract furniture seemed like an ideal setting. Though the employees from the unit had work to do and reports to file, Jake knew anytime they traveled to the West Coast there was a semi-vacation attitude about the trip. Jake really couldn't fault the bureaucrats for going luxury; when he had a choice between entertaining the bad guys at Taco Bell or a five-star restaurant, glitter and gold prevailed.

Taking a deep breath and slowly blowing it out, he punched the elevator button for the eighth floor. Let the mind games begin!

CHAPTER FIFTEEN
SATURDAY, APRIL 23
Mexico City, Mexico

Song and Chen stayed one night in Mexico City as was their original plan. Song wanted to party; Chen stopped him. The task at hand required focus, not fun. At the hotel, they were greeted by an unnamed associate who remained long enough to provide each with a Diamondback .380 and suppressor. Their mission called for them to be in the United States as soon as they could cross the border. Chen hoped that would be in a day or two. Since he didn't take the time to check the map before beginning the journey, he didn't realize it would take two days to get from Mexico's capital city to America's southern border.

To avoid too much scrutiny of their false identification papers by a rental car agency or the police should they be stopped, Chen didn't want to rent a car for the long ride from Mexico City. Besides, as a safety precaution, he preferred several tons of steel protecting him on the Latin roadways as they made their way north.

Chinese immigration into Mexico had a checkered history. Sometimes welcomed, sometimes not, early immigrants were seen as a form of cheap labor. As early as the 1500s, thousands of Asian men were brought into Mexico as slaves or *indio chinos*. Estimates as high as 120,000 Asian immigrants arrived in Mexico during the colonial period. Beginning in the 1800s through the 1920s, the Chinese were Mexico's fastest growing immigrant group. Even today there are about 10,000 full-blooded Chinese in Mexicali, a border town ninety miles east of Tijuana. Though the two men's Asian features would distinguish them from the Latins, it wasn't unusual to see Chinese tourists in Tijuana where Chinese restaurants were sprinkled throughout the city.

It was already decided by their handlers not to fly into the border town, neighboring San Diego. The leadership feared their arrival might draw too much attention by the authorities. They assumed the U.S. in some way, probably through NSA, monitored the arrival of all passengers at the General Abelardo L. Rodriguez International Airport—or as everyone called it, the Tijuana Airport.

Song wanted to avoid the Mexican "chicken buses" and hoped to ride in luxury for the two-day trek. From the downtown hotel in Mexico City, Song and Chen took a cab to the Terminal Central Norte, one of four major bus stations in Mexico City. This terminal serviced all travel going north and no reservations were required.

At the ticket counter, Song explained his travel plans and learned there was no direct route to Tijuana, and no one bus company serviced all the way to the Baja Peninsula. Rather than expressing his frustration, he merely smiled, pretended to be on a leisurely Mexican sightseeing vacation, and using cash, purchased two premiere class tickets to Guadalajara. After they completed that five-hour journey, they could purchase additional tickets to Tijuana.

The men traveled in luxury as bus service in Mexico far exceeded expectations. They rode on an air-conditioned bus complete with reclining seats, music, and immaculately clean onboard restrooms.

As the men knew when they purchased the tickets, it was going to be a long ride with several stops and two transfers. They saw a great deal of the Mexican countryside and cityscape as they traveled through Guadalajara, Mazatlán, Nogales, and along the border from Mexicali to Tijuana. The bus ride took twice as long as the flight from Beijing to Mexico City. Each stop along the way was a welcomed opportunity to stretch their legs and grab some food.

In the early evening on the third day, they arrived at the Central de Autobuses de Tijuana, the city's main bus terminal. Located within the Tijuana River basin and surrounded by hills, mesas, and canyons, Tijuana was called the "Gateway to Mexico." It was the largest city on the Baja California Peninsula and with a population of about 1.7 million people, was one of the fastest growing metropolitan areas in Mexico. Though known in the American media for its drug cartel violence forcing many urban residents to move to the outlying areas, Tijuana was a burgeoning industrial hub. It was the medical device manufacturing capital of North America, and its scenic shoreline was no longer a secret. For years, Chinese agents targeted the city's industries seeking to steal production secrets thus reducing manufacturing costs in China.

After gathering their luggage, which wasn't much, two soft-sided bags, they made their way to a taxi stand outside the main entrance to the terminal. Grabbing a cab, they headed north on the Alfonso Bustamante Labastida for Avenida Revolución, the town's main shopping venue for everything from souvenirs to prescriptions.

They were to meet their contact near the arch, a city landmark, visible from miles away. The cab skirted the central business district and dropped them off a few blocks from the familiar attraction.

Song was immediately captivated by the bright, bold colors of the many items for sale hanging in front of the shops. Blankets and serapes were most common but souvenirs and conventional clothing were available at what appeared to be discounted prices. Stopping to gaze at multi-colored shirts hanging on a sidewalk rack, an older lady dressed in a traditional Mexican outfit, grabbed Song's arm, and attempted to hustle him into her shop.

Chen stopped him from going in by grabbing the other arm. "We are not here to sightsee or shop."

"How about to eat?" said Song who stopped at a food vendor's cart.

"We will eat when we make contact."

CHAPTER SIXTEEN

Tijuana, Mexico

Just a few miles south of San Diego's beautiful sandy beaches, Mexican residents experience a Southern California lifestyle for pennies on the dollar. Pedro Bautista's three-bedroom, three-bath condominium was hidden from Baja's tourist traffic. Gringos on their way to Ensenada might not even know the Playa community existed. Yet just a mile from the border, from their balcony, Pedro and his family could see San Diego's skyline and the Coronado Bridge.

Pedro paid cash for the one-floor residence. Though most people assumed he made his fortune in his Avenida Revolución storefront schlepping cheap knockoffs to unsuspecting American tourists, the money really came from northern Mexico's number one industry—drug smuggling.

The "Revo" as the locals referred to the tourist center in historic downtown Tijuana was slammed in recent years. Once billed as the "most visited city in the world," Americans shied away from traveling to the border town even before the pandemic.

The tourist numbers were nowhere near the visitors of a decade ago. Cartel violence headlined the Southern California evening news, and deeply discounted ponchos weren't worth getting caught in the middle of a well-publicized drug war. Pedro's business took a hit as well. He needed to provide for his wife and two children. When the sale of cheap dolls dressed as mariachi musicians in charro outfits and other such detritus plummeted, he looked elsewhere to pay the bills.

His wife, who liked the lifestyle before the COVID economic downturn, begged him to see her brother, Ernesto, who lived in Rosarito Beach, twenty-five miles south of Tijuana. Ernesto, a skilled mechanic and craftsman with nefarious connections, knew his select clients could use the services of a man living on the border and in need of lucrative part-time work.

Pedro now worked for the cartels and his black-market job was thriving. He transported modest-size quantities of cocaine, fentanyl, and methamphetamine across the border on a semi-weekly basis. His newfound riches meant he and his wife could dine out weekly on Boulevard Sanchez Taboada and spend their weekends at Agua Caliente, the racetrack. The part-time work was risky, but blending in with the crowds crossing the border and Ernesto's vehicle modification skills lessened the danger. Pedro was willing to chance fate believing the cartel's deep pockets in the Mexican government could protect him should an alert border agent detect his cargo.

Pedro wasn't in the smuggling business because of his devotion to the craft. For him it was for pure profit, and if Americans wanted to put the white powder up their collective noses, who was he to deny them their pleasures? He saw their greed in the marketplace as they tried to bargain for every souvenir in his shop. He was only too happy to profit from their excesses as the drug abusers could haggle over anything but the value of their lives.

In recent years, the cartels modified their smuggling practices. The terrorist attacks on 9/11 saw an increase in U.S. border security. But as the United States built taller obstacles, the cartels merely bought "bigger ladders." Technology and innovation made the contraband so desired by habituated Americans still available but at an increased price. The cartels weren't about to let a few more border agents adversely impact their multi-billion-dollar enterprise. Those seeking refuge in the States took advantage of what could almost be described as an "open border" policy by the current administration. The U.S. Border Patrol was focused on the flood of human trafficking and asylum seekers from the south crossing at every opening in "The Wall" rather than the recognized border checkpoints. This provided new opportunities for the couriers.

Pedro's Ford F-250 extended cab pickup was tricked out by Ernesto. He introduced Pedro to midlevel traffickers who needed mules to ferry cocaine, fentanyl, and meth across the border. Ernesto reconfigured the dashboard. Though fully operational, it could easily hold a quarter of a million dollars of white powder imported from South America. Accessible through the glove compartment, only a trained investigator or a skilled drug-sniffing dog would discover the secret.

Ernesto also custom built a hydraulic system rear seat "trap." The bench seat comfortably sat three adults. But when the backseat passengers exited the vehicle, the truck was in park, and the cigarette lighter pushed, the rear seat opened. A fiberglass-lined bed could hold hundreds of kilos of contraband or a smuggled adult. Though it was secure, it was far from a luxurious ride, but for the hour or so it took to cross the border, the price of discomfort was worth a new life in the United States.

It was getting late, and Song and Chen had trouble finding the street address they were given. Many of the shops on Revolución were already closed, and the two men had a hard time finding street numbers on the storefronts. Song was told the owner would await their arrival, so the men assumed that meant the lights would still be on. A few stores had numbers either above or on the door. That however was sporadic. The men seemed to be getting closer, but just as they thought they were nearing the location, the numbers above the doors disappeared altogether. They walked past several unnumbered open stores. Their contact in Beijing hadn't provided the name of the store, only the name of the owner—the "coyote" as he was called, the man who would transport them across the border.

When they finally found a number above the door of a business, they realized they passed the store and returned to three consecutive opened stores. One was a convenient mart selling beer, soft drinks, and snacks. The other two stores sold souvenirs.

Standing in front of the first open store, Song shrugged his shoulders and opened his hands in a universal gesture as if to mean, "I guess we give it a shot."

As they entered, Song spotted a short, rotund man behind the counter who seemed restless and eager to close. In Spanish, the two men conversed.

"Are you Pedro?" asked Song.

The man nodded without smiling.

"I am Bing, and this is Ho."

Chen was surprised Song identified themselves by using true first names. He assumed it would be better tradecraft to use the fictitious names on their passports but either Song forgot or just didn't think it important. Chen didn't know Song that well. During the trip, Song shared some of his story but the Chinese man who spoke Spanish was more valuable for his language skills than his espionage talents. He talked too much and projected weakness. Unlike Chen, Song had never been involved in a covert mission. It wasn't like the Mexican merchant was going to ask for identification before smuggling them across the border, so maybe the slip wasn't that important.

"You are late," said Pedro in English, having been told both men spoke English.

"We could only come as fast as the bus would bring us. It is a long trip from Mexico City."

"Then let us go."

"I have rented you a room in a motel just down the street from my house. We will leave early in the morning. It is not an easy trip to cross the border. I can only take one at a time."

"We are aware of the logistics," said Chen. "Everything has been explained to us."

CHAPTER SEVENTEEN

SUNDAY, APRIL 24

Tijuana, Mexico

When President Richard Nixon visited China in February 1972, he hoped to "build a bridge" between the United States and the most populous country on earth—and drive a wedge between China and the Soviet Union. Nixon also believed exposing the Chinese to modern capitalism and democratic political values would be in the economic interest of the people of both nations and hasten the demise of communism. It didn't work out quite the way he intended.

Over the course of the next five decades, the People's Republic of China (PRC) transitioned from a struggling, third-world economy to become a booming competitor of the United States in the global marketplace. The government in Beijing accomplished this while remaining a tyrannical, one-party communist dictatorship—and employing "illicit trade practices" deemed illegal in Western democracies.

Today, the PRC is intent on becoming the most powerful economic and military power on earth by any means necessary. In 2020 the U.S. and our NATO allies estimated the PRC stole nearly $6 trillion of protected intellectual property over the past decade. When the previous administration took action by imposing tariffs on Chinese goods because the PRC failed to halt the theft of U.S. tech innovations and intellectual property, the Chinese declared a "Peoples War."

Some Western intelligence services now argue the COVID-19 pandemic, which killed millions around the globe during 2020–2022, originated from a virus created and/or modified in a Wuhan, China laboratory as part of their asymmetrical "People's War."

In April 1942, Chinese soldiers and civilians rescued survivors of the "Doolittle Raid" over Japan when the U.S. airmen bailed out or crash-landed in China. The grandchildren of those saviors are now governed in Beijing by those who call America their enemy.

The motel just south of Pedro's condo was separated from the Pacific by a small stretch of white sandy beach. From the room's patio, if you had a major-league arm, you could throw a rock and hit the water. The only problem was the motel was crowded and only one room was available. Chen was sharing it with Song whose snoring kept him awake. He'd put a pillow over his head, but it didn't drown out the roar of Song's incessant snorting and wheezing.

Questioning the man's value to the mission, Chen could almost justify what he believed would be an "efficient murder." Song's passable Spanish, the only skill he brought to the table, wouldn't be needed once they crossed the border. There were many pieces to move around the chessboard, and Song was merely a pawn. He was expendable. Chen's skills were in demand and were now necessary in the United States for the immediate undertaking. He needed his sleep, but it wasn't going to come anytime soon. Three times he'd reached across the divide of the twin beds and poked at Song. The noise stopped for a few seconds, then when Song rolled on his back it would begin anew. Finally, Chen gave up. He threw on his shoes and a pair of pants and walked out of the room.

Fresh air and a cool breeze greeted him. The light from a partial moon reflected off the water as the ocean washed ashore. Chen found peace in the breaking surf as the successive waves came without ceasing. As he neared the water, he stopped long enough to take off his shoes and roll up his pants legs to just below his knees. The wet sand massaged his feet as he began slowly walking south allowing his mission rather than sleep to bring him comfort.

Chen didn't have a watch but realized the hour was nearing. He and Song were to meet Pedro at his condominium at four-thirty. He returned to the motel a little after four and startled Song awake when he shook him violently. "Get up," he said in English. "It is time."

Song sat up in bed and rubbed his eyes. Opening the drape and peering out the window, he said, "It is still dark."

"Yes, and it will remain dark for a long time. We have to be at his place in thirty minutes. Get ready."

CHAPTER EIGHTEEN

Tijuana, Mexico

The San Ysidro-Tijuana border crossing was the busiest land port of entry in the world. Seventeen million vehicles passed through annually from Tijuana into the United States. Each day about 30,000 people who lived in Mexico crossed to work in Southern California. Many of those were pedestrians who had SENTRI cards. The "Secure Electronic Network for Travelers Rapid Inspection" cards allowed for easier access for workers and students who traveled daily back and forth across the border. Buses lined the border on each side depositing and picking up the daily passengers. The San Diego trolley had cars running at regular intervals hustling workers from the border to downtown.

In September 2012, the United States opened a new pedestrian crossing on the eastern side of the San Ysidro crossing, and in 2014 Mexico opened a three-level $4.2 million structure. It still could mean hour-long waits but the facilities were nicer than the previous building.

It was Pedro's expertise that Chen and Song required in order to safely cross. He knew the tricks. Pick a middle lane since there was usually less of a wait. During the morning hours—five a.m.—was the best time to cross, even on a Sunday. There was enough traffic at that hour to avoid suspicion, but border agents were intent on keeping the traffic moving due to the anticipated heavy buildup in an hour or so. Questioning was minimal and Pedro made the trip often enough to appear familiar with the procedures, not drawing attention to his truck or its contents. It still might be at least a thirty-minute wait for the vehicle to get through one of the twenty-four lanes, but in a couple of hours the wait could easily be three to four hours.

The men purchased some food at a vending machine before heading toward Pedro's. At each leg of the journey, they had minimized their belongings. Dirty shirts, underwear, and socks were thrown away. On the trip across the Pacific, each man had a soft-sided suitcase only half full of clothes. It was designed more to divert suspicion since international travelers seldom flew with few belongings. Now they were down to the backpacks they kept in the suitcases. They knew whatever items they might need could be purchased in the United States once they arrived.

The plan today was simple. Pedro would take both men back to the shop on Revolución. One man would remain in the back of the store as Pedro took the other across the border. Once he dropped that person off, Pedro would return and take the second man across. Pedro's wife was to open the store at nine, the usual opening time, to avoid questioning by neighboring businesses as to why he would shut down, especially since it was forecast to be a beautiful day, perfect for materialistic tourists from the U.S.

When they arrived at Pedro's two-car garage beneath his condominium unit, Pedro was waiting with the back door of the pickup truck opened. He greeted Chen and Song with "Buenos Dias."

Both responded, Song in unaccented Spanish and Chen less polished.

Without any small talk, Pedro began explaining how the rear seat operated. He pointed out the interior release levers on both sides of the fiberglass-lined bed to be used in the event of an emergency. Both men were pleased with the quality of the human smuggling platform and were anxious to start traveling in order to cross the border with minimum delay.

Chen was not happy with what he witnessed next. Pedro opened the dashboard. He then walked to the other side of the garage and grabbed a large box from inside a locked metal cabinet. When he returned to the truck, he began filling the space with kilos of metham-phetamine. Chen estimated it was about twenty kilos but didn't take the time to count. "No, you can't do that," he said in English.

"What do you mean 'no, I can't do that'?" responded Pedro.

"You are not taking drugs in the truck. We are paying you to trans-port us, not the meth."

"What does it matter? You will be under the back seat," said the overweight smuggler.

"It matters because we do not want to alert the authorities to our presence. They have dogs and machines that can smell the drugs," said Chen as he put down his backpack and began removing the kilos packages.

Pedro grabbed at Chen's arm. "It is the same risk for me to take drugs or you across the border. I am doing both."

"We are paying you for exclusive services."

"And you are getting my exclusive services."

"Not if you take drugs with us."

Chen looked to Song for help, but Song's skills were in travel logis-tics not negotiations with cartel middlemen. Song looked down, a sign of surrender. Chen knew he would have to settle this matter on his own.

"You have been paid in advance to take *us* across the border. You are not transporting drugs. That is final."

Pedro screwed up his courage and confronted the younger, stron-ger man facing him defiantly. "Who are you to give me orders? You are merely the *pollo*. I offer safe passage. If you do not like the arrange-ments, I suggest you try heading east. Find an opening in the fence and begin your walk across the desert. I am sure you are smart enough to avoid the American Border Patrol. They, of course, would never be interested in Chinese illegally crossing into their country."

Chen was at least three inches taller than the squat merchant who was winded from merely loading the 2.2-pound packages in the dash. Physically, Chen could destroy him, but at least for this day, he needed him. The Chinese operative thought for a moment and said to Song, "Watch him."

Song wasn't quite sure what he was to do. He was not a fighter. He, too, was taller and stronger than Pedro, so he merely stood between the two men in an effort to watch him.

With that, Chen walked through the garage and entered the Mexican's condo.

"Where are you going? You can't go in there," said Pedro as Song held him back.

In a matter of seconds, Chen returned with Pedro's wife and two sons. All three were still in their pajamas.

"We have new travel arrangements," said Chen with a smirk. "We will all go to your store now. Of course, your wife and children can get dressed. And while they are getting dressed you will empty the truck of the remaining drugs. You will take me across first and one of your sons will accompany us. Pick one. I don't care. Then I will watch him until you return with Song. Once we are both safely across the border, you will get your son back. I hope I am making myself clear. There will be no deviation from the new arrangement: no drugs and a safe delivery. Once you have fulfilled your obligation, you and your family can go on living."

CHAPTER NINETEEN

San Ysidro, San Diego

Originally a farming community and named after San Ysidro Labrador, the patron saint of farmers, San Ysidro was annexed by the city of San Diego in 1957. Just north of Tijuana, it is where Interstate 5 crosses the U.S.-Mexican border.

After dropping off his wife, younger son, and Song at the family's shop on Revolución, Pedro negotiated through the streets of Tijuana toward the border. His oldest son sat in the passenger seat of the Ford F-250 not quite appreciating the card he was unknowingly dealt.

Though it was a little before five, traffic was already backing up. He maneuvered to one of the middle lanes hoping to expedite the journey, but there was no way to legally rush through the border crossing. The last thing he wanted to do was draw attention to his truck. Song was armed and if anything went wrong at the checkpoint and Chen didn't safely cross, he was instructed to kill Pedro's wife and son.

Thirty minutes later, Pedro's older son smiled uncomfortably as his father handed the U.S. Border Patrol officer their papers. In a matter of seconds, the officer waved the truck through, unaware a Chinese operative was secreted beneath the back seat.

Once across the border, Pedro immediately veered right off Interstate 5, heading north on the 805. At the first off ramp, Pedro exited. When he stopped at the light, Chen hollered from his hidden compartment, "Pull off to the side of the road and make sure there are no police around."

Pedro did as instructed.

"Is it safe?" asked Chen when he knew the truck was stopped.

"Yes," said Pedro.

Chen activated the internal emergency switch and the rear seat opened. He awkwardly unfolded his body and climbed over the seat. Then pushing the bench seat back into place, he sat down and gave more instructions. "Find a motel."

Pedro turned right twice and was heading south on San Ysidro Boulevard. The street was lined on both sides with money exchanges, pawn shops, and *abogados*, the lawyers who specialized in immigration issues. When Chen spotted a motel, he ordered Pedro to pull to the side of the road. Filled with fear of the unknown, the boy began to cry.

"Quiet," said Chen as he displayed the silenced Diamondback .380.

The boy's cries faded to whimpers as Chen watched the activity at the motel. Within a few minutes, he saw a couple heading to their car, pulling two pieces of luggage. After loading up the car and pulling out of the parking lot, Chen waited only a few more minutes before he saw a maid pushing a cart down the walkway. She stopped in front of the room the couple just exited, unlocked the door, and walked in. Within seconds she returned with the sheets and towels, threw them into her cart, and kept moving to the next room that had already been vacated. She continued this ritual until she reached the end of the walkway.

Chen told Pedro to drive over to the motel in front of the rooms the maid just left. The Chinese agent ordered the boy out of the truck and the two walked to one of the vacant rooms. When he turned the doorknob, he smiled. The door opened. He signaled for Pedro who turned off the engine. Pedro cautiously looked up and down the walkway before entering the room and joining the two.

"What are you doing?" Pedro asked with apprehension.

"We will remain here. You go back to your shop and return with my friend. When he is safely here, I will release your son and you can go on with your lives. I suggest you say good-bye to your son. If there are any problems and my friend is not delivered to me, you will never see your little boy again." He paused and said with a wicked smile, "At least not alive."

"Please do not hurt him," begged his father.

"I have no intention of hurting him but if there are problems, I will not hesitate to carry out my contingency plan," said Chen pointing the gun at the boy's head which brought on more of his tears.

Pedro held his son as tears formed in his eyes as well. "Please, I beg of you do not hurt him."

"I suggest you hurry. As you have said, 'traffic will be bad at this hour.' I would hate to think I misinterpreted your delay and killed your son merely because of an unforeseen holdup at the border."

Pedro kissed the boy one more time and raced to his truck.

CHAPTER TWENTY

San Ysidro, San Diego

Chen was still stiff from the time spent in the cramped rear seat cargo container of Pedro's truck. He continued to stretch his back, arms, and shoulders trying to loosen up. Nothing seemed to help but he hoped time and an anti-inflammatory would bring some relief.

He knew it would be several hours before Pedro returned with Song. He ate the snacks he purchased from the vending machine before they crossed the border but was hungry again. Though there was no real need to establish his alpha-dog superiority, he flashed the Diamondback semi-automatic at the young boy. Sitting in the corner of the darkened motel room in a high-backed wooden desk chair with his arms grasping his curled-up legs, fear consumed him as he looked into the throat of the silenced weapon.

"What is your name?"

Tears began to flow again.

Chen repeated, "I said, what is your name?"

Between sobs he said, "Mario."

"How old are you, Mario?"

"Eight."

"Eight is old enough in my country to work in the factories. Quit your crying. We are going to get something to eat. If you try to run, if you cause me any problems, I will kill you. I will also call my friend and tell him to kill your family. Do you understand?"

Mario hung his head, trying to hide his tears but continued to weep softly.

Chen used his free hand to grab the young boy's face and forced him to look at him. "Do you understand?"

The boy's body trembled with fear as he nodded without saying a word.

Chen shook his head in disgust. "Wipe those tears. We are going out."

Chen peeked between the divide in the thick drapes and determined it was safe. Before leaving the room, he tripped the lock so they could easily re-enter. With the number of people he saw checking out of the motel earlier in the morning, he assumed it would be a while before the housekeepers returned to prepare the rooms for the afternoon check-ins. The room would be a safe retreat for most of the morning.

As they walked out into the bright morning sun, Chen shaded his eyes. Sunglasses would also be on his list of items to purchase. He looked up and down the street with confusion. Almost every sign was in English *and* Spanish. Had he not known better he would think they were still in Mexico. The businesses were opening, and the storefronts were preparing for the locals who frequented the area merchants and those tourists who enjoyed shopping on this side of the border.

Chen had money Song gave him when they arrived in Mexico. Thinking it might be wiser to somewhat conceal his face before he began walking up and down San Ysidro Boulevard, he stopped at the first vendor they encountered and, using pesos, purchased a pair of cheap sunglasses and a San Diego Padres baseball cap. Both helped shield the sun and obscure his features.

His next stop was just up the street, a currency exchange. The building looked cheap and temporary, certainly not fortified like a bank. Chen thought it would be an easy touch for robbers, but he appreciated the distressed appearance. Sophisticated cameras wouldn't be capturing his or Mario's photo. Standing on the sidewalk at the vendor's lone window, Chen traded pesos for dollars. He kept his head low as he slid the money through the barred partition. The young Latino sitting on a stool examined the pesos and counted the currency as Chen looked on. Satisfied with the quality and count, the merchant handed U.S. bills to Chen, who quickly pocketed the cash and headed farther up the street.

As they approached the next block, a lone San Diego police officer in a marked black and white drove slowly down the street, watching the people on both sides. Chen grabbed Mario's hand and squeezed it enough to let him know not to make any sudden moves. The unit passed without incident.

Chen wanted to avoid the franchise fast-food places and those businesses that appeared to have surveillance cameras. He needed a low-rent convenience store where the items might be overpriced but security minimized. It didn't take long to find a mom-and-pop market fitting his needs.

He grabbed a bottle of Advil, a pre-packaged turkey submarine sandwich, a large bag of corn chips, and several candy bars.

"Get some food," he told Mario.

The boy stood there without moving.

"That was an order, not a suggestion."

Mario took several candy bars and a bag of potato chips. As they headed to the counter, Chen took a two-liter bottle of Pepsi from the cooler.

"Do you want something to drink?"

He nodded and selected the green apple *Sidral Mundet*, a carbonated soft drink.

"Is that good?" asked Chen.

The boy nodded and Chen took one as well. A small man with weather-worn dark skin rang up the items and placed them in a plain brown paper bag. Chen paid with his American currency and they headed back to the motel. When they stopped at the corner for the light to change, Chen noticed a street vendor selling junk trinkets and children's books.

"Do you want to get a couple of books? It's going to be a long wait for your father," he said without a hint of compassion.

Mario slowly nodded and they walked over to the heavyset woman with jet black hair pulled back into a tight bun. Dressed in a lime green blouse, she sat on a stool at the side of her cart.

"*Buenos dias, señor*," said the woman.

Chen didn't respond but told Mario, "You can have two or three books."

The little boy took only a minute to pick out two books.

The woman waved a multi-colored plastic bird attached to a stick. "Would you like one of these? They are very much fun to play with."

"No, we are fine with the books," said Chen who paid the woman with exact change.

Once again, the two approached the corner and the light changed just as they arrived. With the groceries in one hand and holding Mario's hand with his other, the two crossed the street and returned to the motel. Chen casually looked up and down the walkway and, as if they belonged, they entered the room without being noticed.

CHAPTER TWENTY-ONE

San Ysidro, San Diego

Chen sat at the window with the drapes partially opened, his weapon on his lap. Mario fell asleep on the bed reading the two books Chen purchased from the street vendor. The Advil he took several hours earlier minimized some of the discomfort and the turkey sub and chips satisfied his hunger. He was getting anxious for Song to arrive and kept looking at the clock on the nightstand. The minutes seemed to drag. A mission awaited and he was looking forward to completing the journey to Los Angeles.

Chen ruminated on Song with contempt. He saw the Spanish speaker as weak, undisciplined, and nonessential.

As Pedro pulled into the parking lot, Chen heard the V-8 turbo diesel before he spotted the F-250. Looking out the window, Chen saw Song in the back seat. Pedro pulled in front of the room. The timing was excellent. The housekeeper for this side of the motel was still at the far end of the walkway and no one noticed when the two men exited the truck.

Song stood there on the sidewalk stretching as if he were on vacation and looking forward to a comfortable night in the motel.

"Get in the room," ordered Chen from the open doorway.

When Pedro entered the room, he raced to Mario. The two hugged for a long moment telling each other of their love—tears of relief flooding their faces.

Chen understood the emotion but only from the distant past. He pulled Song to the side and whispered, "How did it go?"

"I am a little sore. It was much longer in the container than I expected. The traffic was very bad, and the wait was long, but now we are both safe on this side of the border."

"I do not care about your comfort. Did you take care of the others?" asked Chen.

Song said nothing as he angled his body away from Chen and looked to the floor.

Chen grabbed him by the arm and twisted him, so they faced each other. In a voice louder than a whisper and his anger evident, he asked, "Did you dispose of the other two?"

Song shook his head weakly, refusing to look Chen in the eye, and said, "There was no time." Pointing to Pedro, he continued, "He did not leave me alone with his wife and the little boy. I never had the opportunity and if he knew I killed them, he would never have transported me across the border. I needed to be safe." He paused for a beat and added, "We needed to be safely brought across the border."

"You fool," whispered Chen in anger.

Chen's plans changed. Since Song did not dispose of the wife and child, it would be futile to kill the father and son. The wife could tell the authorities of the two Chinese men who purchased her husband's services, and law enforcement in the United States would be alerted. In a perverse way, Song saved four lives.

Taking the high road, Chen said to Pedro, "We are men of honor. You and your son are free to return to your family."

Without comment, Pedro grabbed Mario and raced out of the room. They were gone within seconds.

As the truck pulled from the parking lot, Song said, "See, it was not so bad to let the family live. Now, I will be on my way. You no longer need me. You are safely across the border as were my instructions. My handler told me I did not have to help with your plans at the Beverly Hills mansion. I have my own plans."

Chen looked in astonishment. "How do you know my plans?"

"I was told to get you into the United States so you could use your skills setting up the mansion."

The anger was instantaneous. No one outside his immediate circle of operatives was supposed to know about the program. What idiot would share this secret with someone so weak, someone with such poor tradecraft. Incompetence was woven into the Chinese intelligence community. It was just such ineptitude that resulted in his expulsion two years earlier.

Chen turned his attention to Song. "The branch that sticks out gets trimmed," said Chen with his weapon at his side.

"What is that supposed to mean?"

As he lifted his weapon, Chen said, "A lot of problems can be resolved with a bullet."

Chen fired one round only inches from Song's head. A muted sound filled the motel room. The silenced bullet penetrated the side of the skull, exiting through the top of Song's head as a pink mist flooded the immediate area, brain and bone splattering on the near wall. With a population of 1.4 billion, Chen knew his country could easily find a replacement for the Spanish language speaker.

Before exiting the room, he grabbed the half-empty liter of Pepsi. As he closed the door, he hung the "Do Not Disturb" sign on the doorknob.

Chapter Twenty-Two

Burbank, California

The Allan and Carolyn Carpenter Foundation was an anomaly on the West Coast and particularly so in the dark blue state of California. Based in Los Angeles, it was small by traditional think tank standards. It didn't come close to competing with the Rand Corporation in Santa Monica or such giants as the Heritage Foundation, the Council on Foreign Relations, or the Hudson Institute in Washington, D.C. The United States had close to 2,000 think tanks and the conservative Carpenter Foundation was barely on the radar. It certainly wasn't a household name and was only based in L.A. because two of its principal financiers came from the hallowed halls of ultra-liberal Hollywood and provided office space in Burbank.

As demonstrated in every recent awards show coming out of Tinseltown, Hollywood had swung to the far left. Whenever celebrities gathered and took their places behind the podium, they spent more time bashing traditional American values than thanking the people who made their awards possible. Their fabled trophies became little more than battering rams as they forced home their beliefs. Though a few actors with an "R" by their name on the voting registers could still find work because they commanded an audience, many lesser-known Hollywood employees kept their politics to themselves. They only spoke of their beliefs in cloistered settings. Since it was hard enough to make it in the entertainment world, few desired to be ostracized for openly challenging the progressive party line. Those who supported the foundation were as secretive as those working an off-the-books CIA black bag operation.

The foundation's mission was twofold: assist conservative politicians at all levels of government and help produce conservative content for Hollywood. Like all foundations, it was in the business of selling ideas.

Brian Sullivan, a retired Army colonel, was busy, even on a Sunday, researching the foundation's latest project, a documentary on the Chinese enslavement of Uyghur women. Brian almost didn't take the job at the Los Angeles-based think tank because he couldn't get a carry permit. Throughout the state, CCWs, concealed carry weapon permits, were issued by the respective county sheriffs and it was never easy to get the thin paper stock permit that looked as if a teenager created it on a home computer. Pressured by local mayors and city councils, no recent sheriff would easily issue the coveted license in L.A. County.

Sully, as he was known by his friends, would just have to pray his years of on-again, off-again martial arts training would provide the necessary skills to thwart a personal attack. Twice married and divorced, the West Point graduate grew soft since retiring. At 5'10" and 215 pounds, he knew it was time to get back into the gym. Besides, he knew his military pension and salary from the think tank might not be enough to attract some struggling Hollywood starlet who would most likely end up being ex-wife number three. He needed to thin down and muscle up.

Working with General Peter Newman, the CEO of Centurion Solutions Group, Brian was viewing covert surveillance video furnished by the general and his international intelligence-gathering organization. The laptop computer screen displayed a Chinese factory where running shoes were being manufactured. Surrounded by barbed wire, cameras, and heavily armed police, the building looked more like a prison than a factory. The workers were young Uyghur girls, a religious minority, who according to Chinese officials "graduated" from detention camps.

The documentary Brian was researching would shed light on the reality that these girls were bought and sold by local governments to work for the shoe company and other American-owned businesses in the PRC. Government officials, private brokers, and company officers profited from every worker placed. American companies posing as social justice warriors, caring about macro-injustice with politically correct advertising campaigns, bowed to maximizing profits at any cost. Sully hoped to expose the human rights hypocrisy of U.S. companies benefiting from what was essentially slave labor.

CHAPTER TWENTY-THREE

Beverly Hills

It had been two years since the intelligence agents worked together in Texas. With only seventy-two-hours notice, the Chinese mission in Houston was closed in July 2020 by the previous administration. Allegations of cyber espionage and unfair trade practices, both violations of the Vienna Convention, were the basis for the extraordinary action. A member of the Senate Intelligence Committee, called the Houston consulate a "central node of the Communist Party's vast network of spies and influence operations in the United States."

Others referred to the diplomatic mission as the "epicenter" of intellectual property theft and commercial spying. The actions of the U.S. government did little to enhance an already fragile relationship between the two economic superpowers. The work beginning with Richard Nixon's efforts to engage China and the eventual granting of "Most Favored Nation" trading status was in a tenuous state. COVID-19 and a change in the White House did not result in improved relations. The world now knew China was no longer sleeping. A giant has emerged.

For Chen Ma Ho, his expulsion was immediate. He was identified as a member of China's Ministry of State Security and was forced to leave the country before the consulate was officially closed. Lin Xu Ping, who maintained a lower profile in Houston, moved to Los Angeles, assuming a similar role he held in Texas and attempted to remain below the FBI's radar. This latest singular mission, approved by Beijing, brought them together again in the United States.

Just a few blocks north of the Beverly Hills Hotel, known as the "Pink Palace" and home to the legendary Polo Lounge, the People's Republic of China purchased a 12,560 square-foot home. Using an LLC cutout to hide the Chinese government's ownership, the spacious residence with nine bedrooms, ten baths, high ceilings, and marble floors was more than just another property investment for the communist state. Hidden behind high walls and serving as a luxurious Airbnb-type retreat, the estate was also designed as a place for CCP representatives to entertain the Hollywood elite and political leaders. Only China's Ministry of State Security knew the mansion's primary purpose was more than just entertaining American notables.

Lin greeted Chen at the door as the Chinese covert operative marveled at the sheer opulence of the two-story home spreading over a half-acre of valuable California real estate. Zillow valued the property at $21,000,000 and that was in a down market as Southern California companies fled to more business-friendly states. Lin offered his hand, "I am glad you were able to make it."

Looking in all directions, gaping at the modern splendor, Chen said, "It was not easy, but I could not take a chance on facial recognition software at the airport."

"It is always easier to come in through the front door, but I understand the need for stealth. Is Song with you?"

Chen shook his head wanting to spit at the sound of the name but didn't want to damage the sheen of the marble flooring. "He knew about our mission here at the mansion. Some fool in Beijing let it slip. We were to be the only two in America aware of the project. His amateur tradecraft made him a liability. I left him dead in the motel room. I stripped him of all identification and what few valuables he possessed."

Lin smiled. "We cover San Diego. The consulate will decry his death as another Asian hate crime."

"It was a hate crime," said Chen without a smile. "I hated his arrogance and stupidity. He was worth little to us after he got me across the border."

"I have no issue with what you did. We knew from the beginning of the mission he was a throwaway."

"Will the consulate identify him, once the body is discovered?"

Lin shook his head. "He has never been in the United States. You took his identification. We may not even be able to confirm he is Chinese. We will see how the authorities play it, but I will be handling the matter if the consulate is notified. I will deflect with the accusation of a hate crime. The mere allegation quiets the press."

Walking through the expansive living room and glancing into a kitchen equaling something in a five-star restaurant, Chen said, "I see your living arrangements are a little more glamorous than we had in Houston."

Lin laughed. "I wish they let me live here. As in Houston, I have a two-bedroom apartment a few blocks from the consulate. Since I do not rate a driver, I walk on most mornings. At least, the weather here is better than in Houston. It never rains. Besides, I do not mind the exercise, and I figure the FBI assumes an espionage agent would be a little less overt."

"Yes, but did not Confucius say, 'Only the nail that protrudes gets hammered'?"

"You were not protruding in Houston—"

Chen interrupted with an imperceptible smile, "And I got hammered."

"You got hammered, but I do not think Confucius said it."

Walking out onto the patio, Lin pointed out the Olympic-size pool and sprawling outdoor pavilion with a large stone fireplace marveling anything featured in *Architectural Digest*. As the men continued the tour of the furnished home bathed in extravagance, Chen said, "I have been told you have all the technical equipment I need."

Both men were born in China after the implementation of the one-child policy designed to stem the ever-increasing population issue plaguing the People's Republic of China. Their fathers were pleased when they had sons and more pleased when their boys were selected for government service. The parents would be bursting with pride if they knew their sons were members of the PRC's elite Ministry of State Security. Known to U.S. intelligence as the MSS, it was a combination CIA and FBI responsible for foreign intelligence and counterintelligence missions. Within China, MSS served as a security and police agency suppressing internal dissent. Both men were assigned to Bureau 3, the Political and Economic Intelligence Division, headquartered in Beijing.

Chen, five years senior to Lin, was a gifted, technically trained officer who spent much of his time when previously in the U.S. secreting recording devices against targeted individuals, corporations, and government installations. Phone taps, bugs, video surveillance, illegal entries, and blackmail were all part of his arsenal.

Nodding, Lin, a human asset manager, answered, "I guess we could have used the Geek Squad from Best Buy, but the mission is too important to leave to chance or discovery. I have purchased everything you requested. It is in the garage."

"Only one?"

"Only one what?" asked Lin confused by the question.

"A place this big should have more than one garage."

Lin smiled. "Only one, but it holds five cars. We need this place wired so we capture video and audio in every corner of the house."

"It is what I do best."

Nodding with concern, Lin said, "We need to be careful. Even though the FBI's focus is on the consulate in San Francisco because of our efforts in the Silicon Valley, the Bureau has expanded its efforts here as well."

Chen let out an uncharacteristic laugh. "For all the work we did from Houston, this administration made our job easier with last year's surrender of Afghanistan. As I understand it, Beijing not only has the plans for much of this country's top technology but now the actual equipment. Billions of dollars' worth of sensitive items we were committed to stealing fell into our hands thanks to cooperative efforts with the Taliban."

"Maybe their leaders should have read Sun Tzu?" said a smiling Lin.

"The greatest victory is that which requires no battle," said Chen.

"The Taliban win was our win as well."

"What about our battle here? What do we know about our enemy?" asked Chen. "The new supervisor of the Chinese squad came from FBI Headquarters where she sat on the desk which oversaw the Houston investigation. She and the Assistant Director in Charge, who is also new, hope to duplicate that success here."

"It took many years before their White House acknowledged our efforts."

Lin sneered, "The last administration was an anomaly. This administration, like previous ones, recognizes our value to the world economy and the balance of power."

"So, the current president will not manufacture the intelligence for some government oversight committee?" asked Chen.

"Are you suggesting they manufactured the intelligence in Houston?"

"Of course not, but we were doing what every other mission does throughout the world."

Lin offered a smirk but said nothing.

"Okay, we were doing a lot more or at least, I was doing a lot more." Chen then added with a brief smile, "They do make it easy here to spy. Their open-source intelligence and calls for transparency expose more than we would ever disclose. Their freedom has a price."

"And we are willing to pay that price," responded Lin.

"Big money buys big secrets," said Chen aware of his success while in Houston.

"How about a swim? We have suits upstairs and some Yanjing on ice."

"Will there be any other entertainment?" asked Chen.

"Not now, but we have places set up in Monterey Park if you are seeking companionship."

Chen smiled, ready to relax and enjoy his first day back in America before the real work began. "Have you provided me a driver's license and identification?"

"Michael Yang has supplied you with a proper legend," said Lin, pleased he delivered on all Chen's demands.

Michael Yang was born in the United States to immigrant parents: his childhood normal, his education impressive. He was given every opportunity to succeed and succeed he did. His family was proud of his many successes, though a failed marriage to a dutiful wife from his parents' hometown baffled them. He won awards for his charity and civic accomplishments. He was recognized by the mayor and featured in the Sunday *Los Angeles Times*. By all accounts, he was living the American dream.

But Michael Yang, U.S. citizen, was caught by a foreign dangle. The Chinese intelligence services routinely scoured pornographic websites identifying purveyors and purchasers. Yang's name popped up as a frequent purchaser from several sites catering to men attracted to underage females. With very little background investigation needed, he was identified as a potential agent, valuable to the PRC. He was a prosperous entrepreneur in a business that could be utilized on many different fronts. More importantly, he frequented a world of successful and respected men with aberrant desires—Americans who could be easily exploited.

Rather than confront Yang directly seeking his cooperation, the MSS did what it did best. It offered a "dangle," an underage girl with whom Yang could engage in sex. Yang bit and one evening in a West Los Angeles motel room, he was caught on video tape molesting a thirteen-year-old female runaway. It was a binary choice: he could cooperate with the country of his ancestors or risk public exposure and humilia-tion. With no real love for America, no sense of patriotism, no loyalty to anyone but himself, the decision was easy. He chose to maintain the status quo with one exception. He brought a new partner onboard, The People's Republic of China.

Yang Printing expanded to include the production of falsified doc-uments and counterfeit identification for Chinese operatives in the U.S. Thanks to Yang's work, Chen Ma Ho could travel freely throughout Los Angeles for as long as he needed before the mission was complete.

Chen nodded, "Good, let us swim first. Then we can head out for an evening of entertainment."

CHAPTER TWENTY-FOUR

Monterey Park, California

There was no easy way to get from Beverly Hills to anywhere. The freeway system didn't come close to touching the city limits of one of the nation's most famous municipalities. Time considerations were always a factor, requiring the allocation of thirty to forty-five minutes just to get to any of the freeways traversing much of Los Angeles.

Since Chen had spent little time in L.A., Lin drove down Sunset Boulevard through Hollywood to the 101. The glacial pace of the traffic was annoying, but it allowed for seeing some of the sights so commonly associated by outsiders with Los Angeles: Whiskey a Go Go, where the Doors got their start; Chateau Marmont, where John Belushi overdosed; The Laugh Factory whose first performer was Richard Pryor; even Hollywood High School whose graduates included Carol Burnett, Cher, Judy Garland, Mickey Rooney, and other media notables. Chen was familiar with all the names because of the decadent Western entertainment he secretly consumed.

Once they got on the 101, they headed east toward the San Bernardino Freeway and Monterey Park.

"Have you been to this location?" asked Chen.

"No, they just opened at this spot a couple of weeks ago."

"Are they paying?"

"Yes, just as in the other apartments, Franklin is collecting $2,500 a month."

Chen smiled. "They pay us to do what we want them to do."

"What a country!" said Lin.

Both laughed out loud.

It took almost an hour to get to the apartment complex near Garvey Avenue and Atlantic Boulevard.

Chen and Lin were pleased to see the complex was fenced, needing the combination to the security gate or to be buzzed in by a resident. Customers preferred a location they believed to be more secure, at least delaying a breach by law enforcement until everyone was prepared. Though neither man nor their government was directly profiting from the business, more customers meant a continual pull at the thread of America's moral fabric. Without a shot ever being fired, the Chinese intelligence community recognized a nation could be most easily taken from within.

The townhouse-style apartment complex was maintained; no chipped paint, no overflowing trash cans, no debris strewn across the neatly trimmed grass surrounding the narrow walkway to each unit. It was quiet, more conducive for business. Only the noise of the street traffic a block away broke the serenity.

The two men approached the front door, painted fire engine red, an appropriate Chinese color, but maybe ironic, for the business they were about to enter.

Ben greeted the men with a bow and a welcoming smile. "Mr. Michael said you would be coming. Thank you."

Though each could speak Mandarin, English was the preferred language. Since many of the customers were American, it was important to continually practice. Hospitality meant profit.

The downstairs was neat with minimal comfortable furnishings, a loveseat, two overstuffed chairs, and a big screen TV attached to the far wall. The furniture's muted colors were unusual for an Asian household, but most visitors would not be spending much time downstairs. The action occurred upstairs in the three bedrooms.

Three young women, two Asian and a Hispanic, remained seated at a table near the kitchen. They said nothing, averting their eyes, not scrutinizing the strangers.

Looking at Chen, Ben said, "All my girls are very good, but many Asian and American men like my new Mexican daughters."

Though his "Mexican daughters" were from El Salvador and Nicaragua, neither Ben nor his customers cared.

Chen looked over the three. All had black shoulder-length hair and were slightly built, almost waif-like. "Do your daughters speak English?"

"They all know a few words. But few men engage them for talking."

"Have you had your daughters long?"

An astute businessman, Ben recognized the need to expand opportunities for his customers. "My Chinese daughters have been with me for several months. My Mexican daughters arrived three weeks ago. I traded two daughters for my new arrivals. I think they will provide a variety most customers will like. They are very well behaved and appreciate what they have to do to repay me for my generosity."

Chen dealt with men like Ben. Though prostitution was only legal in certain counties in Nevada, the business flourished throughout the States. "How long have you been in America?"

"I have been here many years but only recently moved to Los Angeles. I have been working in San Francisco, Sacramento, and Phoenix. The work there was very good, but I was told there was a greater need for the services here."

Chen nodded. "I am new to Los Angeles, so I am unfamiliar with their needs, but I believe you will succeed."

As Chen was saying this, a Hispanic girl was making her way down the stairs, followed by a middle-aged Asian man who looked satisfied following his upstairs adventure.

"How was your encounter?" asked Ben.

"It was most unusual."

With that, the Mexican girl presented a paper cup filled with water to the man. The presentation represented the Asian culture as she bowed and pushed forward the cup with both hands.

The customer quickly drank the water, handing back the used cup to the girl.

Ben ushered the man to the door inquiring as to whether he would return.

Offering a huge smile, the man replied, "yes, soon."

Turning to Chen and Lin, Ben asked, "Would you like to try one of my daughters?"

Chen spoke for both. "No, our tastes are little older, but we will see you again soon."

CHAPTER TWENTY-FIVE

MONDAY, APRIL 25
Westwood, Los Angeles

"You can go on in," said Barbara Nolan.

"Am I late?" asked Jake.

Barbara looked across the room at a large clock centered on the wall above the couch.

"No, you're actually three minutes early. The other three are already in there."

"A couple of lions in the den to take on the beleaguered Christian?"

"Don't inflate your self-worth, Jake. These are more like pussycats, and we're still trying to teach Boy Wonder to use the sandbox."

"Wow! I wonder what you say behind my back."

"Just get in there and behave yourself. If you play this right you can coast for a few more months before they figure out you are wasting our tax dollars," she paused, then added, "again."

Jake walked through the anteroom and headed into the ADIC's office. As he entered, no one rose and without even a greeting, Valerie Carlisle said, "Take a seat we were just talking about you."

Somewhat strangely, the chair directly in front of Carlisle was open and the chairs on either side were occupied by the prim and proper. Jake sat, knowing he might be auditioning for an undercover assignment and knew if he didn't get it, he would be working applicants or poring over ledger sheets on a bank fraud squad. At least for the near term, he planned on obeying orders and presenting himself as a professional.

Carlisle began, "Do you know Charlene Taylor, Timothy O'Connor, and Tonya Rodriguez?"

"No," said Jake reaching to his left toward the female dressed like management and offering his hand, "I'm Jake Kruse."

"Charlene Taylor."

Jake then turned awkwardly in his seat and offered his hand, "Jake Kruse."

"Timothy O'Connor."

"Nice to meet you, Tim."

"Timothy," said the FBI poster boy dressed in a blue suit with a paisley print silk tie.

Oh brother.

Finally, Jake extended his hand to Tonya, "Jake Kruse."

"Tonya Rodriguez."

Jake noted she was less than enthusiastic in her greeting, dressed more street agent than administrator; skinny jeans and a baggy sweater designed to conceal a weapon.

The ADIC began, "I received the paperwork from Thursday's psychological evaluation, and it looks like you passed. You must be right. You can fake sanity. I'm sure Charles Hafner will be disappointed."

There was not even a hint at a smile as the words left her mouth. Jake said nothing, sitting there stoically, biting his tongue to prevent some smart-ass comment from slipping through his lips and destroying an opportunity to get out of the office for an extended UC assignment. He had seen it before. Undercover agents, though likely the most valuable investigative tool in the Bureau's arsenal, were underappreciated and viewed by some in management as a liability. Though they were in fact the eye behind the sniper scope deciding whether to pull the trigger, they were almost viewed as a necessary evil. Jake didn't really care how he was perceived as long as he was able to pursue the adrenaline rush. It never failed. Not always appreciated by upper management, those same administrators were quick to take credit for a successful UC operation, fighting for shine time on TV.

Carlisle focused on Jake, her penetrating eyes underscoring the seriousness of the discussion. "Everything we are about to discuss this morning remains in this room. If you decide not to take the assignment, you may not discuss this with anyone. Do you understand?"

Jake nodded.

"I don't want just a nod. I want a verbal confirmation."

Is this being recorded? Somewhat confused by all the cloak and dagger, Jake said, "I understand. Nothing we discuss this morning goes beyond these four walls."

"If you don't take the assignment, nothing leaves this room. If you take the assignment, obviously, all of this will be discussed in greater detail during the course of the investigation."

"Of course."

"Charlene and Timothy are on the FCI side of the house, the Chinese squad. She's been in the division for little over a year now and came to us from Headquarters where she sat on the Chinese desk. She's handling the desk here."

Foreign counterintelligence was a unique animal within the FBI, differing from the criminal responsibilities most people assume when hearing "FBI." It wasn't bank robberies, kidnappings, white-collar or organized crime. The focus was foreign penetration of our government, military, and economic institutions. Some in D.C. called for a complete separation of the two factions, requiring distinct agencies reporting to independent government bureaucrats.

Every Director since Hoover fought to maintain organizational integrity arguing the crossover in investigations required both houses reporting to a single director. Within the Bureau, the squads were separated from the rest of the office by secured doors requiring a code to enter. The FBI's Counterintelligence Division was housed within the National Security Branch. Known inhouse as the "Secret Squirrel Division," most agents who worked in the Criminal Division avoided FCI like the latest COVID variant.

Though the term "counterintelligence" seemed like investigations reserved for the Cold War, the division's work increased over the past several years, particularly with China targeting our most valuable secrets. It was no longer reserved for military intelligence or weapons technology. It was more than bombs, bullets, and weapons of mass destruction designed to kill Americans. Beyond protecting the secrets of the U.S. Intelligence Community, the Counterintelligence Division was tasked with protecting the nation's critical assets, like advanced technologies and sensitive information in all aspects of our economy to include banking, manufacturing, finance, and public health.

China was attempting to steal trade secrets which impacted the economy. To China, "R&D" meant "rip off and duplicate." Any shortcut was viewed as an asset. Just as the Japanese learned to reverse-engineer our cars decades ago, China was attempting to reverse-engineer our entire technological community. Why spend millions developing expertise and know-how when it's cheaper to just steal it? Universities and businesses were fair game. Much of the espionage was cyber-based.

Now it looked like Jake was going to be in the middle of a new venture, taking him past the boundaries of the Criminal Division.

"Charlene and Timothy need a certified undercover agent. Right now, you are the only agent available that fits their needs. Frankly, if I had someone else, I would probably move him or her into the slot, but like I said, you're the only agent available in the division and I'm not willing to expend division funding to bring in an outsider from another office."

Not quite the ringing endorsement Jake expected based upon his career successes. He thought Carlisle was going for the Olivia Knox brass ring, but even without her full support, it beat the applicant or bank fraud squad alternatives.

"What exactly do you have in mind?" asked Jake.

Charlene Taylor, the supervisor, rotated in her chair toward Jake and began, "We've recently come across some intelligence identifying a local businessman with ties to a Chinese I/O who previously operated in Houston before we closed the consulate."

Jake knew the initials I/O meant intelligence officer. *Maybe this could develop into something.*

"We believe in excess of 3,000 businesses in the U.S. are providing cover for China's Ministry of State Security activity. A Chinese American businessman, Michael Yang, owns a print shop in West L.A. and had numerous phone contacts and business dealings with Chen Ma Ho who worked out of the Houston Chinese consulate. Chen was expelled two years ago for suspected espionage activities here in the United States. Yang is also associated with Lin Xu Ping who works at the consulate here in L.A. Due to fortuitous circumstances recently falling into our laps, we have an opportunity to insert an undercover agent as an office supplies sales rep."

Jake smiled. "A sales rep? I can play profoundly ordinary. I know how to talk about the unimportant until nobody cares, and nobody remembers."

Charlene continued, "We are in the preliminary stages of this investigation and are seeking probable cause for a FISA warrant."

There were two types of court-approved wire taps at the FBI's disposal. One was under the auspices of the Foreign Intelligence Surveillance Act of 1978. The seven-member FISA court met twice a month to approve requests from the intelligence agencies, including the FBI. The purpose of a FISUR, as it was called in the Bureau, was solely to gather intelligence. The requirements for obtaining such an order were less restrictive than the criminal wiretaps issued under Title III authority granted under the Omnibus Crime Control and Safe Streets Act of 1968.

Thanks to Comey and the Russian collusion fiasco, the American public was all too familiar with FISA.

Knowing it was about power, not some abstract higher good, Timothy O'Connor struggled to assert his authority as case agent and needed to include, "The faster you can provide me the intel, the faster we can be up on the phones."

"How do I take the first step?" said Jake.

Carlisle then looked to Rodriguez and said, "Why don't you explain your source."

Tonya slowly crossed her legs before she began speaking. It was almost as if she were hesitant to get involved and wanted to be any-where but in this meeting.

"I'm not on the squad. I work child exploitation. Two weeks ago, we picked off Preston Brookside who downloaded some very graphic images of men having sex with pre-adolescent girls. Brookside owns an office supply business here on the Westside. After confessing to down-loading the images, a confession we really didn't need because all the images remained on his hard drive, he decided to play a 'get out of jail' card."

Jake interrupted, "We are letting a damn pervert walk?"

"It wasn't my choice," responded Tonya, a hint of anger in her voice.

Charlene Taylor added, "He provided information about one of his customers that may have greater implications than mere pornographic images."

The ADIC jumped back into the conversation, "Obviously, Jake, we take kiddie porn seriously, but this information provided by Brookside could be very important and have national security impli-cations. He is not getting a complete pass. If everything pans out, he's looking at probation, but probably not jail time. With a plea, he'll have to register as a sex offender."

"So, what's his information?"

Before Charlene Taylor or Timothy O'Connor could explain, the ADIC said, "Michael Yang runs Yang Printing. It's not your run-of-the-mill print shop. It's much more than business cards and PTA fliers. This is a major, highly successful operation. He services many of the inde-pendent production companies reproducing their scripts and produces most of the political campaign materials you see every election cycle. Though he stays somewhat under the radar, he is a very influential cog in the Los Angeles political machine. He has been in some of the largest campaigns both at a state and local level. Though he hasn't made much of a dent on the national scene, he has been involved in area congressional elections. His influence has been substantial in the last two mayoral campaigns and last year's gubernatorial recall effort. I guess you could call him a force in local politics."

"Do you believe this Michael Yang is an intelligence officer?" asked Jake.

Valerie Carlisle shook her head. "He's second generation. Based upon what we have seen so far, we believe he is an asset reporting to Chen or Lin."

In FCI speak, an asset was the Bureau's equivalent to a CHS, a confidential human source, an informant, or cooperating witness, not a trained espionage agent.

"So how does Brookside fit in?"

Carlisle looked to Charlene Taylor for the answer. "Brookside owns an office supply company. Yang is one of his largest clients. Brookside supplies all the office needs for Yang who in turn supplies the consulate and every political campaign in which Yang has a financial interest."

"I still don't see how this involves espionage."

The supervisor continued, "Brookside has been present at Yang's office when Lin Xu Ping was there. Based upon information Brookside has furnished, we believe Lin is a Chinese intelligence officer working out of the Chinese Consulate here in L.A."

Jake's eyes opened wide, "Whoa, that sounds big time, but I thought the consulate was in San Francisco."

"There is one here in L.A. It's in the Wilshire District near 6th and Vermont."

"What information do you have that makes you think Lin's an I/O?"

Once again Timothy O'Connor asserted himself into the conversation. "Brookside has been present in the office after hours when he, Yang, and Lin have been smoking Cuban cigars."

Jake laughed out loud. "I guess I'm in trouble. I've smoked a few of those myself."

O'Connor asked, "But were yours smuggled into the United States through the use of diplomatic pouches?"

"No, mine came across the border thanks to targets of my last investigation."

O'Connor continued, "Lin has bragged in Yang's office while Brookside has been present that he can get almost anything into the United States."

Jake cocked his head questioning the importance of this supposed I/O. "It sounds as if Lin has a tendency to run his mouth. That doesn't seem like great tradecraft for a well-trained intelligence officer."

O'Connor nodded. "I would agree, but according to Brookside, once Lin gets a little too much mao-tai or Fenjiu in his system, his lips are loosened, and he probably talks more than he should."

"So, what's my role in all this?"

Tonya stepped in. "Preston has decided to take an early semi-retirement. Thanks to his wife's money, inherited from her father, they own a nice place up in Big Bear. He's decided to begin spending more time in the mountains and is bringing in a new sales rep."

"And I'm that sales rep?" asked Jake.

"Yes," said the ADIC.

"Sounds fairly simple. It won't take that much backstopping. I've been sheep-dipped at Headquarters with several covers. This one won't require much. Probably just a good credit score which is easy. No need for a criminal history or anything fancy. My last cover documented stays in a couple of cities enough to get me an apartment and utilities," said Jake.

All agreed. Just a routine citizen back story.

"I'm ready to green-light the operation," said the ADIC.

"I'll just need to spend a few days with Brookside. I'll try not to wipe the floor with his pervert ass as he teaches me everything he can about reams of paper, bulk pencil sales, and paperclips."

For the first time in the conversation, a smile crossed Tonya Rodriguez's face.

Chapter Twenty-Six

Agoura Hills, Los Angeles

As Natasha walked out of the kitchen with two plates of pie topped with vanilla ice cream, she said, "What's with the beard?"

"I'm going L.A. grunge for my next fashion shoot. Eurotrash is still the rage."

As she dropped off the pie and returned to the kitchen for the iced tea, Jake asked, "How are you and Joey getting along?"

"We're doing well," she said with a slight hesitation.

"You don't say that with much conviction."

Sitting at the table, she brushed a stray hair behind her ear, just like Katie used to do. Jake smiled at the familiar mannerism.

"I know people mean well, but one of the ladies at church yesterday morning said something that set me off and it's still eating at me."

"Did you clock her?"

"No, of course not."

"You want me to have her whacked? I know a guy."

"Yeah," Natasha said with a faint smile, "I bet you do. It's not that. I'm not even sure she knows how upsetting her words were. But the sermon was about Christians grieving and how it's not the same for us as it is for those who don't believe."

Jake didn't say anything as he took a bite of the strawberry pie and recalled Paul's words in the Bible in his first letter to the Thessalonians.

"I didn't say anything, but I still grieve, and it's been almost four years since Joe died. I know healing will come but for now I need to live with my pain. Finding someone new won't diminish the loss, just as moving forward won't diminish the memories Joe and I shared for far too short a time.

"Sometimes I think grief is so deep it can never be erased. It just wasn't losing my best friend. I lost the life Joe and I planned to share and the family we planned to have. The pain is personal as it is for everyone. We all grieve in our own way. Being a Christian makes it different than, as the Bible says, 'those without hope,' but it still hurts. There's an empty place in my heart.

"Someday, I'll be ready to write a new chapter in my life, but that doesn't mean the early parts of the book are forgotten."

As a tear tracked down her cheek, there was much Jake wanted to say, but this was not the time.

When Natasha said, "Jake, there is a weekly Bible study I have been attending that meets tonight. If I can get the tenth-grader gal next door to babysit for Joey, would you please come with me?

The feelings intensifying in him were not the same feelings she was experiencing. An awkward silence hung over the room until he replied, "I've never been to a Bible study, but I will be glad to accompany you to wherever you want to go."

Chapter Twenty-Seven

MONDAY, MAY 2
Santa Monica, California

With the undercover operation approved, Jake would restrict his trips to the Westwood office. It was just too dangerous. He might be spotted by a target of the investigation or someone with whom he might have contact during the op. Since there was a belief Jake might eventually encounter a Chinese intelligence officer, there was another fear. It made sense China would have surveillance cameras focused on the entrance to the Wilshire Boulevard federal building hoping to identify the agents working there. Years ago, it wasn't as big an issue because there were few buildings with direct sight to the entrance. The FBI kept a constant vigil, sweeping the area for video surveillance devices, figuring the Russians, our biggest nemesis at the time, might be tracking the employees. With advanced facial recognition technology, it was virtually impossible to guarantee the anonymity of the agents going to and from the office and the garage.

It's not unreasonable to assume if Jake could gain entry to the target's inner circle and confirm China's participation, the PRC would be using facial recognition software to match up Jake with anyone entering the federal building. In anticipation of that ever happening in any of his undercover operations, he rehearsed his response—he went to the passport office located on the premises.

This afternoon, Jake was meeting with Tonya Rodriguez and, for the first time, Preston Brookside. He and Jake needed to prepare their back story to successfully introduce Jake to Michael Yang, the print shop guru, who apparently had his hands in the muck and the mire.

Tonya picked a deli in Santa Monica's Third Street Promenade, three blocks of open-air shopping and restaurants just a five-iron shot from the Pacific Ocean. The Promenade was blocked off from vehicle traffic, so it was easy to navigate from store to store. The Seaside Market Deli located just off Wilshire Boulevard had outdoor seating as well as limited seating in the rear of the restaurant.

It was two o'clock in the afternoon and Tonya staked out a place in the back of the cafe. She was already seated when Jake arrived.

"It's just you? Where's our boy?" said Jake as he took a seat across from her.

Before Tonya could answer, a college-age server approached the table offering a broad smile displaying perfect teeth framed by her year-round tan and shoulder-length blonde hair. "Hi, Tonya, what can I get you guys?"

"Hi, Kilee, bring me an iced tea and an order of shrimp nachos which we will split. Jake, what do you want to drink?" said Tonya taking charge of the ordering.

"I guess if we're having shrimp nachos you better bring me a diet something."

Kilee smiled hesitantly, "Diet Pepsi?"

"Yeah, Diet Pepsi's fine."

After Kilee left the table, Jake cautiously asked, "You must be a regular here. She doesn't know what you do, does she?"

"No, she thinks I'm a psychologist and if I do bring a source here, she just assumes they have a personality disorder I am trying to help them resolve."

Jake laughed. "Any hint as to my disorder?"

Tonya placed both her hands on the table interlacing her fingers and leaned forward. Almost in a whisper she said, "I've asked around and it doesn't appear as if I can limit you to just one. Management throws around terms like borderline personality disorder, narcissistic, antisocial, mood swings, impulsive, arrogance. Others assume a dissociative identity disorder."

Displaying a manufactured frown, Jake said, "Man, you're starting to hurt my feelings. One of my alters is highly sensitive."

Tonya nodded, "You might take up a couple chapters in a postgraduate textbook."

Without a hint of a smile, Jake responded, "You must have gone back in and talked to the ADIC after we concluded our meeting. I'm not sure she's sold on my sanity. Is this all part of a ruse to get me fired? Fake a UC op and see how I screw it up."

Tonya stifled a laugh and said, "Maybe we should add PPD, paranoid personality disorder. Actually, if we're going down this rabbit hole, I'd rather target management and their behavioral aberrations instead of you."

Jake was beginning to like Tonya. Anyone who questioned management's sanity was on his good list until they proved otherwise. He liked to joke that if you're in management or have management aspirations, you have to prove you belong. If you're a street agent dedicated to taking out the bad guys, you have to prove you don't belong. It looked like Tonya might have made the "belong list."

"I will tell you though I've been warned you've learned to evade Bureau protocol," she said unapologetically.

Jake gave a slight shrug of his shoulders. "I used to try to follow the manual, then I learned it was written by idiots."

"That can lead to some issues. I have a family and need this job. Don't shower me in your sewage without at least a heads-up."

"I admit I've participated in every bad decision I've ever made. My life isn't a Hallmark movie, but I'll keep you clear of the swill."

"Fair enough," she said.

"So, where's our boy?"

Once again before she could answer, Kilee returned to the table with the drinks and shrimp nachos smothered in melted cheese and the deli's secret sauce. Kilee gave Jake an extra-long look as if sizing him up to determine his psychological issues. He met her inquisitive gaze with an irreverent Jack Nicholson smile, causing her to abruptly leave.

"I told Preston to be here around 2:30. I wanted to meet you a few minutes early just so we could talk."

Before Jake reached for the nachos, he picked up his Diet Pepsi and offered a toast to Tonya who smiled as they "clinked" paper cups. "To all who serve in the defense of our values."

"I like that, thanks."

"I meant it," came Jake's reply.

Tonya got down to the business at hand. "I've worked sources, but usually they aren't registered sex offenders or about to be. Although Brookside was one of the less egregious men I've arrested, I still wasn't too excited to give him an opportunity to work off his beef. The images he downloaded were pretty bad."

After swallowing a couple of chips, Jake said, "These are good."

Tonya nodded and before she reached for the chips said, "But the Chinese card Brookside was willing to play took the decision out of my hands. When he gave me the information, I was obligated to let the FCI guys know. I was hoping it wouldn't amount to anything, but they jumped on the name of Brookside's cigar-toting Asian friend, Lin Xu Ping. Then it was just a matter of trying to work out the best deal for the government and Brookside. What makes this interesting and forgotten by the other side of the house is Brookside thinks Michael Yang is into little girls."

Jake put down his drink. "What! Why didn't that come up in the ADIC's office?"

"I was playing by their rules. I was told to focus on the I/O not Yang's possible kiddie porn fetish."

"Have you pulled his records?"

"I was told I couldn't get a subpoena because of the FCI conflict. I think there's a fear if we identify this guy's criminal actions too soon, it won't allow us to explore the espionage aspects of the investigation which is their bigger concern."

Jake shook his head. "What did your AUSA say about this new wrinkle with Yang?"

"She doesn't know. I was told not to discuss it outside the Bureau."

"Thanks for telling me. I need to understand the routines and habits of everyone involved. It reduces our chances of failure. We find the flaws and weaknesses rather than concentrating on their advertised strengths. I'll want to explore Yang's issues with Brookside. All of this can play into my cover story, though at this point, I'm not sure how."

Tonya slowly nodded. "I understand the Chinese implications and the danger that country plays in our national security, but it's personal for me. I have children. I don't like seeing sexual deviants skate."

"Did you have any trouble with the AUSA going along with Brookside's agreement?"

"No, she agreed to the probation as long as he registered."

"Is that a public registration?" asked Jake knowing some RSOs, registered sex offenders, aren't known to their neighbors

"No, it would be a class III only available to law enforcement. I think the way he's playing it, even his wife is unaware of what went down. She still thinks this is some white-collar matter. She's a piece of work and will probably cut him off at the knees, if she knew what really happened."

"If the images are as bad as you suggested, I'd be willing to cut off something other than his knees."

Offering a smile, Tonya said, "It may come to that." After taking a sip of her iced tea, and as she reached for more nachos, she said, "And speaking of degenerates, here he comes now."

Jake stood as Tonya introduced them. After a quick exchange of pleasantries, they both sat, Brookside with his back to the door, Tonya and Jake practicing situational awareness.

Before they could get started, Kilee approached, asking Brookside what he wanted to drink and offered to bring refills for Tonya and Jake. Kilee gave Tonya a brief inquisitive look as if to ask, "Are you counseling two sociopaths at the same time?"

Tonya betrayed nothing to the server as Brookside ordered Pepsi, full strength. Jake silently noted if anyone should be drinking diet, it should be Brookside.

After a second plate of shrimp nachos and more drinks arrived, Brookside and Jake worked out a cover story as to why Jake would be taking over sales responsibilities for Michael Yang's business.

Before ending the afternoon meeting, Jake asked about Yang and the basis for Brookside's belief he was into little girls.

"We traded images."

"That's it?" asked Jake.

Brookside shrugged and nodded.

CHAPTER TWENTY-EIGHT

TUESDAY, MAY 3
Agoura Hills, Los Angeles

Jake and Natasha were relaxing on the couch watching a rerun of *Longmire*. Though he knew the show was filmed in New Mexico but set in Wyoming, there were times he longed for the wide-open spaces. Sometimes, he wished he could find a deputy position in a small Western town, fairly crime free except for a homicide every week. Maybe even Cabot Cove, a small oceanside town in Maine with a murder rate rivaling Chicago, where Jessica Fletcher solved a weekly slaying in *Murder, She Wrote.*

"I'm thinking of buying a ranch in Wyoming. Maybe I could find a sheriff's position and wear the boots full-time," said Jake, with Joey asleep beside him.

"And leave the crowded freeways and shopping malls of Southern California? No way," said Natasha with a smile.

Jake's undercover phone erupted with the "Folsom Prison Blues" ring tone. It was on the table on the other side of the couch.

"Do you want me to get your bat phone?" asked Natasha.

"Please," whispered Jake, hoping not to disturb Joey.

As she picked up the phone and looked at the caller ID, she saw "Tonya" displayed. "Is this your new girlfriend?"

Jake responded with a smirk, "Probably one of them. Who is it?"

"Tonya."

"I'll take it," he said as she handed him the cellphone.

He awkwardly answered the phone on the fourth ring before it went to voicemail. "Yeah," whispered Jake.

"It's Tonya, are you okay?"

In a soft voice, Jake responded, "Yes, why wouldn't I be?"

"Why are you whispering?"

Jake answered, "Because I'm cradling a preschooler and he's asleep."

"Oh, I'm sorry. I didn't think you had any fatherly instincts."

"Is there a reason why you're calling?"

"Yes. Did you hear about Timothy O'Connor?"

"No, what happened to Boy Wonder?"

"He just got transferred."

"What?" said Jake, a little too loudly as Joey jumped before nodding back off to sleep.

"Yep. He just got orders back to Headquarters. He picked up a supervisory slot on one of the Chinese desks back there."

Jake offered a muted laugh, "I thought he was going to ride this case to the top. I didn't realize he would get there without saddling up. Have they named a new case agent?"

"Not yet. Charlene Taylor, the supervisor, just called me and asked if I wanted to transfer off the kiddie porn squad and bring the informant with me."

"And your answer?"

"Not just no, but hell no."

Jake laughed. "So, they're looking for a case agent?"

"Yep?"

"I think I have just the man. Should I call Taylor or go straight to the top?"

"You got more time than I do and probably more pull. If you have someone in mind, I'd go straight to the top."

"Thanks, Tonya, for the heads-up. I need to make a few phone calls."

✕ ✕ ✕

After Jake ended the call, he immediately punched in Tyrone Greer's number. The former Ranger answered on the third ring. Jake turned on the sales charm, using the skills he often employed while convincing targets of undercover operations to engage in criminal admissions. Jake laid out all the positives for the two of them teaming up again. "Salt and pepper and condiments to be named later."

By the time the call was over, Rone wasn't sure he should have answered the phone. As much as he wanted to get away from the ledgers he was poring over every day on the bank fraud squad, he was still debating whether he wanted to move over to the "Secret Squirrel Division" of the FBI. Agents who went to the "dark side" were known to never be heard from again. For some agents, it was like an early retirement. Out of sight, out of mind. They merely spent their days interviewing foreign travelers and eating in ethnic restaurants. For others, it meant never being able to transfer back to the criminal side of the house. But Greer was looking forward to working with Jake and figured with his SWAT team leadership and experience, he could return to the Criminal Division after the undercover operation terminated.

Every undercover operation required an accountant. In Tyrone Greer, the FBI got a two-banger. He could serve as the case agent managing the day-to-day operations of the investigation and perform the minimal accounting responsibilities. Because of the nature of this UC op, there wouldn't be any project-generated income like some investigations produce. The accounting responsibilities for this approved operation would not be that arduous.

When undercover operatives were handling millions of dollars in money laundering investigations or producing income through government-sanctioned criminal operations, the accounting tasks required a full-time specially trained agent. As Jake explained the assignment to Rone, there was little chance Jake would be making any money. Brookside wasn't paying a salary or sales commission for whatever work Jake generated. The accounting duties would merely be seeing that routine expenses such as travel and entertainment were within budget and properly expensed. Jake even promised to encourage his target to pick up the tab whenever possible, citing tax deduction opportunities. Rone wasn't grabbing at all the carrots being dangled in the slick sales pitch, but he was ready to sign up.

Jake promised his first call in the morning would be to the ADIC Valerie Carlisle, then maybe a courtesy call to Charlene Taylor, the squad supervisor. Carlisle wielded the power. If she signed off on Greer hopping the fence to FCI, he was in. Jake might even play the "career-enhancing" card for Greer, which apparently Carlisle liked to play.

CHAPTER TWENTY-NINE

THURSDAY, MAY 12
Los Angeles

Tyrone Greer spent the next couple days shadowing Timothy O'Connor while coming up to speed with the investigation. Because Preston Brookside brought this issue to the attention of the FBI only within the past couple weeks, the file was not papered with many reports. Mostly, what O'Connor did was run preliminary background information on Michael Yang and obtain his bank and phone records. The squad analyst was busy evaluating those records and would prepare her initial report in a few more days.

O'Connor had one foot out the door and couldn't wait to get back to Headquarters, what he referred to as Mecca. O'Connor had only been an agent five years. The Brown graduate with a degree in East Asian Studies spent his first year on a bank robbery squad before transferring to the Chinese counterintelligence unit. That year on banks provided a little street experience but not much. Basically, it familiarized him with the necessary paperwork to prepare a criminal case for trial; important knowledge for any FBI agent, but of little use to someone more interested in the James Bond stuff of identifying those hoping to steal our secrets.

His time on the FCI squad involved mainly interviewing Chinese students at UCLA, Pepperdine, and USC, tech executives dealing with the Chinese, and U.S. citizens who traveled to Hong Kong and China for business or pleasure. While the work helped him with his

Mandarin language skills and a greater appreciation for Chinese culture, it did little in ferreting out spies. It wasn't for a lack of enthusiasm.

Timothy O'Connor was a true believer and willingly educated Tyrone Greer on what he deemed "the Chinese menace." China became a communist state in 1949 following a civil war led by Mao Zedong. After Mao assumed power, becoming a communist dictator, he joked about killing thirty million people in his own country. "We have so many people. We can afford to lose a few." With what Mao described as his "great leap forward," even greater numbers of Chinese died. Never relinquishing power, under his rule, sixty-five million Chinese were murdered or starved to death. It is said "the bigger the state, the smaller the god." With Mao, the state became a god. The individual was nothing.

O'Connor railed about the Chinese communist government's inability to control the deadly coronavirus and its failure to warn the rest of the world. Thanks to their willful neglect or outright sabotage, more than 950,000 Americans were already dead from the virus.

But what O'Connor saw even more threatening were the trained Marxists operating here, just like communist revolutionaries in Russia and China during the 1900s. These radicals captured the attention of the media and demonized every attribute that made the United States the greatest nation on earth. He watched these leftists incite violence, divide people based on the color of their skin, impose identity politics, and terrorize the public with arson, looting, and demands to "defund the police." Though his education at Brown was "liberal," O'Connor understood the goal of socialism was communism. As Rone noted, "The boy could preach it."

Rone appreciated O'Connor's enthusiasm for the job. There were two types of agents in the FBI, those who worked and those who didn't. O'Connor was a worker and established some early career goals. He was recruited by the CIA while still at Brown but chose the FBI in deference to his father who spent a career chasing Russian spies during the Cold War. Thanks to his own studies and his father's influence,

Timothy recognized Communist China as America's #1 adversary. Hence, his concentration at Brown on East Asian Studies.

He thought heading back to the Hoover Building would allow him to help counter the threat posed by the PRC on a national and international level rather than just what was happening in Southern California. O'Connor believed he could make a difference in the slot at the Headquarters which could also vault him to his ultimate career goal: legal attaché, or as it's referred to in the FBI, "Legat" at the American Embassy in Beijing.

Greer never heard a young agent ordered to Headquarters say anything positive about the experience. In fact, most agents complained about the bureaucratic treadmill but knew they had to get on it if they planned to ride the incline to FBI management hierarchy. After spending a few days with O'Conner, Rone sincerely hoped the Brown grad could fulfill his dreams.

CHAPTER THIRTY

MONDAY, MAY 9
West Los Angeles

Usually, the pre-briefing for an undercover operation took place in a secluded locale. Often that meant motel rooms. For Tyrone Greer, now the case agent and accountant, a motel room meant more paperwork. He wasn't interested in making this any more difficult than it had to be. Because it was just going to be Preston, Jake, Tonya, and Rone, the four decided to meet at Brookside's offices. He had a small conference room off the main entrance to the West Los Angeles office space. Since Jake was going to be spending time at the business, it made sense for him to be present. Tonya and Rone's presence merely looked like a typical business meeting, which in fact it was. Today's business, however, was not the purchase of office supplies. It was preparation for the first meeting targeting Michael Yang.

Jake already had the recording equipment he would need for the meeting. There was no need for a technically trained FBI agent to assist in strapping on any complicated high-tech devices. It was not unusual for an initial meeting not to be recorded. If the undercover agent was unfamiliar with the targets and uncertain as to how he would be received, often no technical equipment was taken into that first meeting.

In UC work, Jake had experienced the wand as targets slowly ran a device over his body. Commercial grade RF detectors could find most wireless cameras, microphones, routers, and phones whether analog or digital. Fortunately, the equipment used by the FBI could defeat any over-the-counter device. Jake had also experienced a full pat down, sometimes as thorough as the one the Bureau gives when taking a suspect into custody. Had any of the devices been discovered, Jake probably wouldn't be around to tell the story.

This afternoon, Jake wasn't concerned about meeting with Michael Yang. Preston Brookside did a good job laying the foundation for introducing his new sales rep. In the past, Brookside brought other employees to Yang's offices either delivering supplies or explaining the intricacies of the equipment Yang leased or purchased. Brookside told Jake that Michael saw nothing unusual about someone new servicing his needs. Neither the undercover agent nor the CHS, the confidential human source, anticipated a problem this afternoon.

For the source—cooperating witness, asset, snitch, rat, whatever you wanted to call them—introducing an undercover agent was a stressful situation. Though Jake wasn't expecting any problems, he understood how nerve-racking the initial meeting could be. Preston had already pitted through his dress shirt and was in the process of changing. As a result of the nervous perspiration, Brookside was also emitting strong body odor.

Jake did not notice the odor in his two previous meetings with Brookside and mentioned the issue to Tonya. It didn't take over-sensitive olfactory nerves to detect the smell. Jake, not so gently, suggested Preston double up on the anti-perspirant deodorant.

You could never take any undercover meeting for granted, however, there was nothing to suggest Michael Yang would prove to be a danger in this afternoon's meeting. Jake had infiltrated some dangerous groups often with the aid of a cooperating witness. In those situations, stress levels were off the charts. Informants introducing Jake to cartels, organized crime groups, or gunrunning gangs had much more reason to be nervous then Brookside. All three FBI agents attempted to put the businessman at ease. No one was succeeding.

Though Jake had worked with some heinous individuals both as targets and cooperators, few rose to the level of those who exploited children for their own sexual gratification. It was going to be important for the undercover agent to sublimate his desires for "justice" so the case could proceed.

Tonya provided some last-minute paperwork for Brookside to sign acknowledging his cooperation and consent to be recorded. He carefully read over the documents and asked several questions. After the third or fourth question, Tonya reminded him the documents weren't open to negotiation, and if he wanted to call off his cooperation, she would gladly contact the U.S. Attorney's office and they could begin criminal proceedings and a guaranteed prison sentence.

Jake liked her handling of the situation. Brookside had little "redeeming social value" and the agents were less than enthusiastic about working with an informant who enjoyed downloading graphic images of men having sex with adolescent girls. Brookside was lucky he had the Chinese card to play. Few pedophiles got the opportunity to work off their arrest, though he was still a long way from probation and a class III registration as a sex offender. It was going to take more than a mere introduction.

If Michael Yang didn't bite and take Jake into his confidence, Brookside's cooperation would not result in lessening the punishment. It was going to take Jake gaining an inside track into Yang's operation and his affiliation with the Chinese government. It wasn't going to be easy. This wasn't some hand-to-hand drug deal where the exchange of cash for contraband resulted in a solid criminal case. This undertaking was going to require a lot of skill and maybe even more luck.

Because the initial encounter was going to take place at Michael Yang's office, there was no need for surveillance. There was no need to take any of the principals away after the meeting nor a need for a QRF, a quick reaction force, should the undercover agent need rescue and protection. This first meeting was going to be about as bland as you could get, like avocado and mayo. Just an introduction and setting the stage for future interactions.

With the plan for the afternoon summit solidified, the four left Brookside's office and headed toward the parking lot. Brookside said he would drive, and before he and Jake climbed into the 2021 Maserati GranSport, Rone said, "Make your own luck."

Jake replied, "I always do."

CHAPTER THIRTY-ONE

West Los Angeles

It was a beautiful day for an undercover meeting, but for Jake there were no bad days for any UC meet. Even innocuous meetings generated a rush. Ever since he had his first undercover meeting shortly after joining the Bureau, he had been chasing the "adrenaline dragon." Like a drug addict seeking to recreate the original high, Jake was hooked on the excitement of pretending to play for the other side.

He wanted to recapture the thrill of that first weapons deal where he walked into a darkened barn at midnight with a briefcase full of cash and negotiated for the purchase of ten AK-74s. When he gave the signal, an FBI SWAT team raced in and "proned-out" three members of a minor league outlaw motorcycle gang trying to elevate itself to varsity status. That quick hit solidified his desire to remain in the FBI's stable of certified undercover agents. Every opportunity to go behind the curtain was a chance worth taking.

He loved the dark side. He loved the half-truths and outright lies, the perfect recipe for misdirection. Though he wasn't sure whether this operation was headed for the shadows, at least he wasn't tethered to a desk. He would make the most of any venture outside the confines of the federal building. He would live his cover and embrace the mediocrity, his new life as paper products salesman.

There were just enough clouds to filter the warmth of the California sun; almost a Chamber of Commerce–style day, perfect for welcoming out-of-state visitors to the City of Angels. Though the air conditioner was running at full tilt, beads of sweat trickled off Brookside's bald head down his cheeks to a graying goatee. This was nerves, not heat. Fear washed through his body. Puffy eyes demonstrated sleep was not coming easily to the capitalist as felony charges hung over his head like the blade of a French guillotine.

"Nice set of wheels," said Jake remarking on the black Maserati trying to relax the cooperating witness before adding, "The air conditioning works well."

Brookside didn't immediately respond, as if he didn't hear the comment but then said, "I've been successful."

"You need to relax. Unless you typically sweat like a turkey at Thanksgiving, you better turn off the glands. You're a salesman. Today is a great day to sell it."

Almost in a whisper, Brookside said, "You have never done anything like this."

Without suggesting the informant pop a few Valiums, Jake attempted to reassure him. "That's where you're wrong. I've been here plenty of times. I've got your back. Just make the introduction and step back. You've provided enough grenades for me to start the war."

Nearing tears, Brookside choked out an immediate enraged response. "A war! I'm not looking for a war. That's my biggest fear. You guys are going to get me killed. I watch enough TV to know snitches get stitches. I should have never agreed to this. All I wanted was a way to get out from under all those charges."

Jake had nothing but contempt for this man who with cooperation might end up skating on a minimum mandatory federal sentence. "Not to put too fine a point on the argument, but you should've thought of that before you downloaded the images. I can handle this for both of us, but if you can't, we can head back to court and let the judge decide your fate."

Brookside said nothing as he rubbed the sleeve of his shirt across his brow and swallowed his whimpering. Turning into the parking lot to Yang's business, he slowly drove into a visitor slot just to the left of the front door.

From the outside, the concrete stand-alone building in the industrial park was nondescript, only a modest sign "Yang Printing" centered above the double-door entry identified its tenant. There were no windows facing the front to give a view of the parking lot and street. There was nothing demonstrating this to be a cog in the machine to bring down America. Jake questioned whether this was one more figment of the FCI imagination where investigations often go to die.

Brookside sat in the car for an extended second wiping perspiring hands on his trousers, taking a deep breath easing the tension building in his chest.

"Maybe you better give him a fist bump and tell him you think you might be coming down with a cold. I guess we can always play it off as a new strain of COVID. That might encourage him to keep his distance and engage only with me." The UC said it with a smile, but Brookside wasn't laughing. Jake's logic was clear, as was his sarcasm.

They stepped out of the Maserati and headed toward the front door. Jake held it open as they entered.

Both were immediately greeted by an attractive young receptionist who looked as if she were still in high school.

"Good afternoon, Mr. Brookside. He's expecting you. He said just to go on back to the conference room."

"Thanks, Madison," mumbled Brookside.

"Sell it, Preston," whispered Jake.

CHAPTER THIRTY-TWO

West Los Angeles

Heading down the hallway, Jake noted dozens of pictures of teenage girls. Most appeared to be Hollywood-style headshots, the kind agents submitted to casting directors, others a bit more provocative.

Though smoking was prohibited in California workplaces, upon entering the conference room, Jake was immediately greeted with the smell of bold tobacco smoke.

Michael rose from behind an elongated mahogany table capable of seating twelve. He was less a Bruce Lee and more an Asian Danny DeVito. An inch shorter and about ten pounds lighter than Brookside, starch and carbohydrates were his obvious favorite food groups. Jake was liking his chances if this went a few rounds in the ring or one-on-one on a basketball court.

"Welcome," said Michael with a wide toothy grin of yellowing teeth as he lifted a pack of Xiongmao cigarettes off the table. Michael's blue dress shirt was starched to perfection and probably custom tailored to fit his Humpty Dumpty physique. The khaki trousers' girth far exceeded the inseam. His plump and prosperous wardrobe contrasted with Jake's fresh off the clearance sales rack at T.J. Maxx.

The conference room was large and exceeded Jake's expectations based upon the business's sedate concrete frontage. Though without windows and thus fresh air to dissipate the smoke, it was tastefully decorated with a full bar on the far wall. Had you not known it was a print shop, you might think a Hollywood boardroom.

The three exchanged hasty greetings as Brookside slipped back toward the wall like a freshman at his first high school dance, allowing Jake to take the lead.

Michael gestured toward Jake with the yellow cigarette pack featuring two Pandas, "Would you like one? I know Preston doesn't like cigarettes."

Jake shook his head. "No, thanks. I will occasionally enjoy a good cigar with an adult beverage, but I'm not much into cigarettes. I assume they are Chinese."

Michael tapped the pack on the palm of his hand as a cigarette popped up. "In English, we call them Pandas. It's a popular brand with executives in China. Prior to '97, they were only available to government leaders. Deng Xiaoping made them popular. He smoked several packs a day. The cigarette smoke has a distinct aroma, the fragrance of affluence and power."

When Jake acted as if he didn't know Deng, Michael asked, "Are you familiar with him?"

Jake shook his head. "Sorry."

"Americans should study more Asian history. He rose to power after Mao's death. He is called the Architect of Modern China."

Jake merely nodded.

Michael took a few seconds to light the Panda, inhaling deeply before blowing out the smoke. Throughout the meeting, he smoked a steady stream of the imported cigarettes, the ever-present haze was like that produced by a cracked cylinder head on an old V-8.

"So, Preston tells me he's decided to cut back a little bit on his hours and you will be handling my business from now on."

Jake nodded. "Yes, I guess that cabin in Big Bear keeps calling him. I can understand why he would prefer to spend a little more time up there than down here. I appreciate him giving me a chance."

Looking to Preston, Michael remarked, "Are you okay? You look pale."

Without verbally answering, Preston threw his hands up as if signaling surrender.

Jake jumped in. "I told him it might be his gall bladder. On the way over, he was complaining about a pain on the right side just below the ribs. Of course, it could be indigestion. For lunch, he wolfed down a cheeseburger lathered in mayo, a double order of fries, and a large shake."

Sometimes working with amateurs required a quick recovery. They skipped lunch because Preston was afraid, he couldn't keep anything down.

Embarrassed, Preston merely shrugged.

Michael warned the equally overweight associate, "That diet will kill you. I should know. I had my gall bladder taken out four years ago. Rich fatty foods were my downfall. I still need you healthy. You've always done a great job of making sure I got everything I needed. If this guy can't meet all my expectations, I'm calling you, gall bladder or no gall bladder," Michael said without smiling.

Jake jumped back, "He's done a great job of explaining your needs, and I'm sure there won't be a problem."

"He tells me you were a Marine."

"Yes, that's correct."

So far, Brookside held to the setup.

"Were you in the service?" Jake knew the answer, but it came from an intelligence briefing and not from the lips of Brookside.

"No, I was never in. My father wasn't much of a dad, but he gave me something that has stuck with me all my life."

"What was that?" asked Jake.

Michael laughed, "Flat feet."

"That will do it."

"What did you do in the Marine Corps?"

"Infantry."

"Did you deploy?"

"Yes, to Iraq."

The key to a successful undercover was to lie as little as possible. It was difficult enough keeping the back story straight. If you got caught slipping, make sure it was a big lie, not a little one.

"Were you an officer?"

It was a lie, but Jake shook his head saying, "No, just a grunt who took orders. I think that's why Preston hired me."

"If you were infantry, you must know something about guns."

Brookside mentioned Yang owned guns and Jake was hoping this might provide a common interest. Jake offered a huge grin. "That's the one thing the Marine Corps gave me, an appreciation for weapon systems and the opportunity to play with a lot of guns."

Brookside, who was yet to participate in the conversation, was still nursing a sick throbbing in his stomach and pleased Jake was fielding all the dialogue. Maybe he could get out of this alive.

"Do you carry?" asked Michael.

Whether to carry or not was always an issue while working undercover. With California's position on guns, particularly the L.A. County Sheriff's reluctance to issue concealed weapon permits, there would be little reason for Jake in this undercover capacity to legally carry. If he were playing the role of a hardened crook, he might carry, knowing it was illegal. The other side doesn't respect gun laws no matter how restrictive. In this investigation, playing the role of a law-abiding white-collar salesman, it made no sense for him to be carrying, legally or illegally.

"No, getting a CCW in this city is next to impossible. My military background didn't help. In fact, it probably hurt. I think most people believe the reports that any of us who served overseas, especially Marines, are somehow flawed. They assume if we saw combat, we have TBI or are suffering from PTS. Maybe, someday I'll move to a state where they issue carry permits, but I have no plans to leave anytime soon. It's a trade-off. I'll take the weather and leave the guns at home."

With that, Michael Yang lifted his shirt and a layer or two of fat to flash a semi-automatic from his appendix-carry holster inside his waistband. "This is what I carry."

"You have a CCW permit?"

"Sure."

"That's great. What reason did you give?" asked Jake knowing there were only a limited number of reasons for the permits to be issued, most dealing with handling large amounts of cash or valuables being transported daily.

"You don't need a reason if you know the right people. I know the right people."

Michael carefully removed the holster from his belt, then slid the weapon out of the leather encasement.

"Is that a 19?" asked Jake, immediately recognizing the weapon.

"Yes, it's a Gen5."

"A Gen5. You *do* know the right people. Gen5s aren't even on the California gun roster."

Brookside was completely lost in this conversation but decided to join. "What's a gun roster?"

Jake wasn't about to launch into his argument that California's gun roster was unconstitutional. Since only about a third of the most common handguns available to the rest of the country can be legally sold in a California gun store, the argument goes Californians are denied their Second Amendment rights to purchase handguns available to those living in other states.

As Michael was lighting another cigarette, he took the lead in the conversation. "California passed legislation known in gun circles as the microstamping law. The state said every new gun imported into California must have microstamping technology to be considered for the roster of handguns certified for sale in the state."

"What is microstamping?" asked Brookside still perspiring despite the conference room air conditioning.

Michael continued without waiting for Jake to respond. "From a practical standpoint, this technology doesn't exist, but what California wants is for a microstamping to be on the firing pin of a handgun so when it's fired, the serial number for that weapon would be imprinted on the shell casing and primer. Though the legislators said the law was designed to identify those handguns used to commit crimes, it was really just a way to make it more difficult for gun manufacturers to sell guns in California."

Jake decided to jump back into the conversation, "I don't believe California has added any new handguns to the approved list for the past seven or eight years."

"It's been at least that long," said Michael, knowledgeable about Second Amendment issues.

Jake smiled, "and the Glock Gen5 isn't on the approved list."

"No, it's not, but I have mine. Do you want to take a look at it?"

"Yes, I've never seen the 5. I have a Gen3 which is the last model on the list."

Brookside looked pale and pitting out his shirt but believed he needed to participate in the conversation to maintain a presence. "What are you guys talking about when you say Gen?"

Again, it was Michael answering: "It means generation. So, with Glock each new upgrade became a new generation. Jake has the Gen3, and I have the Gen5."

With that, Michael dropped the magazine and cleared the weapon, pulling back the slide and ejecting a round from the chamber. He wasn't fast enough to catch it before it fell to the carpeted conference room floor.

Jake bent, picking up the round, noting the hollow-point cartridge before handing it to Michael.

Michael offered the weapon to Jake who began carefully examining the upgraded model.

Like most politicians, there were half-truths in everything Jake said. He did have a Gen3 which he bought while still on active duty in the Marines, but he also had the 19M, a model developed for use by the FBI. The M resembles the Gen5 in many respects. Since Jake spent time comparing his Gen3 with his newly acquired M, he was about to launch into a semi-rehearsed response.

"I've always liked the 19. It has the full finger grip so all three fingers can rest comfortably, and it's compact enough that if I could carry it, it would fit inside the waistband."

As if preparing to write an article for *Guns and Ammo*, Jake detailed the differences. "It really doesn't matter to me because I'm right-handed, but it has a reversible magazine catch and an ambidextrous slide stop lever. The texturing on the grip is different. It looks like you could mount a different backstrap on the grip, something I can't do on mine." Then looking down the barrel, he added, "I like the sights. Even with the naked eye, I can tell the backside is wider and lower. I noticed when I first got my 19, I had a tendency to aim high with that front sight."

Michael nodded, "I know that was one of the issues with the Gen3. I think they changed that with the Gen4, but I never had a 4, so I really don't know."

Tracing his fingers around the front of the barrel, Jake said, "They claim this beveling makes holstering easier, but it's not like I'm Wyatt Earp, so I'm not too concerned with holstering. Does it break down the same way?"

"Yes," answered Michael.

"Do you mind if I disassemble it? I would just like to take a look at the barrel and spring. By looking at the footprint, I can tell the spring is larger."

Michael Yang nodded.

Within seconds, Jake disassembled the Glock separating the barrel and spring from the slide. "The barrel looks the same, but the spring is much different from mine. I'm not sure how much of a difference that makes."

Jake quickly reassembled the Glock and returned it to Michael.

As Michael inserted the magazine and chambered a round, he looked toward Preston and nodded with approval. Then he said, "Let me show you one more thing I like about this model. The magazine well is bigger and flared just a little more than previous models. That makes it a little harder for concealed carry, but it isn't that much of an issue for me. Watch this."

With that, the target of the investigation and possibly Jake's new best friend hit the magazine release and the magazine literally sprang from the magazine well. "I had a Gen3, and it was more of an effort to get the magazine to release. Rather than popping out, the mags more or less dropped out from the well. I like this better. It allows for a quicker exchange of magazines when I'm shooting rapid fire."

Michael topped off the magazine with the round he dropped when initially clearing the pistol and slammed the magazine into the well.

"I'm impressed. You must shoot a lot. Where do you go?"

"I have a membership over at Shooter's Paradise. Do you ever go there?"

"I've never been. I live in the Valley, so I usually go to a range off Ventura Boulevard in Tarzana."

Looking at his Rolex, Preston Brookside said on cue, "If you gentlemen will excuse me, I need to make an important phone call. I have the quotes in the car and need to call a customer. Michael, maybe you could show Jake the operation while I take care of this other matter."

"That's a good idea," answered Michael.

Brookside excused himself and headed out to the Maserati. He and Jake planned this twist to the initial meeting, but Jake was hoping Brookside wasn't going outside to throw up. Though Brookside held it together in the conference room, it was apparent he was uncomfortable playing junior G-man.

Jake responded with the enthusiasm of a lottery winner, "Preston has given me the basics, but I sure would like to see how it all fits together."

The two headed down a short hallway before coming to a set of opaque double doors. Michael punched in a code to a security device mounted on the wall, and the distinctive click of the locking mechanism could be heard. As the doors opened, it was obvious the steel doors were soundproof.

The warehouse was larger than Jake would have estimated based upon the entrance to the business. Dozens of machines were systematically laid out and people were busy working at each. Jake had to give Michael credit, it looked like a United Nations workforce: male and female, black and white, Anglo, Hispanic, and Asian.

"This is much larger than Preston led me to believe."

"If it goes on paper, we do it," said Michael. "We do everything from postcards to programs, from mailings to neighborhood weekly newspapers. We service several independent production companies who find it cheaper to employ our services to print their scripts than to lease copying machines and all the problems that go with them."

"It is my understanding we are leasing the machines to you."

"Yes, originally, I was dealing directly with the manufacturer, but found it cost me about half as much going through Preston. When I told the company I was switching out service plans and going to be leasing through a third-party broker, it was as if they didn't care. Frankly, I found better servicing from Preston than I did the manufacturer. I've never had a machine down more than a day. He has been very responsive to my needs."

"Well, I won't let you down. I promise we will continue the gold star service you are used to receiving. His Big Bear retreats won't impact the quality of care you can expect from us."

"About 80 percent of our business comes from our top twenty customers. We still get walk-ins, but the onesies and twosies don't keep the lights on. I prefer not to even deal with them, but occasionally we will do a small job such as wedding invitations for someone who happens to be the purchasing agent for a Fortune 500 company. Before I know it, we're taking them on as a major client."

"Any major projects on the horizon?"

"With the upcoming elections, we can anticipate a much greater volume. We handle most of the campaign literature for most of the winners," Michael laughed out loud as he added, "and a few of the losers."

"How does that impact the volume of needed supplies?"

"During campaign season, we will triple or even quadruple our paper and toner purchases."

"I promise to be here for you. You can count on Brookside to supply all your needs, even if I have to deliver the supplies myself."

"I'm going to hold you to that. I have a standing reservation for a lane at Shooter's Paradise on Thursday at noon. Why not meet me Thursday and we can shoot? I want to see what an ex-Marine can do." He paused waiting for an answer then said, "Don't tell Preston, but we will expense the ammo to his account."

Jake cringed at "ex-Marine" but held his tongue, saying, "Once a Marine, always a Marine. I'll see you Thursday."

Though Jake sometimes went weeks or months before establishing a relationship with a target of an investigation, the undercover agent was confident he sold himself at this initial meeting.

CHAPTER THIRTY-THREE

Koreatown, Los Angeles

In the L.A. area, the highways aren't referred to as interstates but rather freeways, and many are given a geographical rather than a numerical designation. Interstate 5 is known as the Golden State Freeway; Interstate 10, the Santa Monica Freeway. The multi-lane Hollywood, Ventura, and Long Beach freeways are always crowded with cars at any hour of the day or night.

Brian Sullivan set up his appointment for 10 a.m. hoping he could avoid the bumper-to-bumper traffic of the early morning commute. Unfortunately, an accident in the number two lane of the westbound Santa Monica Freeway clogged the traffic to a snail's pace. He was two exits from the Vermont Boulevard offramp and slowly making his way to the far righthand lane. Since arriving in Los Angeles, he couldn't recall a time where he wasn't an hour early for every interview or an hour late. Traffic was as unpredictable as the Tigers' pitching. Only when the governor issued COVID "stay-at-home" orders were the freeways manageable.

The Chinese consulate general in Los Angeles was headquartered in Koreatown at 443 Shatto Place, one block east of Vermont between Fourth and Fifth Street. Opened in 1987, the 33,000-square-foot building sitting on a half-acre lot serviced Southern California, Arizona, Hawaii, New Mexico, and the U.S. Pacific territories of American Samoa, Guam, and the Northern Mariana Islands.

The consulate was not without its controversy. Protesters frequently stood on the sidewalk railing at some PRC government policy. In 2011, a sixty-seven-year-old activist from Shanghai, protesting China's human rights record, fired a 9mm into the consulate. In 2017, a Chinese national fired multiple rounds into the front of the building then returned to his car and committed suicide.

As Brian turned down Shatto, seeking a parking spot on the street crowded with cars, he noted dozens of protestors in front of the consulate marching up and down the sidewalk.

After parking several blocks away, he navigated his way through the growing crowd of Asian male and female picketers. Bypassing the visa and passport line, he headed to the front door, presented his identification, and was ushered into the consulate.

Once inside, a second consulate employee directed him to a small office just off Passport Hall. Sullivan took a seat waiting only a couple of minutes before a small, well-built man in his early thirties entered. He carried himself with the confidence of a warrior.

Extending his hand, the man said, "I am Lin Ping. I am an attaché representing the consul general."

For Brian Sullivan, it was a familiar face, not one he had previously met, but one he might have viewed in an intelligence briefing furnished by Centurion Solutions Group. Brian focused on the facial features of the Chinese representative trying to memorize them in hopes he could recognize the face in an intel report.

Taking several minutes to explain his project and seeking the cooperation of the Chinese consulate, Brian explained he didn't believe in "hit pieces." He wanted to provide an opportunity for a Chinese official to comment publicly on camera regarding the Uyghur issue. Though Sully already formed a position on the issue, he presented himself as a disinterested third party seeking a balanced examination of the issue.

With Lin remaining expressionless as Brian presented his case, Sullivan decided on a different tact. He opened his laptop computer and played a snippet of the covert surveillance video. It was a damning portrait of the conditions under which the Uyghur women and children worked as slave labor at a Chinese shoe factory.

Without commenting on the video, Lin excused himself for several minutes, promising to return with an answer. Once outside the conference room, he made a phone call alerting the person on the other end of the call of the immediate need to retrieve the laptop.

When he returned, Lin responded with the company line, dismissing the allegations of slave labor. Though he didn't threaten Sullivan, Lin stated it would be a mistake to go forward with the documentary since the allegations would be false. He emphasized such a project would harm the rather fragile relationship his country had with the United States and the timing of its release would only hurt businesses and trade in both countries.

Suggesting Brian should consult with the PRC embassy in Washington and State Department of the current administration before rolling tape on the project, Lin requested to see the footage before the documentary was complete, giving the Chinese government the opportunity to comment.

Sullivan had no problem agreeing to that concession but explained commenting officially before the completed project would add credibility to the Chinese position.

The two agreed to remain in contact as the project progressed.

Satisfied, Sully left the meeting and headed toward his car.

Chapter Thirty-Four

Burbank

After getting back on the freeway, Sullivan called General Peter Newman's number at Centurion Solutions Group and left a message on the general's voicemail. Sully failed to notice the tan Camaro following several cars back throughout the trip.

Since Sullivan could work from home or the foundation, there was no need for him to check back into the office. As he neared his apartment, he decided to stop at a grocery store to pick up something for dinner.

Pulling into the Vons parking lot, he found a spot at the far end of the crowded lot. He hopped out of his car and headed for the store.

The Camaro parked next to Sully's Mercedes. The smoked-out windows on the tan Camaro made it impossible to determine who was inside. Just as the driver of the Camaro prepared to complete the mission, he spotted Sully doing a U-turn as he was about to enter the store.

This was California and besides not celebrating gun rights, grocery stores and the state had a love-hate relationship with plastic bags. In 2016, California voters approved Proposition 67, a statewide ban on single use plastic bags. Within days of the proposition being approved in the November election, consumers were required to furnish their own shopping bags or purchase bags from grocery stores. When COVID-19 hit, it was determined reusable plastic bags could be carrying the virus and soon many California communities outlawed the use of reusable plastic bags, not even allowing customers to bring their own bags into the stores. With the pandemic on an apparent hiatus, some cities went back to the Proposition 67 edict. The sign on the front door reminded customers "Don't Forget Your Bags." Brian returned to his Mercedes to grab his canvas grocery bags. He clicked the remote and the annoying sound shrilled once as lights flashed and the car unlocked.

The driver-side window of the Camaro retreated into the door frame as Sully reached the door handle. Two quick shots rang out. A male dressed in black leaped from the Camaro and grabbed Sully's wallet and watch. He then reached inside the Mercedes and retrieved the laptop computer on the back seat. To ensure the success of the mission, the driver fired one more shot into Brian's head. Returning to the Camaro, the driver sped from the scene with the retired Army colonel lying dead in a pool of his own blood.

CHAPTER THIRTY-FIVE

West Los Angeles

The Bureau provided many of the tools Jake needed to be success-ful in any undercover assignment. Sometimes, it was clothing specially equipped with concealed cameras, or weapons not traditionally carried by law enforcement, maybe it was expensive jewelry or watches, but always it was a seized or leased automobile fitting the needs of the cover story.

In the past, when Jake was a "baller," a high roller, his vehicles were high-end Mercedes or Porsches. When he played a low-level street dealer, the car was a dinged-up, rusted-out Oldsmobile that, thanks to Bureau mechanics, ran to perfection. If he were a cowboy, it was a pickup truck.

He had to admit sometimes he used the opportunity to check out a car he was thinking of buying. His personal vehicle was a Jeep Wrangler, but he was looking at the new Ford Broncos. For this assignment, Rone approved a like-new, leased 2021 Ford Bronco Sport. Jake was looking forward to taking the four-door SUV for a multi-month test drive. Thanks to FBI backstopping, the registration came back to a lease by Preston Brookside's office supply company.

Jake arrived at Shooter's Paradise twenty minutes before the scheduled meeting with Michael Yang. The parking lot was about half full, but each vehicle reflected West L.A.'s power elite. There were Range Rovers, Audis, and BMWs. Not a domestic car in sight.

Jake called Rone earlier in the morning after setting up the Shooter's Paradise "shoot" with Yang. Rather than taking a chance of blowing out the sensitive equipment with the explosive concussions of rapid-fire shooting, Jake said he wouldn't be recording the meeting once inside the range. Rone agreed, asking Jake to keep any conversation while on the indoor range semi-innocuous with the promise to get Yang to repeat criminal admissions made while shooting once they got outside. Jake didn't see that as being a problem.

Since Shooter's Paradise required a membership, Jake wasn't too concerned about running into any FBI agents he knew. The indoor range was only a few miles from the office, but agents' propensity to be frugal and the requirement by the range to pay annual dues probably made membership a nonstarter. This was especially true because agents could shoot for free at the FBI ranges.

Though most agents knew not to acknowledge another agent in public, there was always that chance a Bureau employee looking too much like a cop and openly displaying his badge and credentials could say the wrong thing at the wrong time. Even a subtle nod or acknowledgment might mean the termination of an operation. Jake was hoping not to see any feds this close to the federal building and wished he could somehow relocate the op to another city.

At about five minutes before noon, Michael pulled in the parking lot driving a silver Lexus LX 570. The luxury SUV probably retailed for three times the value of Jake's Bronco. It was easier playing a humble servant, and in this role, Jake was in no position to go toe-to-toe matching accoutrements.

Jake grabbed his lockbox and hopped out of the car extending a hand to his newest target.

Michael warmly greeted him as he removed a shooting bag and two gun lockboxes from the back of the SUV.

"Have you been waiting long?" asked Michael.

"I've been here a few minutes. I didn't want to be late for our first date," said Jake with a smile. "It's just always hard to predict traffic in this town."

"I'm spoiled. I think most of my driving stays within a five-mile radius."

Jake laughed. "I think sometimes in this town, a five-mile trip might take all afternoon."

Michael smiled as they headed toward the entrance.

Once inside, they were greeted by an older white man with a large revolver holstered on his hip. "Good afternoon, Mr. Yang, you're right on time as usual. I see you brought a guest."

"Yes, this is my friend Jake. He's going to be shooting with me today."

"That's fine, sir." Then turning to Jake, the older man said, "I'll just need you to sign a release form before you go back to the range."

Without even reading the fine print probably written by an attorney absolving Shooter's Paradise of everything, including a nuclear holocaust, Jake signed the form.

"Your inventory still seems low," said Yang.

"We're trying to catch up from the robbery."

"What robbery?" asked Jake.

"One night a couple of weeks ago, they got wiped out. Every gun and all the ammo. The guard took a savage beating," said Michael.

"Wow. I'm so sorry. Did they get the guy who broke in?" asked Jake.

As the man patted the holster on his hip, he said, "Not yet, but they wouldn't dare hit us in the daytime. That's why we are always packing."

"You'd have to be a fool," said Yang. "Give me four boxes of nine and a box of 44 Magnum."

Jake looked at Yang and said, "I just brought my 19. What's the 44 Magnum for?"

"I brought us a little toy to play with."

At the cost of ammo, Jake was glad either Yang or Brookside was picking up this expense.

Before heading back to the range, both men put on eye and ear protection. Each was wearing Peltor Tacticals amplifying conversational sounds while suppressing gunshot noises.

When they arrived at their lane, Yang opened both boxes, first displaying the Glock 19 Gen5 and then surprising Jake with the Desert Eagle Mark XIX.

Jake offered a huge smile. "Now, I understand why you needed .44 Magnum."

Michael nodded as both men began loading their magazines.

From his shooting bag, Michael pulled a large *Walking Dead* target that didn't quite fit the mold of a man in possession of weapons with a total value in excess of $2,000. Jake was expecting a little more professionalism in the choice of bull's-eyes but played along.

Jake was a skilled marksman, but the former Marine infantry officer never sought the regimentation of SWAT. It was just too much teamwork, too much repetitive training. He preferred being on the highwire alone without a net, singing the aria *a cappella*. He played lonely well and liked holding the success or failure of any operation in his own hands, not relying on teammates. He did, however, like his guns and the opportunity to hone his skills.

For the next hour, the two traded off weapons and enjoyed shooting anywhere from five to twenty yards at stationary targets. Jake wasn't quite sure how to play it and had yet to determine how competitive Michael was. Michael wasn't bad, but his shots were inconsistent and spread out all over the bleeding zombie silhouette. Jake's groupings were tight, but he always managed to throw a few rounds to prevent it from looking like he was trying to show up his new "best friend."

The hour of range time was about up, and Michael offered a challenge as he posted a clean target. "I'm going to set it at seven yards with two seconds facing then spinning for five rotations, ten rounds total. Loser buys lunch."

Jake smiled, "You go first. I hope you brought your wallet."

The results were predictable. Michael managed to put most of the rounds on target, but they were spread across the post-apocalyptic urban creature dripping venom and foam from a gaping mouth. Pleased with his performance, when Michael brought the target home, he counted only nine hits. "Damn, I thought I got them all in."

Jake offered his assessment. "Good shooting. You threw your fourth shot, but the other nine were in the kill zone, assuming zombies have a kill zone."

Michael slapped a clean target on the cardboard backing. "Let me see what you got when the pressure's on."

"This is still for picking up the lunch tab, right?" asked Jake as he slammed a fully loaded magazine in the Gen3.

Michael nodded, pushing "enter" on the control panel.

The target ran out to seven yards, teased with a partial twist, then faced Jake for two seconds, before turning. After five rotations, it was clear who was paying for lunch. All ten of Jake's rounds were headshots centered around the nose.

Michael could only smile. Slapping Jake on the back, he said. "You use that gun like you understand it."

As they were leaving the range, Michael's phone rang. Jake could only hear one side of the conversation, but the printshop entrepreneur wasn't happy.

"Sorry, Jake, but lunch is off. My driver called in sick, and I need to make a delivery out to Monterey Park for a wake this evening."

Attempting to gain further inroads, Jake quickly offered up his help. "I needed to go downtown this afternoon. I can run over to Monterey Park for you."

"That would be great. I've got a potential new client coming over at two and didn't want to postpone that appointment."

"But you're not off the hook for lunch. I'll just take a raincheck for next week."

"I always pay my debts. Meet me at the shop and I'll give you the programs."

Not quite sure where all this was heading, Jake was gaining street cred as the investigation evolved.

CHAPTER THIRTY-SIX

Monterey Park

In an earlier FBI investigation code named "Operation Counterfeit Lies," Jake spent a lot of time in Los Angeles's San Gabriel Valley. Though mostly in San Marino and Pasadena, he had several meetings in Monterey Park. Located seven miles east of downtown Los Angeles off the San Bernardino Freeway, Monterey Park was described in a 2009 survey as having the largest concentration of citizens of Chinese descent in America. Almost two-thirds of the city's population was Asian. Anglos were clearly in the minority.

Then, as now, Jake drew stares as he drove down Atlantic Boulevard through the center of town. Focused more on listening to the directions from his GPS app, he was still cognizant of the looks he received from passing motorists as he slowly made his way through traffic.

With a right turn into a residential neighborhood, a few more rights, and finally a left, he drove down a cul-de-sac of modest homes built shortly after World War II. The yards were neat. The homes painted. There was pride of ownership and few "homeless sidewalk dwellers" often seen in older neighborhoods scattered throughout the greater Los Angeles area.

Jake spotted the house numbers attached to a plaque near the front door of the residence and parked on the street. Grabbing the box of funeral programs, he headed toward the front door, not quite knowing what to expect. Because Jake was a Marine who saw combat, Michael said he wasn't worried about Jake's personal safety, but warned the undercover agent he was delivering funeral programs to a Wah Ching member whose cousin was recently killed.

Most office supply salesmen would be apprehensive about making such a run, but for Jake, this fact added a little bit of excitement to the first couple of mundane, if not boring, UC meets. To date, the case was as exciting as reheated oatmeal. Maybe that was about to change. On the drive through downtown L.A. in the Bronco, Jake talked with Rone about this early twist in the investigation.

Like Jake, Rone was enthusiastic about expanding the investigation beyond an intelligence gathering mission. "We may end up making something out of this yet."

Jake promised to capture the meeting on his secreted recording device.

After knocking twice, a slightly built Asian female answered the door. Not more than twelve or thirteen, she had long black hair, almond eyes, and a porcelain complexion. Maybe a cover girl for the latest teen fashion magazine, she was that striking.

"Yes," she said a little too loudly.

"Hi, I'm Jake. I'm here to see Danny. I have a package from Michael Yang."

She smiled broadly showing perfect teeth, then said enthusiastically, "Danny's my brother." Turning toward a bedroom, she shouted, "Danny, it's for you. It's a big white man. He has the box of programs for Calvin's funeral."

She returned to Jake. "Calvin was my cousin. He just died. Do you have a cousin?"

Recognizing her interaction was not the result of cultural differences, Jake smiled and said, "Yes, I have a cousin. I'm sorry your cousin died."

"It's okay. He was mean. He did things to me that weren't very nice."

Jake wasn't sure how to respond, so he said nothing.

She yelled again, "Danny, a big white man is here for you."

"Let him in, Annie. I'll be right there," came a shout from the back of the house.

"Come in and have a seat." Signaling kindness not often seen in a teenager, she asked, "Can I get you something to drink? I just made some iced tea."

"Yes, that would be nice. I'd like some tea."

"I put lemon in the tea. It is my own special recipe."

"That sounds great. I'd like to try it."

Jake took a seat on a bright red couch accenting the colorful Asian decor. The house was small but orderly, possibly employing the Asian principles of feng shui, but maybe just neat, simple, and efficient.

Annie quickly returned to the living room with a glass of her special recipe and the rapid-fire discussion began. "I'm Annie. Danny is my brother. He's older than I am, so I am his younger sister. Do you work for Mr. Yang? I know him. He smokes. I have been to his business with all the big machines. Have you been there? The machines are very noisy."

Jake took a sip, noting a strong taste of lemon, maybe more lemon than tea. "No, I don't work for him, but I was with him earlier this afternoon, and he asked me to deliver the programs."

Danny walked down the short hallway and extended his hand to Jake. Again, if this were going to be a cops and crooks one-on-one basketball tournament, Jake thought he held the advantage and might have to spot the other team points. Danny was about 5'4" and weighed somewhere south of a buck twenty. He was young, late teens or early twenties and his left arm was fully sleeved with tattoos. "I'm Danny. Thanks for bringing the programs."

"You're welcome. Sorry for your loss. I understand he was your cousin."

Danny shrugged his shoulders as if to say it wasn't much of a loss.

"Danny, I gave the man some iced tea. Would you like some?"

"No."

"Please, Danny. I just made it. I put lemon in it. The man likes it." Looking at Jake, she asked, "You do like it, don't you?"

Jake glanced toward Danny before answering.

She repeated, "You like it, don't you?"

"Yes, Annie. It's very good. I can taste the lemon in your special recipe."

She smiled.

Danny appreciated the compassion the undercover agent offered. "Annie, you can get me a glass, but then Jake and I need to talk."

She abruptly turned, delighted to play hostess or waitress or just a dutiful little sister.

"Thanks for bringing the programs."

"It wasn't a problem. When's the funeral?"

"The wake is tonight at the funeral parlor. The funeral is Saturday. In our tradition, Saturdays and Sundays are considered the luckiest days to have a funeral."

Jake offered a weak smile.

"I know, no day is a good day to have a funeral unless you're well into your eighties or nineties."

Annie returned with the iced tea.

"Thank you, Annie. Now please go to your room and get ready."

Danny choked on the iced tea as Annie headed to her room. "Annie, I think you put a little too much lemon in the tea."

Without looking back, she responded, "It's my own special recipe. I can't change it."

Shaking his head and smiling, Danny whispered to Jake, "Thanks. Fetal alcohol syndrome. I was born before our mother began drinking. Our father was killed in a robbery a few months after mother got pregnant with Annie. No one warned her about what the abuse could do. Our mother died three years ago. It's up to me to protect her."

"It looks like you're doing a great job."

Abruptly changing the subject, Danny said, "Michael tells me you were a Marine and you are a pretty good shooter."

"News travels fast. I do okay. At least, I was good enough today when lunch was on the line."

"What do you carry?"

Jake laughed, "I don't carry. This is California."

"Okay, what do you own?"

"I have got a Glock 19."

"That's it?"

Jake wasn't about to provide an inventory of his Bureau-approved weapons, but answered, "I have a Remington 870 and a Smith & Wesson five-shot model 36 my dad left me when he died."

"Is the Glock a Gen5?"

"No, a Gen3."

"Would you like a 5?"

Back to the same discussion earlier in the week with Michael Yang. "They aren't too easy to get in this state."

"I could probably get you one if you're willing to pay. I have access to a lot of guns."

"Did you get Michael his? We shot it today. I really liked the action."

Danny nodded, his head not rattling hard enough for the recorder to pick up his response.

Jake decided not to press the issue this early in the investigation. Sounding a little naïve, unfamiliar with gang culture, he asked, "Do you work at a gun store or have a federal firearms license?"

"No, but if you're looking to expand your collection, let me know."

Not wanting to appear too anxious, Jake took a short sip of his iced tea cringing as the lemon exerted its sourness. "What's available now?"

"About an hour ago, I got my hands on a Kimber Raptor II."

"New or used?"

"Practically new, not right out of the box but only a few rounds through the barrel."

"Sure, if the price is right, I'd be interested in a .45."

"Wait right here."

Danny retreated back into the bedroom. In less than a minute, he returned with the Kimber. As Jake examined it, it appeared new, but as he ran his index finger around outer edge of the barrel, gun powder residue proved it had been recently fired. The Raptor II retailed for about $1,600, had a magazine capacity of eight, an ambidextrous thumb safety, and Jake could see it had tactical wedge tritium night sights.

"This is a good-looking weapon. Why do you want to sell it?"

"It's not mine. A friend asked me to get rid of it. I need some quick cash."

"How much is he asking?"

"I'm asking seven fifty," answered Danny without hesitating.

"That's a little rich for me, right now. Can you come down any?"

"What are you willing to pay?"

"Would you take five?"

"How about six fifty?"

Jake hesitated for a moment as if calculating the balance in his checking account and determining the total payout for upcoming bills. Though he and Rone hadn't anticipated the need for a large contraband budget in the UC op, they figured in a sizeable amount just in case. He could easily justify a $650 expenditure chalking it up to cred building in the overall investigation. Since Danny was brokering it without going through a third-party who had an FFL, it was a criminal violation in California. At least, they would be putting up some early points on the scoreboard.

Before Jake said anything or countered, Danny belted out, "Six."

"You got a deal. I don't have the money on me. Can I come back tomorrow?"

"Sure."

"You won't sell this out from under me, will you?"

"If I say we have a deal, we have a deal. But this is just between us. No one else needs to know, especially Michael."

"I have no intention of telling anyone."

CHAPTER THIRTY-SEVEN

FRIDAY, MAY 13
Los Angeles

The day before, the two exchanged phone numbers and talked earlier this morning. Jake was willing to meet at the Monterey Park home, but Danny said he had business in downtown Los Angeles and suggested Denny's. Jake was all too familiar with the location on Ramirez Street just off the Hollywood Freeway east of Union Station. On May 6, five years earlier, Jake shot two midlevel drug dealers in the Denny's parking lot on a transaction that went south in a New York minute.

The negotiations for ten kilos of crystal meth seemed to be going well until one of the brokers nodded to his partner. Within seconds, violence erupted as the two men tried to rip Jake for the money he had in a gym bag. Timely, accurate shooting proved a plus as Jake gave new meaning to the restaurant's advertised Grand Slam Special.

Since Jake was wearing a hoodie, the incident took place outside, and the surveillance cameras didn't work, Jake assumed he was still welcome at "America's diner." Agents flooded the parking lot that May evening, yet business boomed as locals followed the news copters overhead and dropped in for a late-night snack. Jake avoided the restaurant since that evening but now was cautiously returning.

He was a little early for the appointment and rather than wait outside as the noon sun pounded the bench by the front door, he walked inside. He searched the dining room but didn't see Danny. He asked

the server to seat him near the windows so he could see the cars entering the parking lot. Glancing over at the hostess stand as he walked to
the table, he didn't see his photo on the wall of shame—those customers whose business was no longer appreciated. Forgive and forget!

Denny's was doing a healthy lunchtime business and just as the
server brought him iced tea, he spotted Danny pulling into the lot.

Danny showed little concern as he hopped out of the car carrying
a cardboard box large enough to conceal the Kimber. As he walked
into the restaurant, he looked to his right and spotted Jake giving him
a slight wave.

Jake started to get up to shake hands, but Danny waved him off and
Jake remained seated.

"I was hoping you would be here," said Danny as the server, a
woman in her fifties, brought two menus.

Before opening the menu, he ordered iced tea.

Jake smiled. "I was hoping you would come. I'm looking forward
to increasing my arsenal."

The server returned with the iced tea. "Are you guys ready to
order?"

Jake took the lead. "Give us a couple of minutes." Then looking to
Danny, he asked, "How was the wake last night?"

"Have you ever been to a Chinese wake?"

Jake shook his head.

"Last night was tame compared to some I've been to. Just some
incense and a few white envelopes filled with cash to help cover the cost
of the funeral. There can be lots of wailing, chanting, and praying. I've
seen them last several days. Family and friends can attend but pregnant
women are supposed to avoid wakes because it's bad luck. Maybe my
mother went to a wake when she was pregnant with Annie."

"Do you believe that?"

Danny shook his head. "All of this tradition is more for the benefit
of the living than the dead. I don't believe any of it."

The server returned and both men ordered.

Danny went on, "Tomorrow's funeral will also be tame. There will be some flowers, the traditional iris wreaths. Calvin was a nobody. He was punk. I don't think anybody other than his mother cares he's gone. I sure don't. Had he been someone important in the community, you might see as many as a hundred different flower arrangements. Tomorrow will just be the burning of a lot of incense and paper products representing his possessions, like fake money, drawings of jewelry, clothing, his electronic products like his cell phone, computer, and his Camaro. In China, they believe you can take it with you to the next world."

Jake slid an envelope across the table and Danny looked inside. Five $100 bills and five twenties.

Danny handed him the used Amazon cardboard box. Putting the box on the booth's bench seat, shielding it from the customers, Jake glanced inside. The FBI just put the first points on the board. This Friday the 13th was turning out to be lucky for the good guys.

CHAPTER THIRTY-EIGHT

TUESDAY, MAY 17
Beverly Hills

The two men sat outside on the mansion's poolside pavilion. Rivaling anything either ever saw indoors or out, the exquisitely furnished patio with an extended barbeque island, large outdoor kitchen, and protected big screen TV could compete with any place in China.

The project was Chen's idea, but the plans were thwarted when he was expelled from the United States two years earlier. Bureaucracies, whether manned by communists or capitalists, moved slowly and the expulsion buried the proposal under more layers of approvals. Upon his return to Beijing, Chen campaigned for the idea with the Ministry of State Security leadership. Thanks to Lin's support and doing much of the initial groundwork, the plot would soon become a reality. Within two weeks, the inaugural voyage would be happening. If successful, it could be replicated over and over.

As the two men drank their mao-tai and puffed on Cohibas, Lin lowered his voice as if the neighbors might be listening, "I had a problem the other day. The first I have had since coming here."

"And you handled it?"

Lin nodded, "Franklin Lee is capable of providing all the brutality we require."

"He is a strong ally. He always provided quality service when I needed something done in Southern California. His insights into the street culture exceeds the training we received in China. I trust his instincts."

Lin added, "He makes sense out of violence."

Chen agreed. "He has survived because he is wise in ways in which we have not been tested. His crew cares little about our cause but honors his commands."

"Their obedience to him is all we can ask. The actors in our play for influence and dominance need only obey without understanding the reasons."

Chen nodded. "And as to Franklin's violence, was it a manual override?"

"Yes," said Lin smiling then breaking out in a laugh.

While working together in Houston, they always joked that targeted killings, almost always with a gun, were "manual overrides." Like Machiavelli, they saw assassination as a legitimate tool for control.

"And the problem?"

"A filmmaker doing a documentary on the Uyghur. He is no longer a problem. From everything I have read in the paper and heard from our sources inside the legal community, it is being treated as an armed robbery."

"Excellent."

CHAPTER THIRTY-NINE

West Los Angeles

The workday was over. Jake delivered five reams of Astrobrights pulsar pink paper for a project Michael promised to complete first thing in the morning for a local elementary school.

"What's with all the pictures of those cute girls in the hallway?" asked Jake as the two men sat in Michael's office drinking Tsingtao while Michael was also knocking down successive cigarettes.

"I work with a lot of independent filmmakers and helped finance several movies featuring some of those actresses," said Michael, his eyes lying as were his words.

"I'm not much of a film buff, but what were the names of the movies?"

Michael hesitated, taking a long, thoughtful pull on his beer, trying to come up with an answer. "Oh, it's nothing you would've seen. They were only distributed overseas and never made much money. Hollywood is a crapshoot and most of what comes out of there are tax write-offs," said Michael with an insincere chuckle.

"Well, those young actresses are certainly alluring but until you start buying a lot more paper, I won't need to worry about investing in any tax write-offs."

Michael asked, "When you were overseas, did you see a lot of men with younger talent?"

"What do you mean?"

"You know what I'm asking. A lot of those countries aren't as moralistic as we are here. Older men can date younger women."

189

"Older men can date younger women here," said Jake.

"I mean younger than that."

Jake understood what Michael was trying to say, but for the benefit of his hidden recording equipment, he wanted Michael to say it. "Do you mean girls?"

"Yes. The age of consent in the United States is sixteen, seventeen, or eighteen depending on the state, but overseas in some countries, it's a lot younger. In China and Macau, it's fourteen. In the Philippines, it's twelve."

"I had no idea. The only overseas country I was in was Iraq and during that time I was too busy fighting a war to study the dating habits of Iraqi men."

"Would you be interested in dating younger women?" Michael asked cautiously, his cigarette down to a hot nub.

"I guess that would depend upon how young. How young are you talking?" said Jake not trying to sound too interested, but with enough interest to continue the conversation.

"I just heard the gangs have taken advantage of some of the unaccompanied minors crossing the southern border and now they've set up places in Los Angeles. Somebody said Mexican, El Salvadorian, Nicaraguan, you know those Central American girls. I've also heard there might be some places in the San Gabriel Valley catering to men who appreciate a younger Asian demographic."

"I'm not sure I'd want Preston to know unless you were fixing him up. He might not understand."

Maybe it was his weight, but Michael was economical in his gestures and moves. Even now there was just a cold hint of a smile. "You would be amazed to know how understanding Preston is. I just know you are new to Los Angeles, and if you were looking for something along those lines, I could ask around."

"Let me think about it. It's always about taking chances though only the necessary ones. That might be a big step for me, but I really appreciate you asking."

CHAPTER FORTY

WEDNESDAY, MAY 18
Santa Monica

It was still early. The lunch crowd would begin to arrive in about thirty minutes. Most of the tables were open. Tonya was already seated as Jake entered the deli. Like any experienced agent, she chose a table in the rear and took the Wild Bill Hickok seat with her back to the wall. The seat received its name from the Western folk hero who was killed on August 2, 1876, in Deadwood, in what is now South Dakota. Hickok was known to always take the seat with his back to the wall so he could see anyone entering the saloon.

The day before, he was playing cards with Jack McCall who was losing heavily. Hickok encouraged him to quit and even gave him some money for a meal. The next day, Hickok returned to the saloon for another game. The only seat available at the card table didn't put him with his back to the wall. He asked twice to trade places with another player but was refused. While holding two pairs and what has become known as the "dead man's hand, aces and eights," McCall entered from behind and shot Hickok in the back of the head at point-blank range. Lesson learned.

Jake gave Tonya a brief smile and said, "I guess I should've gotten here a little earlier to get the best seat in the house."

"If you snooze, you lose."

"Actually, about the only time I don't sit with my back to the wall is when I'm undercover. Even the bad guys know the cops always grab that seat."

With a slight nod, Tonya said, "Yeah, but I've been on enough surveillances to know the best criminals always plant themselves with a good field of vision."

"Your point is well taken," he paused before saying, "thanks for meeting me."

"Hey, I'm always up for a free meal. I figure you can take this out of your undercover budget. Besides, on the phone you sounded as if there's a problem."

When Kilee, the college-age server approached, she gave Jake a look as if to ask, "Still dealing with all those psychological issues?"

Looking too much like the crazy uncle everyone kept in the attic, Jake offered a wide-eyed, tilted smile and a fake facial tic.

Trying to avoid interacting with him, Kilee turned to Tonya for their orders.

After she left, Jake looked around to ensure no one else could hear their conversation. "This op is going in a direction I wasn't expecting. I'm not saying Brookside was involved, but what began as a possible Chinese I/O, has evolved into cross-border human sex trafficking."

Tonya didn't say anything but tilted her head demonstrating an interest in learning more.

"Based on some things you said earlier, I think this may fall within your expertise."

"We work sex trafficking off our squad. I've had a few cross-border cases. Human trafficking seems to be the crime de jour, but most of what we've seen is the old-fashioned pimping of out-of-town runaways frequenting Hollywood Boulevard."

"What can you tell me about human trafficking from Central America and elsewhere coming up through Mexico and across our southern border?"

She offered a slight grin. "You're talking to someone whose Sunday family get-togethers could fulfill ICE's weekly quotas, if the feds still cared."

Jake laughed out loud, "I'm not interested in rounding up your relatives unless you want me to."

"I might take you up on that with a couple of my cousins."

Jake smiled, "Just tell me where and when."

Kilee interrupted the pseudo contract killing with an iced tea, Diet Pepsi, and two Reubens.

Between bites, Tonya said, "Look, we have a crisis at our southern border. In 2020, the Border Patrol had fewer than 500 people in custody, a year later, there were more than 6,000 in custody, almost half were unaccompanied minors. DHS is overwhelmed. There are just too many people trying to get into this country illegally."

"I wasn't aware the numbers were that high."

"In 2014 and 2015, it was a convergence of DACA, the Flores Settlement Agreement, and the TVPA."

"What's the TVPA?"

"It's the Traffic Victim Protection Act. Essentially, it provides T-visas and protection for victims smuggled into the United States primarily for sex trafficking. The one caveat is the victims must agree to testify against their trafficker. Sometimes, they aren't willing to go that far fearing their families back home will be killed."

"And the Flores Settlement Agreement?" asked Jake.

"Years ago, the vast majority of those illegally crossing the border were single adult males who could be easily returned to Mexico or Central America when captured. But there were also minors and unaccompanied minors in the mix. Essentially, the Flores Settlement Agreement, decades old, was the result of a Supreme Court case. With several different federal court decisions, the FSA said we couldn't keep unaccompanied minors for more than twenty days.

"It wasn't possible to process the children that quickly and they were released into the United States to family members or those

designated by the family. Then in 2015, the agreement was reinter-
preted to include families. Now, those seeking entry into the United
States by claiming asylum through the 'credible fear of persecution'
claim, could be expedited if they were accompanied by their children.
The families were essentially released into the United States and told to
report at a later date for an asylum hearing.

"The previous administration implemented the Migrant Protection Protocols or MPP requiring those seeking asylum and wishing to
enter the United States through Mexico had to remain in Mexico until
they could obtain due process. The MPPs no longer exist."

Jake seeing the fallacy of the policy said, "So, regardless of the
validity of an asylum claim, families with children who report to the
Border Patrol or a port of entry claiming asylum are part of the 'catch
and release' program and allowed to remain in the United States."

Tonya nodded. "The cartels aren't stupid. They know the changes
in the immigration regulations particularly with the new administration. They know how to exploit our laws. The cartels and smugglers are
back in business. Their bank accounts are overflowing.

"Again, the cartels were coaching those seeking asylum on the
magic words needed to be said. In fact, Border Patrol agents have found
what amounted to cue cards in the possession of those at the border.
These cards provided the keywords necessary to establish their fear of
returning to their homeland. Adult immigrants are essentially buying
and renting children so they can pose as families and enter the United
States under the Flores Settlement Agreement.

"These children became commodities. With a child in hand, the
adults literally walk up to Border Patrol and surrender knowing they
will be released and told to report for an asylum hearing. Literally,
these 'families' are taking Ubers to the border stations."

Jake could only shake his head.

"There were plenty of documented cases in which the children
weren't even related to those claiming to be their parents. Obviously,
those people coming from wherever across our southern border aren't

bringing with them documentation such as birth certificates or a marriage certificate. There was no way to prove these groups are not families.

"Again, the cartels exploit our immigration rules and regulations. For many of these children, once they got across the border, they were either on their own or working at the behest of the cartels. The promises made south of the border were breached and now the kids are part of labor and sex trafficking organizations. They're required to pay off the smugglers' fees as either sex slaves or working as virtual slaves in minimum wage jobs throughout the United States."

There was compassion in Jake's voice when he said, "They aren't necessarily bad people, but they're cutting in front of the line."

"The wall worked. Not 100 percent, but as part of a multi-layered protection system. Where the wall was built, illegal immigration was down. It allowed the Border Patrol to focus on other less protected areas. It reduced human trafficking. It made sense. Is the thief going to enter your house through the locked door or the opened patio sliding glass door?"

For the cost of lunch, reimbursed by the undercover budget, Jake was educated.

CHAPTER FORTY-ONE

Beverly Hills

Though not a household name, Christopher Edmonds was known by most of the movers and shakers in the entertainment industry. He wasn't an actor. He wasn't a writer or director. He was a facilitator. He was a top executive at a couple of the major studios and currently managed an investment group financing independent films. Occasionally, his name would be listed as a "producer" or "executive producer" on big budget productions, but his job was convincing investors and cajoling A-list performers to sign on the bottom line for Hollywood's next blockbuster.

He was present at most red-carpet affairs usually with a stunning starlet his granddaughter's age on his arm. Their beauty distracted from his failed comb-over and lack of height. Thanks to decades of influence within the industry, he always snagged a seat in the first ten rows of any televised awards show.

His was a cautionary tale of arrogance. Though not physically imposing, the sixty-year-old was financially commanding. Edmonds made money for his investors—lots of money. His bachelor's degree from Harvard and master's from the University of Pennsylvania's Wharton School provided him with the technical know-how to work monetary miracles. People wanted to invest with him. They wanted him to do with their money what he did with his.

Chinese firms were increasing their portfolios of entertainment-related companies. Names recognized by many such as AMC

Entertainment, Carmike Cinemas, and Dick Clark Productions were just some of the businesses linked to China's biggest investors. Dream-Works, the studio that produced *Shrek*, *Madagascar*, and *Kung Fu Panda* invested $350 million in Pearl Studio in Shanghai. Hollywood's productions were huge in Asia, and China's middle-class flocked to the movies.

Edmonds was successful in getting American films on China's big screens. He put together foreign distribution packages which saw all parties making a handsome profit. Each of the independent films in which he had a financial interest, generated more profit in Beijing than any U.S. city. He was on a roll and those in the know wanted to follow in his footsteps.

But Christopher Edmonds had a secret. It was a secret few knew. He had a flaw and if that shortcoming were ever made public, his empire would crumble.

The routine was the same every two weeks. The same day of the week. The same hour. The same cottage in the same luxury hotel. Chris-topher Edmonds had a standing reservation at the sprawling facility catering to the rich and powerful. It was his biweekly staycation. No one in hotel management who mailed the invoice nor the auditors at the investment group who paid the billing on the corporate credit card questioned the expense. If asked, he would always say it was his chance to get away and relax from the unending burdens Tinseltown threw at every executive. As part of his cover, he went to the hotel spa precisely at three for a deep tissue massage, leaving a generous tip on the corpo-rate card, then a swim in the indoor Olympic size pool. At six, room service delivered a meal for one: always the Japanese Kobe steak. But his venture began precisely at noon.

Edmonds chose the hotel for its many amenities, but primarily because during regular hours it was easy to gain access to any of the buildings spread throughout the twenty-acre venue. His cottage, sur-rounded by eucalyptus trees providing shade and secrecy, was near the rear of the facility. A short distance from the cottage was a maintenance gate with a combination security lock. Edmonds was privy to the combination and shared it with one other person.

All these factors made it easy for Franklin Lee to provide the services Edmonds demanded. There was no need for Lee to check in at the front desk or valet park his vehicle. He drove through the unmanned maintenance entrance and parked near the gate. He could quickly exit his car and be at the cottage within a minute or two of arriving on the property.

Lee was cautious, recognizing the danger. His services were never invoiced. The payment was always in cash. There were no receipts and there was no paper trail. Edmonds worked out all the details. Precision and privacy were paramount.

Thanks to the anonymity of the internet, Edmonds learned of others in Hollywood who shared his desires. He was extremely cautious in revealing his identity. Often, he maintained his secrecy never revealing his true name. Playing the sleuth, he would cobble together facts and innuendos, guessing the names of his keyboard companions. When he and the others with whom he was communicating mutually exposed themselves, it was shocking to learn his fellow Hollywood high-flyers had the same secret. His circle of like-minded associates was gradually and cautiously expanding.

He and Michael Yang met in a chat room and after weeks of chatting, acknowledging the same desires, they guardedly revealed their true identities. Not often, but occasionally, Edmonds invited Michael or one of his entertainment contemporaries to partake in what he called "treasured memories."

Lee never brought the same "merchandise," as Edmonds referred to it, two weeks in a row unless Edmonds requested it. The executive made extraordinary demands, not easily met. The specificity of the required services could only be fulfilled by a limited collective.

Franklin Lee knew the secret. Edmonds dated starlets, but he desired children. Originally, Lee furnished Asian girls brought to the United States under the pretense that they would be receiving a free education. The only education they received was the little bit of English they learned in the bedroom.

For several months, all the girls furnished by Lee were from Latin America. They were among thousands of unaccompanied minors who crossed our southern border and fell into the hands of the unscrupulous willing to make a buck on the bodies of children.

Today, Edmonds was alone. No Michael Yang. No Hollywood cohort.

Lee entered the maintenance facility lot from a residential side street on the other side of the complex. After parking the Camaro, he and the thirteen-year-old El Salvadorian girl headed toward the chain-link gate. Punching in the code, Lee opened the gate and the two made their way to the secluded cottage.

Edmonds greeted them at the door. Fear and revulsion washed over Isabella who was here before and knew what the American demanded.

CHAPTER FORTY-TWO

East Los Angeles

Taking its name from La Mara, a street gang in San Salvador, and the Salvatrucha guerillas who fought in the Salvadorian Civil War, Mara Salvatrucha—or as it is better known, MS-13—originated in Los Angeles in the early eighties. Like most street gangs, the ethnic minority Salvadorians sought protection from L.A.'s inner city black and Mexican gangs who dominated the neighborhoods.

But that was then. The local gang metastasized into an international cancer, leaving its bloody footprints throughout North and Central America. With a membership exceeding 50,000, the group's reputation for brutality made other organized crime groups look like Sunday school classes. MS-13 went beyond defacing enemy gang graffiti; it was a lethal threat recognized and feared by international law enforcement agencies and other criminal organizations.

In Los Angeles, the gang had not moved east into the San Gabriel Valley where the Wah Ching held prominence. Though MS-13 had numerical superiority and could easily assume control of the neighborhood, members of the two organizations had a loose alliance which proved favorable for both gangs.

Though the gang members liked their ink, each group recognized visible tattoos provided hard evidence for the police when attempting to prove either gang affiliation or identifying members in the commission of a crime. Younger members coming up through the ranks did more to hide their gang association by concealing their tats beneath long-sleeve shirts and jackets.

MS-13 moved beyond the face tattoos of its original members. Eduardo Chavez, however, was inked up to his neck. A Roman numeral "XIII," now concealed by a full head of hair, was prominent while in prison when he shaved his head. His brazen tattoos, screaming to the world his gang affiliation, wouldn't get him hired as a greeter at Walmart, but he never worried about gainful employment. Exploiting open borders and unaccompanied minors who poured across the Mexican-U.S. frontier, he built a lucrative business trafficking minors for the sexual pleasures of American men.

Franklin Lee and Chavez recently engaged in a mutually beneficial criminal alliance. Lee moved many of the weapons stolen from Shooter's Paradise through Chavez to south of the border into Mexico and Central America. Chavez was furnishing underage females to Lee to service his customers.

Following the afternoon appointment with Christopher Edmonds, Lee returned the girl to an East Los Angeles beauty parlor. From the front it looked like cut and curl. In the rear of the business and upstairs, Chavez operated a highly profitable sex parlor.

CHAPTER FORTY-THREE
FRIDAY, MAY 20
Malibu

Having spent more than a year away from Los Angeles with undercover assignments in Indianapolis and Dallas, Jake sought every opportunity to get back to the ocean. He set up this late afternoon meeting with Rone at the Paradise Cove Beach Café in Malibu. The scenic restaurant, less than a "third and long pass" from the Pacific, had been the home to the TV show *The Rockford Files* and featured in *Baywatch*, *Lethal Weapon 4*, and a number of beach-themed movies. The irony was not lost on Jake as Paradise Cove was previously known as Smuggler's Cove where in the late 1800s Chinese railroad builders were smuggled ashore.

Jake grabbed a table next to the window and was waiting for Rone, who was fifteen minutes late. With no UC meetings scheduled for the rest of the day, Jake didn't care how late his case agent was. A storm, miles out at sea, was causing huge waves to break in rapid succession. The sound of the surf crashing ashore was a sound he had been missing.

Katie loved this place, saying the waves reminded her that "man could never compete with the splendor and majesty of God's creation."

He was on his first refill of Diet Pepsi when Rone arrived, apologizing for being late.

Jake shrugged it off.

"Twenty-five miles," said Rone, just a hint of disgust in his voice.

"What's twenty-five miles?"

"That's how far it is from Westwood to here."

Jake could only smile. "You wanted somewhere out of the way to avoid meeting up with any of our potential targets. You don't see any Triad members, do you? Besides, you're using Bureau gas, have an ocean view on a beautiful day, and get to hang out with me."

"Oh yeah, I'm just livin' the life."

The college-age server with golden hair, bleached with the help of the sun and a little lemon juice, approached and handed each a menu. As she was looking out toward the water, Jake assumed she would rather be out on her board than taking midafternoon food orders from two forty-somethings.

Rone ordered an iced tea. After the server left to retrieve his drink, Rone explained the latest updates to the investigation.

Technical innovations were developing at warp speed, allowing law enforcement to conduct investigations in ways they were unable to do just a few years earlier. Automatic license plate recognition cameras digitally captured images of license plates as they passed police video surveillance systems. Within seconds, the computers compared the plates to a database of stolen and wanted vehicles, automatically alerting the police when a targeted vehicle was identified.

In years past, the FBI installed pole cameras across from a location to observe traffic in and out. This was a valuable investigative tool not requiring a search warrant as long as the cameras were installed on public property or with the permission of a property owner.

Fortunately, Michael Yang's business was located directly across the street from a utility pole. Earlier in the morning, FBI technical agents appearing to work for the utility company, installed a concealed camera on the pole. With the advanced technology, the camera could not only read the license plates of those cars coming and going from Yang's parking lot but could capture high-quality images of the visitors to the business.

"We won't have anyone monitoring the camera in real time," Rone began. "But we can both download an app which allows us to pull up date-stamped images captured by the camera. As we begin to develop a scorecard of persons of interest visiting the business, we can monitor it in real time. When a player shows up, we can run you in and see where everyone fits on our chessboard."

He was interrupted by the server who returned with his iced tea and took their orders. Jake ordered the grilled steak tacos; Rone, the half-pound bacon avocado burger and fries.

"Did your doctor say you weren't getting enough cholesterol?"

Rone ignored the sarcastic question. "Let's get back to Mr. Hoover's business."

As they began to resume the conversation, the hostess seated an older couple two tables away.

Lowering his voice, Jake said, "I need to be somewhat cautious, but I think I can periodically short the orders, giving me a chance to go back to the business. I need to come up with an excuse that allows me to keep returning."

"It doesn't seem like there would be too many advances in paper products, but has Brookside given you any indication of novelties or equipment improvements that might provide opportunities to keep returning?"

Jake had not discussed this with Brookside, but it was a subject he needed to broach. "I guess I could always talk about guns, but Danny Yu doesn't even want me to tell Michael about the Kimber."

"I haven't run the serial number on that yet. How do you want to handle it? Technically, we should book that into evidence, but is Danny expecting to see you with the Kimber the next time you two guys meet?"

Shaking his head, Jake said, "I haven't set up a return engagement. If we want to pursue more guns, I could set up a meeting. In some respects, I think he's a little far afield from our original ops order. Have you been able to confirm the Wah Ching membership?"

"I have a call into a guy I worked with at the Sheriff's Department. He works in their gang unit. We had nothing in our files matching your descriptors. Maybe, he'll have something."

After the server brought the tacos and burger, the two continued to talk.

Rone leaned forward and said, "This is all new to me. Working gangs and bank fraud never exposed me to the Chinese threat. My entire military training was focused on Islamic terrorism and the wars in Iraq and Afghanistan. I've been poring over intelligence files that Headquarters, CIA, and NSA have prepared. I think when it comes to China and our handling of the COVID-19 pandemic, we exposed our flank."

Jake nodded in agreement.

Rone continued, "Their biggest export wasn't a product. It was fear and disinformation. In fact, they've weaponized both. They've set up campaigns promulgating lies, half-truths, and cooked numbers. We've identified social media pages managed from Beijing. They've hijacked propaganda websites, written op-ed pieces on both sides of an issue, and shared them throughout their entire disinformation networks. Because the fabrications have partial truths with a ring of veracity, the gullible share without checking the source of the newsfeeds. If it sounds legit, people buy it."

Jake interrupted, "Rone, this is well above our paygrade. We are just a couple of Bureau pawns waiting to be sacrificed."

"I know, Jake, but maybe we can make a small dent in China's campaign of global domination. We need to dig deep. Right now, we are only scratching the surface."

"At least, let's make the scratches bleed."

✕ ✕ ✕

Agoura Hills, Los Angeles

He used his elbow to ring the doorbell, holding pizza and antipasto salad in both hands. Natasha and Joey greeted him at the door and his heart melted when Joey threw his arms around Jake's legs and giggled an almost perceptible "Uncle Jake."

"I think he loves you," said Natasha as she took the salad off the top of the pizza box. She was wearing a white sun dress accentuating all the right features and emphasizing her summer tan.

"He has the gift of discernment," said Jake with a big smile. "He knows I love him." *Nuts, why didn't I say "he knows I love you guys" or something a little closer to romantic?*

They spent a quiet evening together: Jake and Joey on the floor most of the night roughhousing and laughing; Natasha watching her little boy laugh harder than she had seen in a long time.

CHAPTER FORTY-FOUR

MONDAY, MAY 23
Los Angeles

Jake didn't recognize the number when the "Folsom Prison Blues" ring tone erupted from his cell phone. The undercover agent answered cautiously, "Hello" was all he said.

"It's Grizzly Six."

Jake smiled. No one who served with Peter Newman ever forgot his radio call sign. Peter Newman was Jake's regimental commander when the U.S. liberated Iraq from Saddam in 2003. He was the kind of leader who knew how to accomplish the mission *and* take care of his men.

Whether he was commanding a regular Marine unit or conducting special operations as he did later, Peter Newman was revered and loved by those who served with him in his many commands. While Jake was recovering in the hospital after being wounded in Iraq, it was then-Colonel Newman who visited him and who tried to talk Jake into staying in the Corps. But Jake needed to move on. Peter Newman understood and wrote a gold-plated fitness report that went in with Jake's Bureau application.

Peter Newman retired as a major general when the Senate wouldn't approve his third star. Now the CEO of Centurion Solutions Group, the private security firm awarded numerous classified contracts with various alphabet government agencies: CIA, NSA, DIA, DHS, TSA, FBI. It was General Newman who was in contact with Jake during the

operation designated Counterfeit Lies, targeting North Korean espionage agents operating in Los Angeles. He provided Jake with detailed
off-the-books intel creating a clearer picture of the undercover op than
anything the Bureau or the Agency disclosed. Jake owed Peter Newman
his life several times over and willingly took the call.

"Sir, it's great to hear from you," said Jake pausing before including,
". . . I think."

The general laughed. "We need to talk."

"Sir, I'm not on a secure phone."

"I understand. I would rather meet in person."

"I don't plan on being in Washington anytime soon."

"No need to travel, Lieutenant. I'm in town."

CHAPTER FORTY-FIVE

Malibu

As the sun set, the howls of coyotes surrounded the tiny Malibu Hills cabin five miles from the Pacific Ocean. Peter Newman stood on the front porch of the secluded wood frame structure taking in the sights, sounds, and smells. Clear skies exposed a waxing crescent moon and thousands of stars as two friends took time to discuss very sensitive matters.

The light from the opened refrigerator door was like a lightning strike in the darkened house causing the visitor to turn from his star gazing. Jake walked out, letting the screen door slam, handing an opened bottle of Modelo Negra to the retired Marine Corps major general.

"I understand why you like it here," said the general.

The men lightly touched the bottles in a silent toast as they sat on matching wicker patio rockers.

After a short pull on the beer, Jake said, "I like the solitude. This is still a great escape from all the world tries to throw at me." He paused briefly taking another sip then said, "Two bedrooms and one bath were about all we needed. Neither of us put much emphasis on possessions." Jake added a smile, "Thankfully, Katie's love language wasn't gifts."

"On a Marine's salary and then a pay cut to join the Bureau, I wasn't in a position to throw a lot of gifts her way. We just enjoyed each other's company. After she died, I wasn't about to move away and leave the memories of the great times Katie and I shared here. This place still brings me a measure of comfort knowing we shared a few years of our lives together in this old cabin. She brought meaning to my life in ways I never anticipated. I still fall back on those times when I hit bumps in the road."

Just then, two coyotes exchanged yaps.

"I'm not sure your neighbors appreciate your presence," Major General Newman, USMC (Ret), added with a smile.

Jake nodded and continued, "This cabin has been here about four decades. Coyotes only live six to eight years. I'm claiming dominion. I think we've come to a mutual understanding with a tentative peace agreement. They avoid me and I avoid them. So far it's worked out."

As he said it, two more coyotes joined in the collective yelping, identifying their territory and posting a powerful warning to any animal seeking to infringe.

"Did you know Brian Sullivan?" asked the general.

"No, sir. Never heard of him. You said 'did' in the past tense."

"He worked at the Carpenter Foundation and was killed eleven days ago in a grocery store parking lot in Burbank."

"I haven't watched the news in a couple of weeks, but L.A. averages a few homicides every day, so it might not have received much media coverage."

"It hit the back page of the *L.A. Times*."

"Was he someone under your command at one time?"

"No, he was Army, but was working on a documentary for the foundation. It involved the Chinese-Uyghur issue, and I was providing him information from our intelligence sources. With your new undercover assignment, I just wanted you to be aware of it in case you hear or see anything."

Jake shook his head in amazement, cautiously asking, "How do you know about our undercover operation?"

"Jake, the approvals for your UC op had to go through FBI Headquarters and DOJ. I'm still wired into both organizations and probably know as much about what is going on at DOJ as your Director or the AG."

Jake slowly shook his head, "Sometimes, General, you scare me. Not only because of what and how you know, but the fact so much intel seems to be floating around back there outside official channels. If you know about it, maybe the other side does too."

The general lowered his voice as if to prevent the coyotes from hearing. "It should be a concern, especially because of your current involvement with the Chinese. It was one thing when you were dealing with the North Koreans two years ago. They are limited in their access to our internal secrets, but the Chinese have their thumb on nearly every aspect of our government, economy, national security, and society. China is an awakening Goliath. That's why I was working so closely with Sullivan. I wanted the information we developed on the forced labor issue out in the public for the world to see. The documentary was going to open eyes internationally."

"So, what happened to him?"

The general began to take another sip of beer but stopped, lowering the bottle, and answering, "I don't believe in coincidence. He called me on his way to the Chinese consulate where he was hoping to set up an on-camera interview with a PRC government representative to discuss the Uyghur concentration camps and slave labor issues. All I've been able to gather is within a few hours of the meeting, he was shot in a supermarket parking lot. Two to the chest, one to the head. .45 caliber. Close range. Though the perp or perps took his wallet, watch, and laptop, it looked to me like more than a simple armed robbery."

"Are the police calling it a robbery?"

Newman nodded.

"Were there any witnesses?"

"No one saw the actual shooting. But witnesses described a tan Camaro racing from the scene. I'm not asking you to investigate it, but just keep your ears open. I know your operation is hoping to snag a couple of I/Os. I'm convinced the Chinese consulate was involved in the killing."

Swallowing a mouthful of his beer, Jake said, "I haven't heard about a tan Camaro in any of the briefings, but I'll keep my eyes and ears open."

"Has the Bureau given you much background on the Chinese issues?"

"Not really. I read a generic intelligence white paper that provided little substance. Typical intel-weenie insights, adding two and two and hoping to come up with something close to a four."

"I understand. Jake, China is our biggest challenge on the world stage. The Chinese Communist Party, the CCP, is out to destroy our nation by any means. Though chickens and terrorists like to cackle when they drop an egg, the Chinese know not to advertise their successes. In fact, for them, it's lie, deny, and make counter-allegations. Have you read the book, *America's #1 Adversary*?"

Jake shook his head.

"It was published in 2020, written by three senior members of Ronald Reagan's National Security Council Staff. Admiral John Poindexter and Bud McFarlane were President Reagan's National Security Advisors. Richard Levine was Reagan's NSC Security Policy Director."

Reaching into his old, well-worn map case, Major General Newman pulled out a copy of the book, handed it to Jake, and said, "If you want the straight scoop about what the 'Chi-Coms' are up to, read this book. In just a few hours you will read about all the PRC is doing to take us down. What happened in Ukraine didn't change any of what's in this book. Putin's goal is to dominate Europe. Xi Jinping's goal is to dominate the whole world including us. Xi is much more dangerous than Putin ever could be.

Jake nodded slowly as he looked at the cover and took a long pull on the beer.

Newman continued, "Xi Jinping and the PRC's politburo view us as nothing but a 'paper tiger' incapable of competing in a conventional war or God forbid, a nuclear exchange."

Swallowing, Jake said, "Let's face it, we have been fighting radical Islamic terrorism for the past two decades and we're not ready as a nation to go toe-to-toe with a peer-level adversary who commits industrial espionage. The disastrous surrender in Afghanistan in August 2021 still hangs over our heads."

General Newman nodded and added, "You're spot-on, Jake, but there is much more in this little book. Our very existence as a free nation, in control of our own destiny, is at grave risk due to the communist government of the People's Republic of China. Absolute power in the PRC is wielded by Xi Jinping. He has succeeded in creating a false equivalence with America's presidency. Xi is frequently addressed as 'President of China' a title he has held since March of 2013. Xi, however, has many other sources of power, which are now virtually unlimited.

"Among his many titles, he is General Secretary of the Central Committee of the Communist Party of China, and Chairman of the Central Military Commission; Xi attained both positions in November 2012. He is also Commander-in-Chief of China's military and combined forces as of April 2016, and Chairman of the Central Commission for Integrated Military and Civilian Development since January 2017. Such a combination of civilian and military authority in one man is daunting in an undemocratic state. Xi Jinping has made clear, his ultimate goal is to make Communist China the dominant economic and military power on earth.

"Xi is employing unprecedented, unlimited levers of power against the Chinese people, the United States, and our democratic allies around the globe. Communist China's military is the largest on earth. They now have more combatant ships and aircraft than we do—and are building new ones three times faster than we are.

"The PRC's theft of intellectual property threatens our national security and that of our closest friends. Xi's willingness to allow tons of illicit, addictive drugs to be dumped on Western populations endangers millions. His false territorial claims over vast expanses of open seas and the erection of man-made islands, which are, in fact, military bastions, provide visual proof of his determination.

"Even more menacing are the PRC's overt and covert actions to thwart UN sanctions against Tehran. As in North Korea, Xi's ruthless geopolitical strategy all but ensures the ayatollahs in Iran will obtain nuclear weapons and the means of delivering them.

"Credible evidence exists that the Communist Party in China was instrumental in the worldwide spread of COVID-19—"

At this point Jake interrupted, "So is this COVID virus a biological warfare agent created in the Wuhan lab?"

General Newman paused a moment before responding, "We know this virus isn't spread to humans by bats like mosquitos spread malaria. We know it was genetically modified to make it more easily transmitted and deadly. That's what the scientists call 'gain of function.' We know the Wuhan Institute of Virology is one of nine laboratories reporting to and regulated by the Chinese Academy of Sciences, or CAS. And we know CAS reports directly to the State Council of the People's Republic of China. And we know the State Council considers this kind of research to be a top national security secret, but we don't know the answer to your question."

Jake responded, "Okay, fair enough. What do you *think*?"

Once again, the general took a breath before speaking. "I can't prove it—yet. But I believe the Communist Chinese have been conducting biological warfare experiments since shortly after the Korean War. And at some point—hopefully soon—we will have a couple of defectors from the Wuhan labs who come over to our side to confirm my suspicions."

Jake shook his head, held up the book and asked, "Is what you just said in this book?"

"Not what I said about defectors, but if you are working undercover against the communist Chinese, there is a lot in those pages that will improve your situational awareness. For example, Xi is cracking down on Christians. Religious freedom in China is nonexistent. Democracy in Hong Kong has been crushed. The economies in dozens of developing countries are threatened by Beijing's 'Belt and Road Initiative.'

"Here at home, the PRC's Confucius Institutes' propaganda and disinformation campaigns have encouraged Marxists and anarchist vandals to torch and loot more than a dozen of our major cities. I have no doubt the 'Defund the Police' movement originated in one of the PRC's human behavior labs. They have succeeded in spewing Critical Race Theory into our schools, even attacking our nation's seminal documents, the Declaration of Independence, and the Constitution as proof of 'White Supremacy.'

"Worse, the pace of Beijing's campaign for global domination is accelerating. If Xi's PRC succeeds, every place on our planet will be plunged into the abyss George Orwell warned of in his masterpiece, *1984*. Our children deserve better than being forced to exist in a totalitarian, all-seeing world where Chinese-built computers, artificial intelligence, surveillance systems, and technology monitor their every move, the words they utter, and with whom they keep company. That's not freedom.

Jake shook his head in disgust. "Meanwhile our leaders are turning our military personnel into social justice warriors."

Newman nodded. "Jake, here's the bottom line. Xi wants Communist China to do everything it can to destroy our economic, political, and moral fabric. Media, politics, culture are their current battleground. They believe economic superiority is a real conquest. In the past decade, the People's Republic of China has stolen $6 trillion in U.S. intellectual property. That's trillion with a 't.'"

"Death by a thousand cuts," commented Jake, referring to *lingchi*, a form of torture used by the Chinese into the early 1900s.

"Exactly!" said General Newman with a clenched fist to emphasize his point. "Asymmetric warfare means the PRC will identify our weaknesses and exploit our vulnerabilities. They have attempted to compromise our tech innovations, medical research, even entertainment from Hollywood.

"Wall Street is betting against us by investing in projects supporting Chinese nuclear enrichment and weapons like the Chi-Com hypersonic missiles. At the same time, China operates a vast intelligence network beginning with a couple hundred thousand Chinese students attending school here. Their laws require the cooperation of Chinese scientists and students working here to be debriefed regularly by PRC state security officials.

"Beyond this intelligence gathering, there are concerted efforts to undermine our values. They are flooding the internet with pornography. They've secretly funneled money to anarchist groups like BLM and ANTIFA. They are pouring their resources into our elections, hoping to fill the seats of local, state, and federal legislatures with politicians promoting a progressive agenda and beholding to Chinese dollars.

"They targeted a U.S. senator's driver who was the liaison with the local Asian-American community. She was on the Senate Intelligence Committee at the time.

"One of the PRC operatives targeted a congressman while he was still a member of city council. This same female PRC agent went after a couple of Midwestern mayors. Your FBI has video of the PRC agent and a mayor having sex in the backseat of his car. Much closer to home, remember Katrina Leung, the 'double agent,' recruited by the Los Angeles field office in the early 80s. She compromised two FBI agents in her bedroom and served as a PRC double agent for two decades.

"Finally, Jake, there's the issue of direct intervention in American election outcomes. Voter fraud is real and has been with us for more years than most are willing to admit. During the 1844 presidential election—James Polk versus Henry Clay—the great issues of the day were emancipation and annexing the Republic of Texas into the Union. In a New York jurisdiction, 55,000 votes were recorded. But there were only 41,000 eligible voters. Polk was elected.

"So, nothing is new in a presidential election, except today there are now issues about foreign powers tinkering in our election technology. Prior to the 2020 election, even Democrat senators expressed concern about the integrity of computerized voting systems. A federal judge identified 'serious system security vulnerability and operational issues with voting machine technology.'

"A PEW study in 2012 found one out of every eight voter registrations invalid or 'significantly inaccurate.' The PEW research determined more than 1.8 million deceased individuals were listed as voters and approximately 2.75 million people had registrations in more than one state.

"California has 'motor voter' registration. When a Californian applies or seeks to renew a driver's license, he or she is automatically registered to vote unless the applicant opts out.

"Consider a tech-savvy country like the PRC accessing DMV records or death records or multiple state registrations. Now, consider this same hostile country accessing voter rolls. It would take very little data mining to determine whether a registered voter voted in previous elections.

"If a foreign power—such as the PRC—can identify registered voters who don't vote, it's now just a matter of casting ballots for the far left's preferred candidate. A sophisticated adversary—like the PRC—recognizes there is little chance a registered, non-voting citizen will inquire into whether he or she already voted. Enough counterfeit ballots can then change the outcome of an election."

At this, Jake shook his head and asked, "How many ballots does it take?"

"Well . . ." the general replied, "back in 2008 Al Franken—a TV comedian—won his U.S. Senate seat by just 312 votes. Lots of elections are determined by a few thousand votes so it wouldn't take that many counterfeit ballots to alter the outcome of a close race. In last

year's gubernatorial election in New Jersey, there were nearly 2.5 million votes cast but the outcome would have been different if fewer than
30,000 ballots were cast for the challenger.

"As you know Jake, the FBI lab can quickly perform forensic tests
on a ballot's paper and ink to determine whether they were printed by
an outside entity. Despite all the controversy over our last presidential election, no investigative, judicial, or legislative entity has required
these kinds of tests to ensure the integrity of our elections."

Jake paused in the gathering darkness before asking, "What better
way to undermine us than to destroy the integrity of our elections?"

"Absolutely, Jake. There is no better way—and it's been going on for
a long time. In the aftermath of World War II, when dozens of former
colonies began voting for independence, one of the 'active measures'
Moscow secretly authorized to achieve outcomes they wanted has been
vbros byulleteney—'ballot box stuffing.' The Soviets still employ this
activity in their own elections as do scores of other countries—including Communist China.

"Over the years the PRC has vastly improved the process. Beijing
now influences U.S. policy through a growing network of people working at the highest tiers of politics, business, education, religion, and
technology. Pedophilia is just one more tool they use to compromise
'leaders' in all those sectors of our society. All this has been done to
increase the PRC's power while weakening our nation.

"Jake, this is no piece of over-the-top right wing propaganda; this
is a real threat to our Constitutional Republic. Too few Americans are
aware of the magnitude or effectiveness of the PRC's efforts."

"Death by a thousand cuts," Jake repeated with a nod.

Peter Newman, whose patriotism could never be questioned and
whose sources topped those of most government agencies, opened
Jake's eyes. Jake suddenly realized he would need to bring his A-game
to this fight.

CHAPTER FORTY-SIX
TUESDAY, MAY 24
Los Angeles

Jake recognized the number displayed on the Bronco's navigation screen and answered on the third ring.

"Yeah, Rone, what's up?"

"Where are you?"

"I'm heading over to Yang's business."

"You guys have a real bromance going on," said the case agent.

"In addition to a couple of incidents in which I've been cleared, my accurate shooting and the ability to translate my skills into teachable moments have made me a valuable commodity at Yang Printing. We have been over to the Paradise range several times and each time he expects a free lesson. He's actually getting better. He would never make it as a Marine, but he can outshoot a lot of Rangers I know."

"Screw you, jarhead," said Rone with a laugh. "So, what is it he needs today?"

"He called me late yesterday afternoon. He needs a ream of Southworth 994C, the gold watermark, and I told him I'd bring it over this morning."

"Wow, listen to you. The Martha Stewart of parchment."

Pretending to be annoyed, Jake asked, "What do you want?"

"When was the last time you spoke with Danny Yu?"

Jake hesitated but only for a second, "I haven't talked to him since we met at Denny's, and he gave me the Kimber. What's going on with him?"

"I just ran the Kimber, and it came back stolen from the break-in at Shooter's Paradise."

"You're kidding," said Jake surprised by the news. "When I first went there with Michael, he remarked to the clerk about the reduced inventory and the guy mentioned they had a robbery."

"What was Yang's reaction?"

Stopped at a light, Jake thought about that day. "He acted surprised. He didn't say anything out of the ordinary suggesting he knew something about a break-in."

There was doubt in Rone's voice. "But then that same day, he asked you to drop off a package to Danny Yu who offers you a stolen Kimber."

"Yep, that just about sums it up," said Jake trying to recall the interaction with Yang and Yu.

"I don't think either one of us believes in coincidence."

Jake didn't, but he responded, "If Michael knew about the theft and Yu's involvement, I'm not sure he would send me over, knowing my appreciation for guns and the possibility Yu might offer me a stolen weapon. I know Michael told him we went shooting that day which is why Yu brought up the Kimber."

"Did Danny say he'd ever been to Shooter's Paradise?"

"I don't recall. It would be on the recording. He may have known Michael was a member at Paradise. I don't think it came up. I don't recall us mentioning where Michael and I went shooting. I have to be a little cautious this early in the investigation because Danny doesn't want me telling anyone I purchased the Kimber. I don't think I know Michael well enough to say something and it not get back to Danny."

"I understand. Do you have a reason to call Danny?"

"Not really unless we want to buy another gun," said Jake.

"Let's do it."

Jake thought for a moment before answering. "I can probably make it work. Obviously, nothing went wrong with the Kimber purchase, and I'll just tell him I'm looking to build up my inventory before the apocalypse. Do you have a list of the stolen weapons?"

Rone read through the list of guns reported stolen. It was extensive, enough to outfit a small army and capable of doing some serious damage.

"I told him I had a Remington 870. Let me check on an AR-15. If he hasn't gotten rid of all the M&Ps, it might make sense I would want one before Congress outlaws them. I don't know that I need to go into a constitutional political diatribe, but if he asks, I can say I think if they outlaw the 15s, they will grandfather in anyone currently in possession of one."

"Yes, but he's not a licensed dealer, so no one will even know you purchased it."

As Jake was pulling up to Yang's parking lot, he said, "Good point. Have you run this past Her Highness, Supervisory Special Agent Charlene Taylor?"

"She's back in Quantico for a two-week in-service."

"So, are we without adult supervision?"

You could hear the smile in Rone's voice. "We are without adult supervision. Let's move before Mother comes home."

CHAPTER FORTY-SEVEN

West Los Angeles

Jake grabbed the ream of paper and hopped out of the Bronco heading toward the business. As he entered, he was greeted by Madison, the receptionist.

"Good morning, Mr. Webb. You're becoming quite a regular around here."

As part of his play, Jake took on the names with meaning. He always kept the same first name. He didn't want a friendly recognizing him in the company of the targets calling him Jake when his UC name was Chuck. Thus, he was always Jake Somebody. For the past several operations, he was Jacob David Webb. Anyone who followed Robert Ludlum's Bourne series knew Jason Bourne's real name was David Webb. Jake loved the irony. *If you can't screw with them, why play?*

"Please, Madison, call me Jake. I don't always answer to Mr. Webb."

"Okay, then. We will start all over. Good morning, Jake," she said with a friendly smile.

"Good morning to you, Madison. And yes, I am becoming a regular. I think he just likes having me around and purposely shorts his orders on supplies so I can make the daily deliveries. I'm sure he thinks I class up the place."

Madison chuckled. "That's what it is. In fact, I heard him mentioning it the other day. He's in his office. You can go on back."

Jake made his way down the hallway past the conference room and knocked on the closed door.

"Yes," came the response.

Jake opened the door without announcing his presence.

"Jake," greeted Michael as if the prodigal son had returned. A cigarette dangling from his mouth, smoke surrounding his face. "Guess what I just picked up?"

Jake shrugged his shoulders having no idea.

Michael opened the top drawer of his executive-looking desk and pulled out a pistol. Holding it up, he said, "A Kimber Raptor II. I thought maybe I'd run over to the Paradise this morning and put a few rounds downrange. Do you want to come with me?"

"Sure, I don't have my gun on me. I guess I could run home and get it."

Stabbing out the cigarette, Michael said, "There's no need to do that. We can trade off with the Kimber."

"Where'd you get it? I didn't see one in the display case the last time we were at the Paradise."

"No, a buddy of mine was looking to get rid of one. It's brand-new."

"Brand-new? What happened? Did his wife find out he used the grocery money to buy a new gun?"

"Something like that."

Michael dropped the magazine and cleared the chamber, handing the weapon to Jake.

Before Jake took the Kimber, he placed the ream of paper on Michael's desk. "Here's your paper."

As Jake was examining the new pistol, he took the opportunity for some small talk. "What's the fancy parchment for? Are you going to start sending out your résumé?"

Michael smiled. "Have you ever had a massage?"

"Sure, I've had trouble with my lower back for years. I've done a lot of physical therapy and every once in a while, the PT was followed up with a massage."

Offering an impish grin as he shook his head, Michael said, "Not that kind of a massage. I mean a real massage. Come on, all that time you spent in Oceanside with the Marines, and you didn't go out in town and get a massage?"

"No, I really didn't."

"Maybe I need to fix you up with one of the places where we provide the paperwork to satisfy the cops and the Board of Health."

Handing the Kimber back to Michael, Jake asked, "What are you talking about?"

"Jake, not every massage parlor in town is staffed by licensed masseuses. A lot of the Asian places have girls moving in and out. It's a little too costly and complicated when they bounce between California, Arizona, and Nevada to keep them licensed. One of my little side specialties is providing licensing certificates, diplomas from nonexistent schools in China, and all the false identification to match the certification."

Jake laughed. "Every time I'm around you, I'm amazed. You do know how to make a buck. I'm going to start calling you Doctor Dollar and sit at your feet learning all I can about every pot in which you have a hand."

"I'm ready to expand my empire, if you want to join me."

CHAPTER FORTY-EIGHT

West Los Angeles

It was another successful morning at Shooter's Paradise. Michael, not the best shot, had trouble controlling the kick of the .45, but with Jake's assistance, he made a few adjustments. By the end of the morning, Michael's groupings on his *Walking Dead* zombie target were a little tighter.

Unable to learn anymore about the source of the Kimber, it seemed too coincidental to Jake that Danny Yu wasn't the seller. Michael avoided answering the question, and possibly like Jake, promised Danny he wouldn't tell how or from whom he obtained the gun. Though it wasn't a matter of distrust, Michael never let the Kimber out of his sight. With too many digits to memorize, it was impossible for Jake to copy down the serial number. Maybe later in the investigation, they would discover the truth.

After Jake left the Paradise and before calling Danny, he called Rone. Every undercover case was different. Often, flexibility was the key. Many of the investigations Jake worked began with drugs and ended with drugs. It was simple A to B. Some investigations, however, went all over the alphabet. In a criminal case, Jake and his case agent typically allowed the targets to dictate the direction in which they wanted to take their lawless activities.

Obviously, there was a common quest as outlined in the approved ops order, but as long as the operation was gathering evidence of federal criminal acts, Jake was able to pursue the varied violations. Because of the nature of this investigation, Jake and Rone weren't sure how far they could expand beyond the narrowly defined borders of the Headquarters-approved FCI undertaking.

With Charlene Taylor out of the office, both men were moving forward as fast as they could. If, when Taylor returned from Quantico, the case agent and the undercover agent were determined to have committed a major infraction in their quest to move the ball down the field, the men would take the fifteen-yard penalty and play it third and long. It was easier to offer a little *mea culpa* after the fact than await approvals which might never come.

Danny answered on the fourth ring and said he was home. Jake stopped long enough to switch out the computer chip on his recording device and headed out the Santa Monica Freeway toward Monterey Park.

✕ ✕ ✕

Monterey Park

Annie answered through the closed screen door. Tendering a big smile, she said, "I know you."

"Yes, you do, Annie. My name is Jake."

"That's right. Your name is Jake, and my name is Annie."

"Is Danny home?"

"Danny is my brother."

"I know that, Annie. Is he home?"

"Yes." Without opening the screen door, she turned and yelled, "Danny, it's Jake. The big white man. He is here to see you."

Now opening the screen door, she said, "Would you like to come in? I made some iced tea. It's a brand-new recipe. My brother said I put too much lemon in my other recipe. Would you like to try it?"

"Yes, Annie I would like to try it."

She really was a beautiful young lady, naïve to a world that might want to exploit her innocence.

Annie's smile was ear-to-ear. "Good. You sit down and I will bring you my new special iced tea."

As she was in the kitchen pouring a glass of her new recipe, Danny walked in from the back bedroom, greeting Jake like a successful business colleague; amazing how an illegal gun sale without an arrest had a way of encouraging fast friendships.

"Good to see you again. What can I do for you?"

"I spent the morning with Michael, and we went to the range. I didn't say anything to him, but I assume you got him the Kimber Raptor II. I didn't have to fake my knowledge of the weapon. It is smooth. I've put a couple of boxes through mine already."

Annie walked in with a glass of iced tea for Jake. "Danny, would you like a glass? It's my new recipe. It's really good."

Danny shook his head.

"Please, Danny. Try it. Mr. Jake is going to try it. He will tell you it is good."

Both Danny and Annie looked to Jake who carefully took a sip. He swallowed slowly trying to soften the sourness so his face would not reflect the fact the recipe still used too much lemon.

Jake turned toward Danny and winked. "Annie, this is much better than your last recipe. It still might not need as many lemons as you are using, but I really like this. Thank you."

"See, Danny. Mr. Jake likes it."

"Okay, you can bring me a glass."

Annie headed toward the kitchen and before Danny and Jake could resume their conversation, she brought Danny a glass. She laughed, "I knew you would want my new recipe iced tea. I already poured you a glass."

"Okay, Annie. Thank you. Now will you please go to your room. Jake and I need to discuss some business, I think."

Annie was all smiles, promising to return if either of the two wanted a refill.

"So, what brings you here?"

Jake was afraid to push the Kimber discussion. Annie's interruption of the conversation made it awkward to go back. Moving forward to pursue a second gun buy, Jake asked, "What else do you have for sale?"

Danny turned the question back on Jake. "What else do you want?"

"Can you give me a good deal on a California compliant AR-15?"

"Why does it have to be California compliant?"

Jake had not really thought through a response, but only brought up the compliance issue because he knew the guns stolen from Shooter's Paradise could be legally purchased and possessed in California. A long sip of the iced tea gave him time to formulate an answer. "The only place I can shoot around here is at one of the ranges. I'm not sure if they have reporting requirements. Maybe if they see me shooting anything not legal in California, they're required to call the cops."

Satisfied with the answer, Danny said he had access to a Smith & Wesson AR-15 M&P Sport II.

Jake nodded. "I've looked at those on the internet. I've never shot one, but Smith & Wesson makes good guns. How much are you asking?"

"I think he's asking five fifty."

"Oh, since you had the Kimber, I thought you had all the guns."

"No, I had the Kimber, but it's a crew with the inventory."

"Based upon what Michael said I thought you were part of a crew."

Danny shook his head. "I have my hands full going to school and taking care of Annie. I don't have time to bang."

"So, I guess you didn't get Michael his new Raptor."

Danny shook his head which the recording device didn't pick up.

Jake didn't want to push it. "Can he go five? I could run down to the ATM and get you five this afternoon."

Danny picked up his cell phone and punched in a speed dial number. When the person on the other end answered, Danny said, "It's me. Hey, can you go five on the AR-15s, the M&P Sport II's?" There was a pause then Danny said, "He can get the money this afternoon—okay, thanks."

Danny ended the call and said to Jake, "You can pick it up this evening."

"Name a time," said Jake.

"How about 6 p.m.?"

Nodding, Jake asked, "Where?"

Danny provided the name of the Chinese restaurant on Atlantic Boulevard with a parking lot in the rear. He suggested they meet inside and could do the exchange at their cars. Jake agreed. Count two of the indictment was about to be written.

CHAPTER FORTY-NINE

Monterey Park

The Asian Bistro was more than the typical fried rice and egg foo young mom-and-pop Chinese restaurant. With subdued lighting and soft music playing in the background, it was more romantic than practical. As Jake walked in, he was promptly greeted with a polite bow by a young lady dressed in a red floral-patterned ankle-length cheongsam dress.

"You must be Jake," said the hostess in heavily accented English.

Jake nodded.

"Please, you come with me."

As he was led toward the back of the restaurant, he noted he was the only Caucasian in the place; possibly, why his hostess had no problem recognizing him as a member of Danny's party. He was surprised to see Annie seated at the table with her brother.

"Hi, Mr. Jake."

"Hi, Annie. I didn't expect to see you here tonight. I'm glad you could join us."

"I'm glad you could join us. I like you, Mr. Jake. They have lemon iced tea here, but it isn't as good as mine."

"I'm sure it's not as good as yours."

This was one of the harder aspects of any undercover operation. Innocent people got caught up in the criminal dealings of friends and family. Jake had to keep reminding himself he wasn't judge and jury.

236   OLIVER NORTH — BOB HAMER

He liked Annie, knew a little of the family history, and appreciated a brother dedicated to keeping what was left of the family intact. If Danny took a fall, she was going to be hurt. Jake was almost reluctant to go forward with tonight's purchase. A second gun count threw the sentencing guidelines into overdrive.

Jake had the money and knew Rone was sitting in the restaurant's parking lot in the rear. From inside a surveillance van, the case agent was prepared to snap pictures when Jake and Danny went to their respective cars. By the end of the evening, the case against Danny would only get stronger.

"Mr. Jake, have you ever eaten here?"

"No, Annie. I haven't. What do you like?"

"I always get the spring rolls and the shrimp teriyaki."

"Well, that sounds very good. If you're going to get that, I'm going to get that. What does your brother like?"

"He likes noodles."

Jake laughed, "Is that all? Just noodles."

"Danny, tell Mr. Jake what kind of noodles you like."

"I get the Singapore rice noodles."

"Danny, let's get the green beans that you chew on."

"You mean the edamame?" asked her brother.

"Yes, the Eddie's mommy."

Both Danny and Jake smiled at her innocence.

When the server came to the table, Annie said, "Li Ming, this is my friend Mr. Jake. He's going to have what I have."

Li Ming smiled, "Annie, do you mean the spring rolls and shrimp teriyaki? That's what you always get."

"Yes. Bring him what you bring me. And bring us both the lemon iced tea. But it's not as good as mine."

The food was good. Jake enjoyed the company and cautiously relaxed in the conversation the three enjoyed. Again, he was touched by the love Danny displayed toward Annie. After they finished eating,

Jake grabbed the check, paid the bill, and left a nice gratuity for Li Ming.

As they exited the restaurant and headed into the parking lot, Rone was snapping photographs as quickly as he could.

Danny made Annie sit in the front seat of his black Honda Accord as the two men conducted business.

"Did you bring the money?" asked Danny.

"Yes, five hundred all in twenties. That's the way the ATM spit it out."

Danny shrugged. "That's okay. They spend like hundreds."

With that, Jake handed over a wad of bills as Danny began counting in full view of the camera. When he was satisfied with the count, Danny opened the back door of the car.

"Wow, still in the box."

Annie intervened. "Mr. Jake, are you buying something from my brother?"

"Annie, Jake and I have business. You just be quiet."

"Is the box for Mr. Jake?"

"Annie, what did I tell you?"

Hanging her head in innocent shame, she said, "I'm sorry."

Lowering his voice, Danny said, "It's never been fired."

Jake reached in and pulled out the AR-15 appearing as if he were concealing it from anyone in the parking lot but displaying it for Rone whom Jake knew was capturing the entire transaction on digital.

"This is great. And it's California compliant, so I won't have any problems at the range."

Danny laughed. "It's compliant, but that stock and grip are ugly."

"Can I mention this buy to Michael? I still haven't said anything to him about the Kimber."

"You can tell him about the AR-15. In fact, he's getting one from us. We might run it over there in the next day or two."

"Let me know when you head over there. Maybe we could all go shoot at the Paradise."

Jake put the weapon back in its box. The two shook hands. As Jake retreated with the box to the Bronco, Annie shouted, "Goodbye, Mr. Jake. I hope I see you again soon."

CHAPTER FIFTY

Los Angeles

Jake and Rone preplanned a rendezvous point at the parking lot of Los Angeles's Union Station, the largest railroad passenger terminal in the western United States. Located downtown, it was an easy exit off the freeway and a quick return once the FBI agents debriefed.

Leaving the restaurant, an experienced Jake did an SDR, a surveillance detection route, to ensure he wasn't being followed away from the deal by any of Danny's watchers. After almost every meet and especially every transaction in which contraband was exchanged, Jake's driving was designed to spot the spotters: left turns; right turns; U-turns; slowing as a light turned yellow, then racing through the red. Jake saw nothing. Though he left first, allowing Rone to watch Danny's actions and reactions, Rone was already at the parking lot when Jake pulled in next to him.

The undercover buy was a success, but Jake was in no mood to celebrate. Rone knew from previous discussions the sister was tugging on Jake's heartstrings and made this transaction difficult. In addition to wearing a recording device, Jake wore a tiny transmitter. Though some of the reception wasn't always clear, Rone heard much of the conversation including the interaction with Annie.

Jake slowly got out of the Bronco without saying a word. Rone went straight to the rear hatch of the SUV, opened it, and began checking the numbers of the rifle with the list of stolen weapons from the Shooter's Paradise burglary. He quickly found a match. The Smith & Wesson

AR-15 M&P Sport II Jake purchased was one of a dozen stolen from the gun range and the first to be recovered.

"It's on the list."

Jake said nothing.

"Did he tell you how the gun was going to get there?"

Slow to respond as if the answer was obvious, Jake said, "No, he just said we would do the deal at the restaurant."

"He didn't bring the gun."

"Yes, he did. It was in the car. Didn't you see me pull it out of the backseat? Don't tell me, you missed it."

"Jake, I saw you pull it out, but he didn't put it in the back seat. An unknown Asian male subject driving a tan Camaro pulled up to Danny's Honda and put the box in the back seat. The doors to the Honda were unlocked and I got the unsub locking the doors at the driver side switch, then leaving."

"Did you get good photos of the unsub?"

"Yeah."

"Let me take a look."

The two men hopped into the surveillance van, and Rone opened his laptop. He snapped hundreds of photos of everyone coming and going into the restaurant. When Rone came to the photos of the Camaro, he stopped the slideshow. The tan Camaro was parked in front of the Honda, blocking it from pulling out. The driver popped the trunk of the sports car, exited, and took the box from the trunk. He moved to the driver's side back door of the Honda and opened it. After placing the box on the backseat, he opened the front door and appeared to activate the remote door lock switch on the door panel. Rone captured each of these movements with a series of photos.

"Do you recognize the unsub?" asked Rone.

"No, but I'm wondering if it's Franklin Lee. I haven't met him yet. Based on what Michael told me, he's older and Wah Ching. Michael called him a *dai lo* which means 'a big brother,' apparently, it's the Asian equivalent of a shot caller. It would make sense he would've been part of the Shooter's Paradise break-in."

"I'll run that information as soon as I get back to the office."

Jake had yet to disclose to Rone his conversation with the general. Until this point in the investigation, Jake viewed the Peter Newman discussion as more of an intelligence briefing. Now, it was beginning to gain traction. Though Rone was somewhat annoyed Jake had not revealed yesterday's meeting, he understood the unique relationship Jake and the general shared. With the tan Camaro now in the calculus, the tentacles of the investigation were stretching beyond the approved operational plan. The war was moving to a new front. The rolling landscape was getting rocky.

As Jake exited the surveillance van, Rone said, "I understand why you like the girl. Let's keep moving forward. We will figure something out. I don't want to see her hurt either."

CHAPTER FIFTY-ONE
WEDNESDAY, MAY 25
Los Angeles

Over the intercom came the words "Dr. Brookside, the call is for you."

"Thank you, Denise."

Picking up the phone, she said, "This is Dr. Brookside. How may I help you?"

"Evelyn, it's Michael Yang."

"Michael, so great to hear from you. Thank you again for printing up our yearbooks. The children love them, and they will create memories for many years to come. I so appreciate your generosity in doing this for free."

With a slight chuckle, Michael said, "You're welcome, but you know there's no free lunch."

"Do you need some checks?" asked Brookside knowing Michael was bundling contributions for their local representative.

"Yes, we are having one of our boys-night-out receptions tonight. If you could give the checks to Preston, I will make sure you're reimbursed."

"I need to be a little cautious, but I have five teachers who are strong supporters of Sylvia Estrada and will gladly provide checks."

"I will see that everyone is reimbursed with a little extra gift for their willingness to help."

Stifling a chuckle, Evelyn changed the subject. "Michael, do you know the vendor who is giving Preston legal issues?"

Genuinely confused by the question, Michael said, "No, I wasn't aware he was having any problems. I haven't seen much of Preston since he brought in the new salesman who is handling our account."

"New salesperson? I wasn't aware he hired anyone new."

"Yes, he hired Jake Webb. Preston said he was beginning to step away from the business and spend more time up at your cabin in Big Bear."

With a hint of concern, Evelyn Brookside said, "That is news to me. I will have to ask him this evening when he comes home. He hasn't been himself lately. I know he isn't sleeping well, and I assume it's because of the legal issues with the vendor. I will make sure he gets the checks to you tonight. Just make sure you get the cash back to me so my teachers can cover them. It doesn't look good when educators are bouncing campaign contribution checks."

"You have my word. Thank you again, Evelyn, for your support."

"No, thank you, Michael, for your continued support of all our printing projects at the school."

CHAPTER FIFTY-TWO

West Los Angeles

Michael Yang had always been Preston Brookside's best customer. Previously, Brookside stopped by the business every week just to say hello, check on the machines to make sure everything was functioning properly, and ensure there were adequate supplies on hand. This erased the burden of Michael monitoring the supplies daily. Brookside could easily determine how much and what products were necessary for the printshop to maintain production and meet its orders.

With Jake assuming Brookside's responsibilities, Jake maintained the arrangement, stopping by the business every few days, avoiding a pattern. Never the same day. Never the same hour. Usually, it meant popping into Michael's office to say "hello," but Michael enjoyed talking guns so a casual greeting, typically meant an hour or so of conversation. It all reflected the personal service Michael Yang expected and played well into the undercover operation.

With the incumbent congresswoman announcing her bid for reelection and other state candidates jumping into the election arena, Michael's business increased significantly. A pallet of paper contained forty cases meaning 200,000 sheets of paper. In a non-election cycle, Michael was running fifteen to seventeen pallets a week. Now, he was doubling that for the beginning of the campaign season. As the election neared, it was conceivable he could double that amount again. Profits and prosperity awaited.

What Jake didn't understand was Michael's business succeeded because he could underbid every printshop in the greater Los Angeles area. Michael Yang was being subsidized by the People's Republic of China. It was a small investment on their part to undermine the framework of a capitalist society.

Because Jake and Rone were monitoring the daily traffic at Yang's through the use of the pole camera, Jake typically stayed within a quick drive to the shop. On this particular day, he noted Danny Yu parked in the visitor slot and was unloading heavy boxes from the trunk of his Honda. Annie was with him and holding the door as he entered the business. The images on Jake's iPhone weren't clear enough to disclose the contents of the boxes but it necessitated further investigation. Jake left a voicemail message for Rone telling him he was making a run over to the office on the pretense of checking supplies.

When Jake walked into Michael's office, he was greeted with a squeal.

"Hi, Mr. Jake." Annie rushed over to give him a hug. "I'm so glad to see you."

"Well, I'm glad to see you too. I didn't realize you and your brother would be here. I just came to see if Michael needed anymore paper. His business is getting very busy."

Annie was waving her arms as if to clear the air. "Michael smokes."

"Yes, he does, but it is his office."

Looking at Danny, Jake said, "What brings you guys clear across town today?"

Michael intervened, "They were just dropping off some ammo. I got tired of paying what they were asking for it at Shooter's Paradise, and Danny got me a great deal. In fact, take a case of nine."

"Wow! Thanks."

With a laugh, Michael said, "Don't worry, I'll bill it to Preston."

Jake glanced at Danny who refused to look at the undercover agent. "We better get going. I have to get to class. Come on, Annie."

Annie gave Michael a reluctant hug, who held her a little too long and a little too tight. He kissed the top of her head as she awkwardly pushed away. Turning to Jake, she gave him a sincere embrace.

As she walked out of the room, she said, "Goodbye, Mr. Jake. Hope to see you soon."

Once Danny and his sister were out of the room, heading down the hallway, Michael said shamelessly, "That is one fine little girl."

Alliances could be easily formed and easily broken. Jake was ready to end this coalition with some immediate justice. *A bullet never lies!*

Before Jake became the hand of righteousness, Michael said, "Jake, I'm glad you stopped by. I was going to call. I need a favor."

Compartmentalizing, remembering the comment, but moving forward, Jake, back in character, said, "I was going to say make it a little one because I'm out of big favors, but you just gave me 500 rounds of 9mm ammo and I'm making more commission off you than anyone else. What do you need? Another lesson at the range? Are we putting together a shooting team for the printshop Olympics?"

"No, that's not it at all. I need to use you as a proxy for some contributions."

"I don't understand."

"As you know, most of the pallets of paper I've been buying recently have been going to several local, state, and a congressional campaign. We have been printing all of the campaign literature to include newsletters, flyers, mailings, and signage."

"I'm aware of that and my paycheck reflected those purchases. Thanks."

"That's why I need your help. We will reimburse you, but I need you to contribute money to each of the campaigns."

"How much are you talking?"

"Don't worry about the amount. Like I said, we will reimburse you. I do this with a lot of my vendors. Preston did it, and he'll be doing it again during this campaign cycle."

"I don't mean to sound naïve, but isn't this illegal?"

"Believe me, this is done all the time. It's a toll we have to pay to keep their business."

"So, you just want me to write the checks, and you will reimburse me?"

"Exactly."

Jake shrugged. "I don't have a problem with that, but I don't have my checkbook with me."

"I understand. Could you come back this evening and bring your checkbook?"

"Sure, just so you understand there's not a whole lot in the account. If I'm going to be writing checks tonight, I will have to cover them in the next day or two. How much money are we talking?"

"For the congressional election, you can donate as an individual $2,900 to the candidate's committee."

Jake really was shocked by the figures. "Wow! You *are* going to have to cover me. I don't have more than a couple hundred dollars in the bank. Who is the candidate?"

"Sylvia Estrada."

Jake didn't have to fake his indignation. "Estrada? If it were up to her, she would abolish the Second Amendment. I'm not sure there's anyone further to the left than she is. Besides, according to the news, her opponent is barely polling at double digits."

"Jake, it's just how it's done. She makes us a lot of money. One representative isn't going to make a difference one way or another as to whether we get to keep our guns. It's just all part of the game. Everyone plays it. She's asked for our financial support, and I'm obligated to contribute. Think of it as 'protection money.' Without paying, I lose a lot of business and so will you. Come on back tonight, bring your checkbook, and I have a friend who will join us. We will have China's 'national liquor' and the best Cuban cigars you've ever smoked."

Once again, Jake shrugged his shoulders as if to say, *I'll play the game as long as the checks don't bounce.* "What time do you want me here?"

"My friend will be here at seven."

"Then seven it is."

Grabbing the ammo, Jake headed back to the Bronco.

CHAPTER FIFTY-THREE

West Los Angeles

Jake wasn't certain who would be at Yang Printing that evening. Rone would set up in the surveillance van around six. Though the pole camera was capturing the traffic going in and out of the business, both agents agreed manning a handheld camera ensured the best evidence. In addition, Rone could monitor the transmitter Jake would be wearing. If it were necessary to call in the cavalry, the former Ranger could move in quickly.

They had not contacted the supervisor, Charlene Taylor, who was in Quantico but Jake and Rone discussed the campaign contribution issue. Under the circumstances, the FBI was not contributing directly to a campaign but merely serving as a strawman for someone to make an illegal contribution. It put the Bureau in the position of appearing to interfere in an election, however Michael left the agents with little choice. If Jake wavered, Michael Yang would find someone else to make the payments. In all likelihood, Jake's refusal to participate, regardless the reason, would end Michael's trust in the undercover agent and the investigation would be effectively terminated. If Jake and Rone papered their decision well in the file, bureaucrats attacking the operation *might* see the logic.

Jake called Tonya Rodriguez who assured him Preston Brookside never told her he illegally contributed to any campaigns in which he was reimbursed by Yang. She admitted she did not directly ask him

that question; her interest was more in exploring the sexual exploitation of children than the vagaries of campaign finance laws. Though
it was outside the parameters of the UC operation, both agreed they
needed another sit-down with Brookside considering Michael's lecher-
ous comment about Annie.

Jake told Rone about the Annie incident and the pictures lining
the hallway of the business. During the investigation, the issue of dating
was yet to be broached. Michael mentioned Jake wasn't wearing a wedding ring, but the conversation went no further. Jake wasn't ready to
commit to being an undercover pedophile to explore Michael's procliv-
ities, but he wasn't going to close off that option. He and Rone agreed
if there were any chance a child would be harmed, the adult dies. It was
plain and simple to two men who were more interested in protecting
children than playing a geopolitical chess game. Never underestimate
ruthlessness. It's kept a lot of societies afloat and psychopaths off the
streets.

When Jake arrived at the business, the parking lot was empty except
for Michael's silver Lexus and a maroon Nissan Pathfinder. Spotting
the surveillance van across the street, Jake knew Rone would have pho-
tographed the vehicle and its occupant. There was no reason for Jake to
risk being caught grabbing a plate.

The transmitter Jake was wearing allowed the conversations to be
heard in the van but unlike Hollywood, Jake wasn't wearing a device
buried deep in the ear canal in which Rome was giving directions or
suggestions. If something important came up and the subject needed
to be explored, Rone would have to make a phone call.

The front door was unlocked and the reception desk unoccupied.
As Jake made his way down the hallway, he could already smell cigar
smoke emanating from the conference room.

"Hey, you're right on time," said a smiling Michael Yang. "This is
my business associate Lin Xu Ping."

"Please call me Ping," said the I/O extending his hand.

Lin was closer to a Bruce Lee and more of what Jake was expecting when he began the operation. Though slender, his tight short-sleeve shirt displayed a well-defined body. The two shook; Jake noting the strong grip.

"I'm Jake. Great to meet you."

Michael, already loose from the liquor said, "He brought us some great Cubans and a couple of bottles of Fenjiu."

"Michael, I thought you were the lead dog on the sled team."

Michael laughed and walking toward the bar said, "It takes more than one dog to pull this sled. Have you ever had Fenjiu?"

"No, but I'm assuming it's an adult beverage," said Jake with a smile.

"The bar is fully stocked. We've got beer, domestic or imported, but I suggest you try either the Fenjiu or the mao-tai which is China's official national liquor.

"When in Rome . . . let me try the Fenjiu, if that's what you recommend."

As Michael was pouring for Jake and refilling the shot glasses for himself and Lin, Lin handed Jake a Cohiba.

"You have some great connections. I haven't had a Cohiba in years. How did you get a hold of these?" asked Jake.

Michael, always wanting to be the center of any conversation, spoke for Lin. "Obama lifted the embargo in 2014, so you can legally bring them in from Cuba, but my friend has another source."

As Michael was handing the glass to Jake, Jake said, "It is always great to have friends in the right places."

The three touched glasses and Jake took a sip of the clear liquor noting its mellow taste with just a hint of sweetness. "This is good."

As Jake began to light the cigar, he felt his cell phone vibrate. Checking the text message, it read "tan Camaro, RAV4, Chrysler 300, Honda Accord." Within the minute, Danny, Annie, and nine other Asian men walked into the conference room. A small box was cradled under the arm of the oldest man, in shape, and in his thirties.

Jake nodded knowingly to Danny but said nothing.

Ignoring Danny and the other men, Michael introduced Jake to Franklin Lee.

Jake opened with, "Michael's mentioned you when we were at the range. It's nice to get to meet you."

Franklin merely nodded. He was more gangbanger than business-man with an observable roughness honed in prison. His eight hench-men, late teens to early twenties, all under 5'8" and in shape, had the air of an urban posse more comfortable on the street than a boardroom. Danny, smaller than any of the others, seemed out of place, uneasy in the company of the Asian scrum.

When Annie spotted Jake, she rushed over and gave him a hug. Then in her rapid-fire way, "Hi, Mr. Jake. Danny didn't say you would be here. I didn't want to come, but Danny said I couldn't stay home at night by myself. I'm glad I came so I can see you. I should have brought my special lemon iced tea. I have a new recipe. It's smokey in here." She saw the cigar poised between Jake's fingers. "Mr. Jake, do you smoke? I didn't know you smoked. Smoking is bad."

Sheepishly, Jake held the cigar to his side.

A second vibration on Jake's phone carried this text, "Maserati."

Within the minute, Preston Brookside waddled into the room. Spotting Franklin first, Brookside embraced the Wah Ching member. At no time in a briefing Jake attended or in the reports Tonya prepared had Franklin Lee's name been mentioned. Franklin whispered some-thing in Brookside's ear, who displayed a huge satisfactory grin but said nothing.

Jake wasn't expecting Brookside. Either he forgot to tell his contact agent or Tonya forgot to tell Jake. Regardless, he was here and would be part of the play.

"Hey boss, I didn't expect to see you here tonight."

Startled, Brookside still at Franklin's side turned to see the under-cover agent and uncomfortably babbled, "I didn't realize Michael had invited you."

Michael choked on the Fenjiu as he attempted to swallow and speak at the same time. "Don't be too surprised. His wife isn't even aware he hired you. Maybe our little Preston has something on the side because she doesn't seem to think he's spending much time up in Big Bear."

With a look of concern, closer to panic, Preston asked, "What are you talking about?"

Michael answered, "I talked to Evelyn this afternoon and she wasn't even aware you hired Jake."

Franklin's attention was fully immersed in the exchange between Michael and the paper supplier. Brookside was visibly rattled by his employee's presence and Michael's assertions.

There was a long pause, too long, as Preston fought to come up with an answer. Finally, he said unconvincingly, "I don't tell her everything about work."

Michael laughed, "Pressy, I don't care what you're doing on the side. Did you bring me the checks she promised me?"

With his hand slightly trembling, Preston handed over six checks, each for $2,900 made out to "Sylvia Estrada for Congress."

Michael was passing out beers to the newest arrivals who were lighting up the Cohibas. As he handed a beer to Danny, Michael said to Lin who was standing at the bar, "Did you see this guy's sister? She is a real cutie."

Lin looked to Danny and smiled.

Danny walked away, as if he hadn't heard the comment, but he did.

Handing Franklin a glass of Fenjiu and acting like a child at Christmas, Michael asked, "What's in the box? Did you bring me what I asked for?"

Again, Franklin merely nodded, handing the box to Michael. Opening it, Michael let out a high-pitch, childlike squeal. A Smith & Wesson M&P .22 Compact with a threaded barrel perfect for the other item in the box, a Ruger Silent-SR suppressor.

Great! Alcohol and guns, the ideal combination.

Pulling the pistol out of the box and holding it up, Michael said excitedly, "Look what Franklin brought me!"

Lin thoroughly examined it after Michael handed it to him. It really was a good-looking firearm. The polymer frame had a flat dark earth finish. With the black slide, it looked like a desert commando's weapon, though not many warriors would be carrying a .22.

As Michael was attaching the suppressor, he said, "Maybe we should do some target practice tonight."

"In a little while," suggested Franklin pouring himself a second glass of Fenjiu.

Jake, a gifted liar, who was standing near the bar, decided to push it with Franklin, "Michael says you have access to good inventory. He says you're a real Guns R Us."

Franklin nodded while taking a drink. "Are you looking for anything in particular?"

"I like the Raptor II you got Michael. That's a great little gun. I like the action. We put a lot of rounds through it yesterday over at the Paradise."

Taking another sip, Franklin said, "I only had one. Michael got it."

Not quite a criminal admission but Jake continued the conversation. "I picked up an AR-15 from Danny the other night. The M&P Sport II. I haven't had a chance to shoot it yet but am looking forward to taking it out to the desert soon and plinking a few vermin. Was that one of yours?"

Franklin nodded—a nod not picked up by the recording device. Jake decided to circle back later in the evening. Maybe Franklin would be a little more talkative after a few more drinks.

Jake slipped over to Danny. "I didn't expect to see you here."

"I didn't have much of a choice. Franklin made me come. It's a business thing, so I came."

"How do you and Franklin fit together?" asked Jake.

"We are cousins. Franklin's father, Calvin's father, and my father were brothers."

"Now, I understand. I guess the one-child policy didn't take."

"That was mainland China. Our fathers were from Hong Kong," explained Danny.

"So, these aren't your homies," said Jake.

"Homies? You've been watching too many Jackie Chan movies. But no, I don't run with these guys. I plan on making something out of my life. Their life isn't anything I want. Right now, I'm just looking to make enough scratch so Annie and I can survive."

"It may be none of my business, but I wouldn't trust Michael around her."

"What makes you say that?" asked Danny as if he knew the answer.

"After you guys left this morning, he made some comments. They may have been innocent, but I took them as inappropriate."

Danny shook his head. "I have to be careful with her. She is so sweet and innocent. She attracts trash and sometimes it comes dressed in expensive threads. Thanks."

"Has she had problems?"

"Calvin touched her."

"She told me he was mean to her. No wonder neither of you cared if he was dead. I would have killed him had I known he hurt her," said Jake with a conviction Danny believed.

"She likes you, but maybe that's because you're the only one who will drink her iced tea."

Both men laughed.

"I thought the Kimber Raptor I bought two weeks ago from you was one of Franklin's, but he said he only had one."

Danny was adamant. "Don't say anything about the Kimber to anyone."

Before Jake could continue the conversation, Michael began to lock and load his new plaything, and Lin suggested they take care of business.

Michael reluctantly agreed and told the others to "get out your checkbooks. In politics, money is the only thing that matters. This happens on both sides of the aisle. I appreciate you allowing me to use your names to prime the political pump. It's good business for me and that makes it good business for you."

Jake wasn't smiling and Michael noted his reluctance.

"Jake, I know you aren't thrilled we are pouring money into Sylvia Estrada's campaign. Don't worry about any of those gun control bills. She just talks that way to get elected. Even if she introduces a bill in Congress, remember, out of the thousands of bills coming before the House, maybe 5 percent become law. If there were a viable candidate running against her, and we were handling their campaign, we would be contributing to both sides. Look at Wall Street. The same people contribute huge amounts of money to all the candidates. For us, this isn't about buying votes, it's about buying business. Just think of it as pay-to-play."

After Jake, Brookside, Danny, Franklin, and the members of his Wah Ching entourage, each wrote a check for $2,900, the next phase of the evening occurred. Lin opened the briefcase and handed each man $3,000 in cash, all crisp $100 bills, the extra $100 a "thank you for playing." You could see a couple of the gang members doing the mental arithmetic, questioning why they didn't just rip everyone. Confident Franklin would keep the men on a short leash, Jake figured a robbery inside the business tonight was not an immediate concern.

A small reception without the candidate even being present resulted in $52,200 into the campaign war chest of an incumbent who had little to no chance of losing. For the Chinese underwriting the evening, an investment in favorable consideration in future legislative proposals and an undermining of the enemy.

"Now that we have our business completed, bring the beer and cigars, let's head out to the warehouse," said Michael attempting to twirl the suppressed pistol on his finger, cowboy style.

Annie ran over to Jake and gave him a hug. "Mr. Jake, Danny and I are leaving. It was nice to see you. Please come to my house soon and I will give you my new special recipe."

Returning the hug, Jake said, "I will do that Annie."

"But you can't smoke at my house."

"I know and I won't."

As she and Danny walked down the hall toward the reception area, Annie turned and waved, "See you soon, Mr. Jake."

With all the men heading the opposite direction toward the warehouse, Jake thanked Lin for the cash and the cigars. "How did you get the cigars? I didn't think any smoke shop in town carried them."

Thanks to the alcohol, which was doing too much of the talking, Lin answered honestly and slightly slurring his words said, "They come in diplomatic pouches."

Jake leaned in a little closer as if his gait were unsteady and asked, "Do you know someone at the consulate?"

Lin smiled but didn't answer the question.

Unbelievably, Michael and the inebriated men spent the next thirty minutes in the soundproof warehouse, shooting the suppressed .22 into eight cases of paper stacked twenty feet away on one side of the room. The rounds spit from the silenced weapon sent brass flying throughout the warehouse bouncing off the copy machines. Even Brookside joined in, peppering the wall more than the reams of paper.

Through beer bottle glasses, Michael scattered his rounds in all the cases, ruining each one. Lin was wobbly even as he walked into the warehouse and his shooting reflected it, popping rounds wildly in the paper. Not unexpectedly, Franklin Lee shot gangbanger-style with the .22 parallel to the ground. His shooting matched Lin's. Each of Franklin's men shot a ten-round magazine, none displaying any real training or accuracy. Jake, who minimized his drinking though the others didn't realize it, put everything center mass, near perfect shooting, and drunkenly admired by all.

While awaiting his turn, Jake caught sight of a stack of anti-fascist newspapers recently printed and ready for mailing.

As the evening ended, Michael reminded them they would need to do it again soon because two state senators and the incumbent district attorney just signed on for the "Michael Yang campaign promotional tour."

CHAPTER FIFTY-FOUR

THURSDAY, MAY 26
Koreatown, Los Angeles

After meeting Jake the night before, Franklin Lee was determined to learn as much as he could about this paper salesman working for Preston Brookside. Brookside's discomfort at Jake's attendance at the event and Preston's bumbling responses were cause for concern. Jake didn't ring true. He wasn't a Brookside or a Yang. He was strong, resolute, carrying himself with the bearing of a leader, not a weak pedophile seeking pleasure by dominating his victim.

While friendly and polite, unassuming to those outside his circle of influence, Franklin was, in fact, a street thug willing to work for the highest bidder. For the past couple years, members of the Ministry of State Security were those bidders. Though not a member of China's People's Liberation Army, Franklin was engaged in the equivalent of clandestine armed combat in the United States.

China, rich in ancient ceremonial tradition, survived a thirty-year civil war to become a titan seeking global dominance. For Franklin, whose ancestors invented gunpowder, the bullet became his weapon of choice. He cared little about politics or patriotism but knew the PRC's priorities in the United States: put friendly people in positions of power, compromise those already in power, damage the morale of America, and weaken the U.S. economy to the point of China becoming the world's economic superpower.

As long as Franklin made money, he was willing to support China's vision. He was encouraged by Chen Ma Ho and Lin Xu Ping to promote the PRC's ideal with the "thousand cuts" strategy. Compromise one American at a time. With enough insiders following the same philosophy, China would prevail, and Franklin would continue to prosper.

Once he arrived at the consulate, he pushed his way past the protesters, walked to the front of the line, and asked to see Lin.

Inside, the two met in Lin's tiny office, poorly decorated with unread books and manuals stacked several feet high. Even those inside the consulate assumed Lin was poring over the reading material performing attaché responsibilities.

"What is so urgent you must see me today?"

"How much do you know about Brookside's employee, Jake?"

"I know nothing about him. I met him for the first time last night. Michael introduced us. Michael has spoken of him and told me of his interest in guns and his ability to shoot."

"Did you watch his performance last night?"

"I saw nothing unusual at the reception. He wrote a check. I paid him in cash. Just like I did the others."

"Did you watch him shoot in the warehouse?"

With a weak smile, Lin said, "I had much to drink last night. I do not recall much about what happened in the warehouse."

"I understand. I too had much to drink, but I watched Jake. He is a good shot, too good. I do not believe he is who he says he is."

"Just so I understand, who does Jake say he is?"

Franklin spent the next several minutes discussing what he learned from Michael Yang about Jake's background. Dismissing several of Franklin's concerns attributing them to the paranoia of the street, Lin also questioned if the opinion was based upon Jake's skill with a gun which bested Franklin's efforts last night. But Lin trusted Franklin's instincts, recognizing one doesn't survive in L.A.'s gang-infested neighborhoods without street smarts not taught at any university. The upcoming mission was too important to leave to chance. The two men came up with a plan of action.

Lin was adamant. "I want this done quickly. Do what you need to do to get answers. I do not want this to impact our plans for tomorrow night."

CHAPTER FIFTY-FIVE

West Los Angeles

Michael Yang looked at his cell phone and smiled. The caller ID displayed the name "Yao Ming," the 7'6" former 2002 first round draft pick of the Houston Rockets. It was an inside joke since Lin Xu Ping barely hit 5'8", but it was a way to disguise the caller. Seldom did Lin call using this number, a phone reserved for sensitive matters.

"Mr. Yao, how are you today? I wasn't expecting a call."

Getting down to business without any pleasantries, Lin asked, "Franklin Lee was just here and is concerned about Jake. How much do you know about him?"

Caught off guard, Yang answered truthfully, "I know very little about him other than what Preston told me. What is the problem? Why is Franklin concerned?"

With a hint of doubt in his next statement, Lin said, "I cannot tell if it is Franklin's paranoia or his jealousy over Jake's shooting ability, but he does not believe Jake is who he says he is."

"What makes Franklin think that?"

"He could not provide a direct answer backed by evidence, just a feeling he has. I would dismiss it, but Franklin has street instincts far superior to most of our assets."

"What would you like me to do?" asked Michael, Lin's best asset in Los Angeles.

"Do you still have the checks from last night?"

"Yes."

"Send me a photo with the account and routing number. We have a number of people in banking who can pull the account and track the activity. I want you to confirm the address listed on his check. Drive there and see if it is Jake's home. But be careful. Have a plan if he is home and sees your car. Have a reason for being in his neighborhood."

Sensing the urgency in Lin's request, Michael asked, "Would you like me to contact Preston? He would have the identifying information Jake would've completed on the W-9 IRS form. That would give us a birth date and Social Security number."

"Check on the address first. Franklin is also concerned about Brookside since he brought Jake onboard. Do this as quickly as possible. We need to get to the bottom of this before tomorrow."

Chapter Fifty-Six

Los Angeles

After ending the call with Lin, Michael immediately left the business, heading over the hill on the 405 to find the address listed on Jake's check. He threw a case of ammo in the back of his Lexus. If Jake spotted him, he would say he picked up a deal on 9mm and wanted to share his success with his "favorite salesman."

With sloth-like speed, Michael's GPS device reminded him he was on the fastest route to the address but still fifty-six minutes from arrival. He wished Lin would have sent one of his Wah Ching lackeys on this mission but didn't want to question his handler. It wasn't as if he had a lot to do. The business almost ran itself since the Chinese were subsidizing the bottom line. He hired a single mother of two school-age boys as his floor manager. She saw that the material was printed, and the orders went out.

As he crested the Sepulveda Pass, the speed picked up some but not much as he made his way to the far righthand lane to transition from the 405 to the Ventura Freeway, one of the busiest interchanges in the nation. He continued traveling on the Ventura toward the west end of the San Fernando Valley until he was directed to the Tampa Avenue offramp. From there, he took a right, heading toward Vanowen Street. At Vanowen, he took a left and soon a right into a shopping center. The GPS device announced: "You have arrived."

Confused, he checked the address a second time. He was in fact at the right location. As he slowly drove through the parking lot, he spotted a privately run mail center featuring post office boxes.

The check Jake provided listed the address as an apartment number and Michael quickly realized the apartment was in fact a private PO box.

Exiting the Lexus, he headed into the small business featuring boxes, packaging, mailing, and private post office boxes. Standing behind the counter was a slightly built, older white woman whose face was wrinkled from years of California sunshine. He assumed she would be of little help but decided to take a chance.

"Hi, I'm sorry to bother you. I was looking for an address. I thought this was an apartment complex and I was looking for the person who lives in unit 222."

With a tired smile, she said, "Well, I'm sorry, but if your friend lives in unit 222, he must be very tiny because that's the smallest box we rent."

Michael thought briefly before saying, "Well, he really wasn't my friend. I was trying to collect on a bad check he wrote, and this was the printed address on his check. I don't suppose you would have an actual address for this person, would you?"

"I'm sorry. Our policy is not to give out information on those who rent our boxes unless we have a subpoena. We won't even help LAPD without a court order."

"Okay, thank you. I understand. I guess I'll have to try another avenue." He paused and said, "I'm just out $2,900."

"Wow. That's a lot of money"

"Yes, it is. I apologize, I don't want you to violate company policy but here's a crisp new $100 bill if you would let me look at the application Jake Webb completed for box 222."

With little to no hesitation, the clerk snatched the new bill from Michael Yang's hand and turned to search a file box located on the shelf behind her. "We don't require a whole lot of information to rent a box, merely some form of identification and payment." Before handing the 5 x 7 application card to Michael, she said, "He paid cash for six months."

Always prepared for such a contingency, when Jake filled out the rental agreement for the post office box, he provided as his previous address, the PO box he used in Dallas. He was using the same UC name for both assignments. There was a notation on the application that he was still trying to find an apartment and was unable to provide a Los Angeles address. There was little Michael could do but copy down the California driver's license number Jake provided as a form of photo identification.

Though not completely satisfied, the information he learned from the application coincided with what Preston Brookside and Jake told him. He wasn't about to track down the address in Dallas, deciding to contact Lin and tell him the latest.

CHAPTER FIFTY-SEVEN

Santa Monica

Often, when Jake went undercover, he had an apartment or office space rented in his undercover identity. It was a place where the targets of the investigation could meet in a location fully wired for audio and visual evidentiary recordings. It also served as a spot where Jake could meet with his case agent and others to surreptitiously discuss the progress of the investigation or solidify a strategy.

Because of the nature of this investigation and the backstory Jake was using, he had no undercover hideaway. He was essentially working out of the cabin and, when necessary, meeting with Rone at restaurants or coffee shops. For today, Rone rented a hotel room on Wilshire Boulevard in Santa Monica. Tonya Rodriguez was scheduled to meet with them but called to say she was running a few minutes late.

When Jake walked into the hotel room, Rone's beefy fingers were busy pounding the keyboard preparing a mandatory update for the operation. He briefly looked up, nodded, and went back to the report. Rather than bother him with the mundane, Jake plopped down on the couch, threw his feet up on the coffee table, and took a swig of his Monster Ultra.

"I got a call from Michael last night. He said Lin was pulled over by the cops for DUI. Were you behind that?" asked Jake.

"No, but let me finish this email and we can talk."

Within minutes, as Jake continued to drink the Monster, Rone completed the email finally pushing "send."

Gulping down the last of his coffee, Rone said, "I had nothing to do with Lin. I debated calling West L.A. and having them pull everybody over as they left the parking lot, but I decided it was too risky. Frankly, with the issues facing the police right now, I didn't want to put anyone in the position of making a routine traffic stop that could end up going sideways. With Franklin and his crew, I wasn't sure how many were carrying. The upside in identifying everyone wasn't worth the potential danger for the patrol officers."

"Probably a wise decision. Apparently, according to Michael, Lin just flashed his diplomatic credentials and they let him go without even taking a breathalyzer. I'm not sure what he would've blown, but he was putting away the Fenjiu and mao-tai."

There was a knock at the door. Jake answered and it was Tonya. They exchanged pleasantries but soon got down to business.

Rone began. "Tonya, the reason I wanted the three of us to get together is because Jake and I have some concerns about Brookside."

Tonya looked at Rone, shaking her head slowly as if to say, *I didn't want to work with this guy in the first place.*

Jake recapped what happened the night before at Yang Printing.

Frustrated, Tonya said, "Preston never told me about the meeting with Yang. I spoke with him yesterday and he said it was going well. He said Michael was pleased with everything you were doing, the supplies were coming in on time, and several times you have made personal runs over to the business when there was a need. Both Brookside and Yang seem pleased with the relationship. Yang especially likes the lessons at the range. From everything I'm seeing, you seem solid with Yang."

Rone asked, "Had he ever told you about contributing to any political campaign and being reimbursed by Lin?"

"No, but I never asked."

Jake joined in, "The other thing that bothered me last night was the fact Preston knew Franklin Lee. They acted as if they have dealt with each other in the past. This wasn't just two ships passing in the night."

"I know that name never came up. Michael Yang and Lin were the only Asian names we discussed."

Rone asked, "Do you think we need to have a sit-down with Brookside?"

Tonya said, "I'm concerned about Jake's safety. Right now, that is my only concern. If I can prove Brookside wasn't playing straight with us, I can get the U.S. Attorney's office to void the plea agreement, and we can send him on a federally paid vacation."

Rone said, "I'm concerned about Jake's safety—"

Jake interrupted, "That's comforting."

Rone smirked, "There's just too much paperwork if you get wasted, but I do think we need to have a sit-down with Brookside. We need to get to the bottom of all this. If we don't, his lawyer might be able to argue he cooperated fully to the extent to which we asked the questions."

All three agreed.

"I've got this room until checkout tomorrow morning at 11. Let's get his ass over here this afternoon and get him straightened out."

CHAPTER FIFTY-EIGHT

Santa Monica

When Tonya called him, Brookside said he would come to the hotel at 1:00. Rather than chancing Jake being seen by any of the targets, Rone agreed to walk across the street to a deli and pick up sandwiches. While eating lunch, the three discussed their strategy with the source and their vision for the rest the investigation. Slow progress was being made but it was hard to tell if this was the beginning of an embrace or the end of the evening without a goodnight kiss.

At 1:15, Tonya called Brookside who still had not arrived at the hotel. He apologized for being late and said an issue came up at work and he would be there shortly. When he walked into the hotel room ten minutes later, Brookside looked like Satan had taken a bite out of him. He was still recovering from the previous night, heavy bags hanging below bloodshot eyes.

The FBI agents got down to business quickly and minimized the small talk.

"Why didn't you tell Tonya about the meeting at Yang's last night?" asked Rone.

Brookside shrugged his shoulders and said, "I didn't think about it. I guess I didn't think I needed to. I don't tell her everything I do during the day. I thought since Jake was dealing directly with Michael, it wasn't necessary for me to fill her in on all the details."

It was a weak explanation, but the agents let it slide.

"How do you know Franklin Lee?" asked Jake.

"I met him through Michael several months ago."

"And what were the circumstances under which you met him? You seemed like old friends last night."

Brookside hesitated in answering, trying to come up with falsified details of their first meeting. "I just can't recall the first time we met. He and Michael are friends, and I would see him over at the business sometimes when I was there." The story wasn't selling.

Jake just stared at him.

"What? Hasn't he been over there when you've been there?" asked Brookside defensively.

"What did he whisper in your ear when you first came into the conference room?" asked Jake.

Brookside stumbled with a response. "I don't recall him whispering anything in my ear."

"You were smiling like the prom queen just asked you to dance."

Brookside shook his head. "I don't recall. Maybe he told me a joke."

"So, you guys are close enough that within minutes of entering the room, he's whispering one-liners in your ear?" said Jake, the sarcasm dripped from the remark hanging in the air.

"I just don't recall." For a successful salesman, he was doing a poor job selling a story reeking of barnyard excrement.

The four spent the next fifteen minutes rehashing Preston Brookside's relationship with Michael. He presented no new information, sticking with the story he first told Tonya.

As he was about to leave the room, Rone reminded him, "Not to put too fine a point on it, but you stepped into this crap with your own two feet. Your plea agreement requires full cooperation. If we find out you've been holding back from us, it could all go out the window."

Brookside seemed incredulous. His response was quick and angry. "I am telling you the truth. I have fully cooperated. You asked me to introduce Jake, and I did. You asked me to back him, and I did. For all intents and purposes, he is on my payroll. That's what my staff knows and that is how everyone in my office will play it, if asked. I promised you Lin and I delivered. He was there last night, and Jake smoked his smuggled Cohibas. I don't know how much more you want from me." He paused catching his anger, then said, "If you have questions just ask. Now that I know, I will keep Tonya more informed about my schedule as it relates to Michael. I'm sorry but I have to go. I have another important meeting to get to."

Brookside left without waiting for a response.

The three FBI agents agreed; he was a problem.

CHAPTER FIFTY-NINE

Santa Monica

Brookside took the elevator to the lobby, fear and anger pulsating through his body. He was actually shaking as he walked outdoors toward his Maserati parked in one of the reserved "check-in" slots. He welcomed the mild ocean breeze carrying some relief but not much. He hadn't slept well since the day Tonya Rodriguez came to his home. Every time the phone rang, he feared it was Michael discovering his betrayal. His wife continued to hound him about the early morning search, demanding to know if the Bureau jailed the vendor. The neighbors saw the cars and the raid jackets that morning. They were asking questions of her, and she wasn't getting answers from him. She threatened to call her brother, Philip, who "knew how to handle the FBI." Those agents had no idea how much pressure he was under, and he was ready to end it—not his life, but his assistance.

Maybe he violated the spirit of their cooperation agreement, but he did not violate the provisions of the contract spelling out his responsibilities. He did what they asked. He wasn't required to disclose every personal secret or covert relationship; that wasn't part of the deal. And he wasn't going to disclose *that* secret ever. He risked his business and maybe even his life by cooperating with the FBI. They put him in this situation by forcing him to introduce Jake Kruse or Jake Webb or whatever his name was. His mind was spinning, his thinking distorted. He couldn't even recall Jake's UC name. *Think!*

If the Chinese determined Jake was an FBI agent, Brookside knew it would mean death for the undercover agent and the person who introduced him. He had no escape from the introduction. Blaming a niece in Dallas would mean little to Lin Ping, Michael Yang, or Franklin Lee. Death was on the menu and if his treachery was detected, he would be served up. Not a symbolic destruction but real destruction—his life.

He knew Michael was more than just a print shop owner. Michael was working for the Chinese government in some capacity beyond printing their travel brochures. Hollywood, in its many political thrillers, taught Brookside about the espionage business and he suspected Lin Xu Ping might be more than just an attaché at the consulate. Lin might be a spy, which made the cooperation even more dangerous.

Though Preston Brookside didn't understand everything about Asian organized crime or gangs or Triads or Wah Ching, he knew Franklin Lee and his posse were the real deal and could snuff out a life without a second thought.

Brookside knew physical and financial harm could result if anyone knew of his relationship with the Bureau. He was balancing his life with too many secrets. He had no next appointment, that was a ruse to get out of the stifling hotel room. Now he needed a drink and not just one.

CHAPTER SIXTY

West Los Angeles

On the drive back to West Los Angeles, Michael Yang called Lin and reported the results of the address search: not an apartment, a post office box. Lin shared what he learned through his connections at the bank, Jake's account had little activity. Less than a dozen checks were written, none for large amounts. Though Lin and Michael acknowledged people use credit cards and cash for many purchases, the paucity of cancelled checks in the account caused concern.

Since no definitive answers were forthcoming, Lin wanted to play out a plan suggested by Franklin. Both agreed to keep Preston Brookside out of the loop until the other avenues of investigation were explored. Tomorrow was coming. If Brookside suspected he and Jake were being investigated, he might say something that would undermine the success of this singular mission.

From his car, Michael called Jake who answered on the fourth ring. "Hey, what's up."

"Well, I guess it's no secret. I need to replace a couple of reams of paper."

Jake laughed. "Reams? I think you probably need to replace about eight boxes of paper. We put a lot of rounds downrange in that warehouse of yours."

"I need a favor. I have a huge political mailing that needs to get out this weekend. Could you get those replacement boxes to me tomorrow?"

"Sure, I have an appointment in the morning, but I can probably get them to you in the early afternoon. Will that be too late?"

"No, that will be fine. I look forward to seeing you."

"See you tomorrow."

Michael immediately called Lin and told him the plan was a go. Jake would be at the printshop tomorrow in the afternoon.

Chapter Sixty-One

FRIDAY, MAY 27
West Los Angeles

It was another perfect Southern California day and Jake enjoyed the drive south on the Pacific Coast Highway. The clockwise circulation of high-pressure winds across the desert brought warm Santa Anas blowing in from the east, driving the morning haze into the ocean. It was cloudless skies as far as the eye could see. Catalina Island, sitting twenty-six miles west of Los Angeles, was clearly visible. Jake had the windows down and Charlie Daniels blasting through the sound system. He called ahead and would have eight cases of Tru Red 92 Bright printer paper waiting when he arrived at Brookside's office.

He wasn't looking forward to seeing Preston. If "his boss" was in the office, Jake would pop in and say hi, just to make a show for the employees who believed Jake was working for the company. The less Jake had to deal with this source, the better. In previous UC assignments, he worked closely with drug dealers, thieves, even murderers, but never a pedophile who got his rush viewing children being sexually exploited. Jake had to sublimate his desires to kick this guy's ass across the parking lot every time they were together. Their relationship was not strong and, fortunately, it wasn't necessary for them to interact daily.

In some operations, Jake was forced to infiltrate the criminal enterprise without the advantage of an introduction by an informant. Those cases typically took a little longer. Unlike television, the undercover agent didn't solidify his relationship with the bad guys during a commercial break. It took time to be invited into the inner circle of a conspiracy: sometimes months. The relationship building required patience, not always easy when some bureaucrats demanded instant results. A good CHS, a confidential human source, could make it happen quickly.

In other cases, Jake worked closely with a source who was an integral part of the investigation. In fact, in some cases, the CHS, a member of a tightly knit criminal organization, was more important than Jake who merely went along as a sidekick recording the conversations and being the upfront man when it came to testifying in court. This was particularly true when the source brought with him more baggage than a family of five on a two-week vacation. In those cases, where the CHS's extensive criminal record called into question his credibility, his testimonial value was marginal without the corroboration of the undercover agent.

For this case, Brookside's role was minimal, merely making the introduction and stepping back. From the Bureau's perspective, it was a simple process for Brookside. Get in and get out. But before retreating into the shadows, he had to make a full disclosure of everyone within the targeted circle. This allowed the agents to understand not only the scope of the investigation but provide the undercover agent the background he needed to direct the operation within the parameters of the law.

With the exception of the reception at Michael Yang's business the other night, the interaction between Jake and Brookside was limited. It worked well, but as the Yang reception showed, Brookside was concealing his relationship with members of the broadening conspiracy. Though the operation was approved for six months, the issue with Brookside made a long-term probe less likely. This investigation was circling the drain.

When Jake arrived at the business, he learned Brookside called in sick. Jake quickly loaded up the eight cases of paper in the back of the Bronco and headed over to Yang Printing.

He called Rone on the way just to check in. Neither had any meaningful updates on the investigation and both vowed to "continue to march."

Chapter Sixty-Two

West Los Angeles

Though Jake could've pulled around through the alley and dropped off the boxes of paper through the rear warehouse door, he parked in front of Yang's. The inconvenience was outweighed by the evidentiary value of providing confirmation of his meeting at the business through photographs taken by the pole camera across the street.

He and Madison exchanged pleasantries as Jake grabbed a dolly from the closet in the reception room. He went back out, propped the door open, and began to load eight cases of paper on the dolly. As he made his way down the hallway, he knocked on Michael's office door. Michael, the immaculately dressed smokestack, came out, cigarette dangling from the side of his mouth, and punched in the access code.

Jake wheeled the boxes to the far side for the warehouse. As he was chatting briefly with two of the workers, he noticed some slick brochures for the political action committee, "For a New America." Michael was making a lot of money from the campaigns.

After returning the dolly to the front closet, Jake entered Michael's office. Madison followed with two cups of coffee: black for Jake, cream and two sugars for Michael.

As Michael smoked one cigarette after another, there was some polite conversation before Michael asked, "Hey, I noticed on your check, you're living at an apartment on Vanowen. For some reason, I thought Preston said you were living in a house."

Sticking with his legend, he said, "No, that address on Vanowen is just a mail drop. When I first got into town, I didn't know where I'd be living so I rented that box. I paid cash for six months and now I wish I could get some of my money back. I thought it was a little more convenient. It can sometimes take me an extra fifteen minutes to get to and from the freeway just to see if I have any mail. I only hit it about once a week and even then, it is mostly advertising and campaign mailers. Probably, some of what you print here."

They both laughed.

Nothing Jake said contradicted what Michael learned at the private mail center. Though Jake had no place to go and wasn't necessarily anxious to leave, it seemed as if Michael was making small talk with no real purpose in the conversation. He brought up guns, the high cost of ammo, and his desire to do some big game hunting.

After about forty-five minutes of the inconsequential, Michael received a text message on his cell phone. He abruptly told Jake he needed to make a couple of business calls.

Jake excused himself and left the building after saying goodbye to Madison.

CHAPTER SIXTY-THREE

Los Angeles

Friday was a new day for Preston Brookside. In the morning, he phoned in sick. Though hungover from self-medicating on a bottle of Scotch the previous night, he *was* sick from the pressure of playing the FBI's game.

Yes, he was caught downloading child pornography, but it was a prudish society that viewed his actions as wrong. He knew history was replete with instances of child love being celebrated. Lewis Carroll had hundreds of little girlfriends throughout his life. What about J. M. Barrie and *Peter Pan*? Edgar Allan Poe married his thirteen-year-old cousin. Each was hailed for his historical and cultural importance.

Though he questioned whether he should still make his scheduled rendezvous, he needed the release Franklin was going to provide this afternoon. Was his every move being tracked by the FBI hoping to catch him violating the cooperation agreement? He didn't realize Jake saw Franklin whispering in his ear at Michael's reception. He didn't realize a grin spread across his face with Franklin's reminder of today's appointment. Though uncertain as to whether he sold his sincerity to his handlers in the hotel room, Brookside was confident he fulfilled the terms of the agreement.

Was he expected to live the rest of his life with the cloud of FBI oppression following his every move? He was tired of answering to them. If only he hadn't tried to navigate this issue on his own. Maybe an overpriced attorney could negotiate with the Bureau, proving the terms of the contract were fulfilled.

Philip, his brother-in-law, certainly wasn't the answer. Where could he find a discreet lawyer respected by the FBI who would never disclose his legal issues to his wife? After this afternoon's engagement, it might be time to begin a circumspect search in a chatroom he anonymously frequents for likeminded men. Someone might know a lawyer, or more likely, someone might be a lawyer who would take on the Bureau.

His desires had deep roots that wouldn't be easily destroyed by pruning. It was only in the past several years he began feeling more comfortable in exploring his cravings. His awkward attempts at grooming family members or the children of friends failed. He was never caught because he was never able to successfully seduce anyone. He even sought out vulnerable children of single parents by offering up vacation and camping opportunities. No one succumbed.

It was only recently Michael Yang learned of his longings and introduced him to Franklin. Thanks to Franklin, Brookside was provided with the opportunities to rejoice in a very special kind of love; this afternoon he was going to again celebrate.

He arrived at the motel a few minutes late and didn't see Franklin's car in the parking lot, but he knew Franklin was cautious and sometimes parked on the street. To call their rendezvous spot a "fleabag motel" was to give it an upgrade. It failed to make the *AAA Guidebook*, but this was where he and Franklin periodically met over the past several months. The owners knew Franklin and never questioned his use of the room. Franklin ensured all Brookside's desires were met and the paper salesman was grateful to Michael for making the introduction.

When he knocked on the door, he heard, "It is unlocked, come in." The smile began to grow on his face as the thoughts of the afternoon's delight raced through his mind.

As he entered the tiny room darkened by the closed curtains, he only saw Franklin sitting in an overstuffed and overused chair. Its fabric was worn and battered, not unlike the motel. There was no real ambience, but Brookside wasn't looking for ambience.

"Is my friend in the bathroom?"

"No, she is waiting in the car. I wanted us to talk first."

"Okay, but I need my special time. Let's talk and get that business out of the way."

Franklin was reminded of something Chen Ma Ho told him several years earlier. Chen tasked him with neutralizing a double agent, a Chinese engineering student at UCLA who was reporting to his consulate handlers but also cooperating with the FBI. Chen instructed Franklin to ask the student "Whose flag are you willing to die for?" In another dank motel room, not far from the college campus, the student begged for his life, claiming he was only providing minimal information to the Bureau to remain in America. The student cried real tears choking out how the FBI threatened to deport him if he failed to cooperate. "If they deport me, I couldn't help my country."

Franklin believed the tears and the explanation. He knew the tactics the FBI employed to gain insider assistance. The Bureau, in fact, approached him when he was arrested several years earlier. Franklin merely smiled at the agents, shook his head, maintained his honor, and spent his time in prison. The blubbering student promised to remain loyal to the five-starred Red Flag. Franklin smiled as he told the traitor, "You will die for that flag" before putting a bullet between the student's eyes. Now it would be up to Preston Brookside to determine if he were willing to die, not for a flag, but for a manufactured lie.

Still seated, Franklin said, "Let us get the financial portion of the afternoon out of the way."

Brookside opened his wallet and retrieved four crisp $100 bills which he handed to Franklin.

As Brookside took a seat on the side of the bed, Franklin said, "I guess we could have taken care of this the other night. It looks like the same bills Lin was passing out like Halloween candy."

Brookside still smiling said, "It came from the same batch."

"What do you know about this Jake who is working for you?"

Brookside's stomach began to churn, the bile rising, tasting like lighter fluid as he wanted to belch but smothered the urge. Caught off guard, he wasn't expecting this inquiry from Franklin. *Stick with the cover story you were prepared to tell Michael if he asked.*

Trying to recall the exact story since he hadn't rehearsed it in weeks, he said, "He is a friend of my niece's. She lives in Dallas, and he recently moved here from Dallas."

"Why did you hire him?"

Brookside nervously shifted his weight while sitting on the edge of the bed. "He needed a job, and I was looking to spend more time at the cabin up in Big Bear."

"Did he have references?"

Brookside, certain his anxiety was betraying him hesitated, trying to recall if they even discussed references. "I didn't ask for any. I hired him on the recommendation of my niece. I had no need to check references. He was enthusiastic and seemed to have caught on quickly to the intricacies of my business."

Franklin paused for a prolonged moment, staring at Brookside, expecting him to continue the conversation providing details of his new hire.

"Is there a problem?" asked Brookside tentatively.

"He shoots good. Too good."

Brookside faltered with a delayed response, "He was a Marine. Even Michael says they all shoot well."

"He asked questions about the guns."

Brookside seemed genuinely confused as beads of sweat appeared on his forehead, "What guns?"

"The gun I brought the other night and the guns I recently sold Michael."

Not used to thinking spontaneously when confronted by a documented gang member, Brookside staggered with a reply, his voice quivering, "He likes guns. He made that clear the first day he met Michael.

I didn't realize he was into guns, but he and Michael hit it off because of their mutual interest."

There was the deliberateness of an assassin with psychopathic ambition when Franklin asked menacingly, "Why are you sweating? This is the same uneasiness you displayed when you learned your employee was at Michael's fundraiser. Do my questions bother you? Have you not prepared your answers?"

Fear washed through him, but his nervous response was sincere, "I'm not used to being questioned by someone like you."

"Do you mean someone capable of killing you, if I don't like your answers?"

"Yes," answered Brookside, his body now quaking.

"I am not satisfied."

Brookside choked out a response. "With me or my answers?"

"With your new employee."

With his heart pounding, fearing it could be seen through his shirt, Brookside grabbed a quick breath. Some of his apprehension was minimized when Franklin's concern was focused on Jake and not him. Believing he might not be killed, he said, "I'm not sure how much more I can tell you. Do you want me to try to find out more about him? I can call my niece."

"Is your niece a cop?"

"No, of course not."

"Is your employee a cop?"

Brookside shook his head.

"Say it!" demanded Franklin.

Panicked, Brookside said, "No. No. No. He is not a cop."

Franklin withdrew a silenced weapon lodged between his thigh and the inside of the chair. "Does this look familiar?"

Brookside had not seen the gun hidden by the cushion. His head hung and he merely nodded.

"This is like the gun you fired the other night. Do you remember how quiet it was? You didn't shoot well, but you shot it. Not as well as your employee and friend. I think Jake is not who he says he is, and you brought him to the party. That makes you responsible. That makes either you a problem or him a problem. Maybe both."

Brookside said nothing as tears welled up and he choked on an answer that never came.

The sadistic monster asked, "Would you like to live?"

Brookside's lifted his eyes, displaying a glimmer of hope as he mumbled, "Yes. I want to live."

"The burden you carry is heavy. I will ask one question. Give me the right answer and you live. Give me the wrong answer and you don't. It is very simple. I am not a violent man. I merely want the truth to tell my superiors. Are you ready for my question?"

As Brookside nodded, he vacated his bladder and bowels; the overwhelming smell flooded the room.

Franklin shook his head at the weakness displayed by the fat man. "Who is Jake?"

Brookside delayed. He stammered. He mumbled, "He is FBI."

Calculate the value of the target, what his death will accomplish, and the costs. After Franklin did the mental arithmetic, the suppressed weapon spit out a single bullet, quickly and efficiently—one more shrine to the Wah Ching death cult.

Brookside's afternoon tryst was canceled.

CHAPTER SIXTY-FOUR

Los Angeles

Franklin's crew, members of the Monterey Park-Side, were successful in a variety of crimes. They were extensively involved in drugs, gambling, and extortion. If an unaffiliated individual wanted to deal meth, run a card game, or traffic in women on their turf, he had to get permission from the Side and pay a "street tax" to continue operating.

The crew successfully burglarized gun stores and businesses, selling much of their contraband south of the border thanks to their association with MS-13. Franklin was personally involved in human trafficking, providing underage females for men who sought perverted sexual satisfaction. But within law enforcement circles, his group was known for follow-home robberies.

What began by staking out ATM machines, watching vulnerable individuals withdraw money, following them home, and robbing them evolved into a sophisticated crime campaign. Surveillance, as law enforcement or felons would tell you, requires manpower to be successful. With technology, manpower needs for successful shadowing were reduced, allowing multiple teams of gang members to function simultaneously.

Two-man crews trolled parking lots, located luxury vehicles, attached a tracker and through an app received a real-time location on their smartphones. Rather than chance being caught conducting a moving surveillance, they waited until the vehicle arrived home. Using the locator, the crew invaded the wealthy residence using violence as an intimidation factor to convince the victim not to call the police. Franklin and his crews had perfected the art of armed robbery.

Initially, the purpose of the two-man Wah Ching surveillance crew was to identify Jake's residence. Once they located it, they were to contact Franklin for further instructions. Though Franklin hoped to covertly enter the home and find more information on Jake, Preston Brookside changed that.

Immediately after disposing of Brookside's body in the motel's dumpster, Franklin contacted Lin with the explosive information about Jake being an undercover FBI agent. It was now a matter of determining what should be done.

With Franklin remaining on the line, Lin contacted Chen who was at the Beverly Hills residence putting the final technical touches on the mansion ensuring the audio and video micro devices provided complete coverage. The operation was set for this evening, and everything was in place. The invitations went out and those invited responded with boyish enthusiasm. Chen's immediate concern was whether Brookside or Jake knew of tonight's event. Lin added Michael to the conference call.

"Michael, I have Franklin and Chen on the line. We have a problem," said Lin.

Michael knew conference calls were outside the norm. "What?"

Lin said, "Franklin has determined Jake is an FBI agent."

"What?" shouted Michael. "How do you know?"

"Franklin questioned Brookside who admitted he knew Jake was working undercover for the Bureau when he introduced him to you."

There was a long silence.

"Did you hear me?" asked Lin.

An incredulous Michael wailed, "That bastard! Yes, I heard you. I'm trying to process everything he knew about my operation."

"Our operation," corrected Lin angrily.

"Yes, our operation," said Michael apologetically.

Lin asked, "Did he or Brookside know about the event at the mansion? We cannot afford any blow back."

"No. I didn't invite Brookside. He wasn't important enough to make the cut. And I never said anything to Jake."

"That is good," said Chen Ma Ho entering the conversation for the first time.

"What are we going to do about Brookside and Jake?" asked Michael.

Franklin answered. "Brookside is no longer a problem. My two best are currently on Jake and will locate his residence."

"What do you mean Brookside is no longer a problem?" asked Michael.

Lin said, "Franklin has terminated his services. He is no longer a concern."

Without asking more, Michael knew what Franklin meant.

"What about Jake?"

"We must terminate him as well," said Chen.

"My men can do it, but they will need to be paid. We will need to buy their expertise and their silence," said Franklin.

"How much?" asked Chen.

Franklin thought for a moment. He knew the men at the consulate had access to money. He knew the importance of the mission. He understood an FBI agent could destroy the plans of an operation months in the making. "I think $50,000 will buy death and loyalty."

Without putting it to a vote, Chen said, "Murder is the most extreme form of conflict resolution; it resolves the issue. Just do it!"

Franklin regretted not going higher in his opening bid.

CHAPTER SIXTY-FIVE

Malibu

Jake believed in per-sec, personal security. At every venue, he quickly identified the exits, the escape routes. He sought out the covers and concealments. His work sent him down enough dark alleys to know danger awaited, even in the light. Always on guard, often presenting a carefree appearance and offering a tired smile, his eyes would be casually sweeping the street—situational awareness. Though on a UC mission, he might have a cover team prepared to assist should things go wrong in a hurry, he recognized he was his own best security team. Combat taught him decisiveness in the face of chaos. If seconds mattered, help was usually minutes away.

When he was heading home or meeting with Rone, he ran an SDR, a surveillance detection route. It took longer but it was safer. It meant taking a freeway exit, then immediately jumping back on. It meant racing through a traffic light before it turned red, observing who else was following. Jake was good. It was hard for the watchers to keep up. He was safer because he was careful.

But today, his precautions were supplanted by technology. While Jake was in Michael's office discussing nothing of consequence, a member of Franklin's posse attached a real-time GPS tracker paired with a magnetic case to the undercarriage of the Bronco.

Traveling surface streets, switching lanes without signaling, jumping off and back on the freeways, though solid SDR techniques, proved useless.

299

He called Natasha and asked if he could bring dinner. He liked the smile in her voice when she readily agreed. After a verbal rock, scissors, paper, his favorite take-out—Three Amigos—won. It was two steak burritos for them and a soft taco for Joey. Jake told her he would stop off at the cabin, grab a quick shower, then head over to Three Amigos. Expecting to be at her house within the hour, he was looking forward to a relaxing evening and a chance to build on a relationship he prayed would go beyond friendship.

Before heading up Malibu Canyon Road, Jake slipped his undercover cell phone into a Faraday bag. Designed to block tracking and hacking, the sleeve ensured no digital trace of movements or location. Though he didn't use the bag in every undercover assignment, he always used it when visiting with Natasha and Joey. It was possible to leave a voicemail message while the phone was enclosed in the bag, but the phone wouldn't ring because no cell tower could locate the device. If important, Rone knew to call on the personal cell phone he kept on him at home and at Natasha's.

CHAPTER SIXTY-SIX

Los Angeles

After the conference call ended, Franklin immediately called the older of the two-man crew assigned to Jake.

"What is your status?" asked Franklin.

"He has parked the Bronco near a small cabin in the Malibu Hills."

"The plans have changed. Are you equipped to eliminate him?"

"Do you mean kill him?"

"Yes. Kill him and anyone in the house."

"We have no long guns. They are back at your place, but I have my suppressed Glock and John has his Beretta," said the leader of the two-man crew.

"Is that enough?"

"We have enough firepower," said the taller man with the cockiness of a killer.

"Good. I was able to negotiate a fair price for you. You two can split the entire $10,000 fee," said Franklin without a hint of deception.

"Thank you. We will do it."

"Don't let me down. He needs to be killed. I'm not concerned about disposing of the body. Leave it. Get in and get out. Do this as you have before."

Though Franklin could not see their faces, he knew the two men were smiling, anxious to complete the mission and collect their fee.

Malibu

Each night before leaving the office, Rone did a quick review of the pole camera results downloading the daily footage. It had been a long day. Sometimes the administrative burdens as a case agent, especially one with an approved undercover operation, seemed overwhelming. The file had to be updated with weekly reports monitored by the various units at Headquarters, each with a piece of the investigation: the China desk, embassy/consulate monitoring section, the FCI program operations, undercover operations unit, Safeguard. These individual units also made time-consuming demands to brief their bosses, typically with questions answered in a previous report which they skimmed rather than studied.

Rone almost missed the RAV4 from the reception as it drove across Yang's parking lot. Stopping briefly at the edge of the monitoring screen, a male jumped out of the passenger side of the vehicle and slapped something on the undercarriage of Jake's Bronco. Within seconds, the man was back in the SUV and gone. The entire episode took less than thirty seconds.

Though he couldn't be certain, knowing the reputation of Franklin's crew, Rone was convinced it was a tracker the man attached. He punched in the speed dial for Jake's undercover phone and the call immediately went to voicemail. Fearing someone might be in the vicinity when Jake checked messages, Rone instructed Jake to call him immediately. He did not provide details of his concern, but the tone of his voice made it clear this was important. Rone dropped down one on the speed dial list for Jake's personal phone.

Jake answered on the first ring. "What's up?"

"Where are you?"

"I just got home. I'm going to shower, then head over to Natasha's tonight for dinner."

"Jake, I just checked the pole camera video. The RAV4 at the reception the other night pulled into Yang's parking lot while you were there this afternoon. A male jumped out of the car and slapped something on the undercarriage below the rear bumper. From everything we know about Franklin's crew, I have to believe it was a tracker. You need to check that now but be careful. They may be onto you. I'm heading your way and will call Tonya to meet us."

"Okay. I think they're just trying to figure out who I am. Michael checked out the mail drop location on Van Nuys. He may have ordered Franklin to check me out. The cabin comes back to an LLC, so they still won't have answers. I'll go look at the Bronco and call you back."

CHAPTER SIXTY-SEVEN

Malibu

Jake had been at this long enough to know no matter how great the plan, the results depended upon how your opponent responded. In the words of General James Mattis, "the enemy gets a vote." Jake needed to be cautious. The enemy might be on the doorstep prepared to cast his ballot.

Franklin Lee and his crew were Wah Ching. Their reputation for violence preceded them. Jake immediately grabbed his Glock 19M and put a second magazine in his left front pants pocket. He slipped his Gen3 in the small of his back. Both weapons were always hot, a round chambered. He really wasn't expecting trouble, but if it came, he wanted to be well-armed with extra fire power.

After shutting off the outlaw country pouring from the surround sound speakers, Jake listened carefully for any telltale noises coming from outside the cabin. Hearing none, he went to the windows. The curtains hung at each opening covering the left and right sides. Rather than stand in front of the windows presenting himself as an easy target to a shooter on the outside, Jake carefully edged the curtain back from the frame. Trying not to disturb the fabric causing movement giving away his position, he peered out. He performed the ritual at each window and saw nothing unusual.

Releasing the deadbolt, he opened the front door but waited before exposing himself by walking out on the porch. Concealed behind the door's frame, he listened for sounds of men racking rounds into weapons or walking on the dried leaves and branches encircling the property. Nothing. From the left side of the doorframe, he scanned the right side of the front yard. Seeing nothing, he quickly jumped to the other side. Still protected by the doorframe, he scanned the other half of the yard. Nothing. Maybe, no one was there. There was caution and then there was paranoia. A slight smile crossed his face as he thought how silly he must look.

Still choosing caution, he moved out onto the porch, seeking the cover of one of the porch beams. It only protected him from a frontal assault. If a shooter were set up on either side of the open porch, Jake was vulnerable. Listening for any unusual sounds, he heard nothing. Searching the area with his eyes, still nothing out of the ordinary.

Not ready to relax, he made his way to the Bronco parked on the gravel driveway. There was no way to lessen the noise as he approached the vehicle. The sounds of shifting gravel echoed against the trees. He headed straight to the back of the Bronco where Rone said he saw the activity.

Squatting with the Glock in his right hand, still watching the yard, he felt along the rear bumper with his left hand. Before he could complete the search, he heard movement about twenty feet to his right, near some California oaks. Scanning, he spotted an Asian male pulling down a black ski mask with his weak hand while holding a suppressed semi-automatic pistol in his right. Just to the man's right was a smaller male dressed in black with a ski mask covering his face and holding a gun in his right hand.

Taking an unconscious deep breath, Jake dropped to his right knee, his mind focused on the two men, not the gravel digging into skin and bone. Two armed men, one with a suppressed weapon faced him: both high threat targets. Jake chose the one with the suppressed weapon as his initial target. Just as the assassin began to take aim, Jake's muscle memory prevailed. His finger moved smoothly to the steel trigger.

Gaining a quick sight picture, his eyes focused on green neon night sights glowing in the sunlight. Centering the front sight circled in orange between the two rear posts, Jake squeezed two shots before his target got off a round. The hollow points exploded from the Glock 19M, spent brass kicking to his right. Seeing the man collapse, Jake immediately turned his attention to the shorter assailant.

Target number two standing in the open had three choices: fight, flight, or freeze. He froze. Failing to seek cover, angling his pistol gangster-style parallel to the ground, he got off some delayed rounds, employing quantity over quality: poor fire discipline and poor shooting. Each shot missed wildly tattooing the pockmarked logs of the cabin.

Jake had seen it before. Elevated heart rate, adrenaline dump, the lack of trigger discipline or muzzle management made even the most expensive weapon useless. Drive-by shootings in the inner city provided little training for a real firefight.

Jake knew he needed to get rounds on the new target. Shifting his weight to his right, his front sight fell on the new target. Jake fired once. The second man folded to the ground but was still alive, his body twitching, attempting to lift his weapon. Jake rose quickly from his kneeling position and fired two more quick shots. The body went limp. He had been accused of reckless shooting, making self-defense a tactical necessity, but this was a righteous shoot. Both men were set on a mission Jake interrupted. As the atheist Voltaire once said, "God is not on the side of the big battalions, but on the side of those who shoot best."

Maintaining his weapon in a high ready position, Jake cautiously moved toward the two collapsed bodies, his eyes scanning in all directions. The gunmen may have friends still in play.

At the first target, he kicked the weapon away. Then keeping the Glock aimed at the second target, kicked the second weapon away. Removing the face masks on each, he recognized the two as members of Franklin's crew who attended the reception at Michael's. Jake felt for a pulse on both men but found none. Their dead bodies lay on the bloodstained gravel.

Before picking up the weapons, he dropped his first magazine, put it in his left front pocket, replacing it with a full second mag. Real combat taught him the fight was never over until it *was* over. It wasn't a time to let down his guard. He needed to determine if others were still in the area.

Jake cautiously circled the area. Near the mouth of the driveway on the main road, he found the RAV4. He could hear sirens in the background and assumed a distant neighbor heard the shots and called the sheriff's department. Jake returned to the dead men and prepared to answer too many questions. A quick call to Rone, determined his case agent was a few minutes out.

CHAPTER SIXTY-EIGHT

Malibu

Three one-man sheriff patrol units were on the scene before Rone arrived.

Jake immediately identified himself as an FBI agent to the responding deputies and answered some preliminary questions. He directed the deputies to the deceased and pulled up the shirts of both, their torsos covered in tattoos. "Wah Ching" in various fonts was inked on each. The deputies instantly recognized this investigation might require delicate handling.

Jake promised to cooperate fully but requested the deputies wait before questioning him further until an FBI representative could be on scene. He also requested they not put out over the air this was an agent-involved shooting. He wanted to reflect on the incident before too much went public. The deputies were in full agreement.

As was procedure, a deputy stretched yellow evidence tape across the front of the driveway allowing only authorized personnel beyond the thin plastic barrier. He stationed himself there granting admission to Rone and later to Tonya Rodriguez who arrived a few minutes after Rone.

At this point, Jake's primary concern was the safety of Preston Brookside. It was obvious, the attack by two confirmed Wah Ching members meant Michael and Franklin's inquiry into the mail drop and his backstory went beyond mere suspicion.

Jake said, "We need to check on Brookside and his wife. We need to get somebody to the house now."

Tonya phoned Brookside. There was no answer, and she left a cryptic voicemail requesting he call her. She also called his business and was told he had been out sick for a couple days. The receptionist suggested Tonya contact him on his cell phone, but Brookside was in the wind, and the FBI needed to locate him immediately.

The two weapons used by the attackers were a Glock 17TB, the threaded barrel supporting the silencer and a Beretta M9. When Rone ran the serial number on the Beretta, it came back to one of the weapons stolen in the Shooter's Paradise break-in.

The fact one of the attackers had a silenced weapon demonstrated the men planned to do wet work. This was no sneak-and-peek mission; this was a termination. There would be no reason to do that unless Michael and Franklin determined Jake was with law enforcement in some capacity. It was still confusing to Jake because he wasn't aware of anything he had done that would've raised their suspicion.

While they were sitting on the porch discussing the failed investigation and awaiting shooting teams from the FBI and Los Angeles County Sheriff's Office, Jake showed Rone and Tonya the GPS device he found attached below the bumper of the Bronco. Available on the internet for less than $50, the inexpensive technology explained why Jake never saw the watchers after leaving Yang Printing.

It appeared the investigation was over. Obviously, if the other side determined Jake was an undercover agent, they would no longer deal with him. What was designed to be a long-term foreign counterintelligence operation ended within a few weeks. From an intelligence standpoint, about all they had were illegal campaign contributions reimbursed by someone attached to the Chinese consulate. In all likelihood, Lin Xu Ping had diplomatic immunity. There were a couple of weak firearms charges against Franklin and Danny, but it might be hard to find prosecutorial interest at the U.S. Attorney's office. You don't get points for trying. It only counts when you score, and this investigation was heading for the loss column.

The agents learned from one of the deputies several news vans were parked on the street requesting permission to come in and get some footage for the evening news. The deputy manning the driveway entrance kept the reporters from legally moving toward the cabin which was situated far off the road, behind scrub pine, California oaks, and chaparral. From the street, their cameras couldn't get any video of value. Soon the news copters would be overhead reporting "breaking news." Since dealing with the media was well above the pay grade of the three, Rone told the deputy to tell the reporters someone from public affairs would be on scene shortly to provide a press briefing.

Rone suggested Jake check his undercover cell phone to see if Brookside attempted to contact him. When Jake removed the phone from the Faraday sleeve, he saw he had one message other than Rone's. Rather than a voicemail from Brookside, it was from Danny. Though they exchanged numbers to set up the gun purchases, they had no other telephone communication and Jake was surprised to see he called.

When he played the voicemail, Jake heard the panic in Danny's voice. Jake put the device on speaker and replayed the voicemail for Rone and Tonya. "Jake, it's Danny. Annie is missing. I don't know where she is, but I suspect Michael has taken her. The house smelled of cigarette smoke when I got back from school. I don't know where to turn, please help me."

Though Danny seemed sincere, real fear in his voice, Rone questioned if this was a setup to target Jake in case the two-man Wah Ching crew failed. Jake voted Rone down. He needed to get over to the house in Monterey Park. The only question for Jake was would he conduct the investigation overtly as an FBI agent or remain below the radar.

Jake offered a suggestion the three agents briefly kicked around. There was no downside other than lying to the media, which concerned no one, but the three decided to call the shooting at the Malibu

Hills cabin a triple fatality, a "three bagger." Let Michael and Franklin believe Jake was killed in the attack. All that would be told to the press was "three men were killed in a shootout. No names were being released until the notification of next of kin." Though no one in public affairs would confirm it, the media would assume the shooting was drug related.

CHAPTER SIXTY-NINE

West Los Angeles

Leaving the investigation to the respective shooting teams, the three FBI agents snuck past the news crews, Jake hiding in the backseat of Rone's Bureau-issued vehicle, a black Chevy Tahoe. Tonya raced over to Brookside's residence as Jake and Rone headed to Monterey Park.

En route to Brookside's home, Tonya called another agent on the squad and asked her to meet at the residence. When Tonya arrived, Sally DePaul who was on the initial search of the house was waiting. As Tonya approached the front door, Sally stood off to the side viewing the garage and driveway and providing cover fire, if needed.

Shortly after ringing the bell, Evelyn Brookside answered. Not being a fan of the Bureau, she didn't invite the agents in and preferred to speak on the front stoop.

Without alarming his wife, Tonya asked about Preston. Evelyn confirmed he had not been to work in several days and said her husband went out for a scheduled afternoon appointment. She was expecting him home soon.

Catching Tonya off guard, Evelyn Brookside asked about the investigation into her husband's vendor. Tonya stumbled in a response until she recalled Brookside telling his wife the day of the search the FBI was investigating one of his vendors. Tonya played off the question with a typical Bureau response, "The investigation is ongoing, and I can't comment on it at this time." Not satisfied with the answer, Evelyn demanded to know why it was taking the FBI so long, pronouncing that since the day of their intrusion her husband had been distant and depressed.

Brookside screeched, "I want the truth."

Not wanting to tell the elementary school principal that the truth was not always your friend, Tonya elected to remain vague with her response.

The wife insisted that without some immediate answers, she was going to have her brother "Philip, a top attorney in town," make inquiries that "would not be pleasant for anyone at the FBI."

Tonya said she would check with the U.S. Attorney's office and inquire about the progress of the case which was being handled by the Grand Jury.

Placated for the moment, Brookside retreated inside the house, slamming the front door.

Tonya returned to her car and called Rone and Jake. After informing them what she learned from the wife, the three discussed whether it was time to clue in Evelyn as to the nature of the investigation into her husband. All three decided it wasn't necessary at this time, but all agreed the wife's life could be in danger if Michael or any of Franklin's crew went to the residence seeking Brookside.

Rone and Jake weren't going to turn around. Believing their investigation into Annie's kidnapping was also a priority, Tonya assumed the burden of getting Evelyn Brookside out of the house and into a safe location; a chore neither man wanted.

As they were wrapping up, Tonya had an incoming call. She put the agents on hold to take the call.

The situation just got worse. An employee at a motel near downtown found Preston Brookside in a dumpster, a single bullet to the forehead. Tonya had an alert on the name and if anyone inquired about him, she was notified. Now, it was necessary to not only give a death notification to Evelyn Brookside but move her to a secure location until all this was sorted out. Returning to the call, she shared the news with Jake and Rone. The string tying this knot continued to unravel.

CHAPTER SEVENTY

Monterey Park

When Jake's personal cell phone chirped, he saw from the caller ID it was Natasha. "Nuts, I forgot to call her and cancel dinner." Jake answered immediately, "Hey, I'm sorry I forgot to—"

"Oh, thank God you are alright. Jake, I saw the news. They have a helicopter over the cabin and are reporting three people have been killed."

"I'm fine. Yeah, there was a problem, but I'm fine. Don't say anything to anyone. I'll explain later. We are in the middle of something, and I can't talk right now."

"Okay, I understand. Just please be careful, Jake." There was a new softness in her voice.

When he ended the call, he realized maybe an emotion was stirring in her heart as well.

✕ ✕ ✕

Once Jake and Rone arrived at Danny's house, it was determined Jake would approach the house alone, with Rone providing cover in case it was a setup. As Jake exited the Tahoe, his eyes swept the street but saw nothing alerting him to a potential problem. He cautiously approached the front door, looking left and right, listening for the unusual. Knocking hard, he stepped off to the side in case someone behind the door opened fire. Danny quickly came to the door. His eyes said it all. The concern was real. This was no setup.

As he opened the door allowing Jake to enter, Danny said, "Jake, you were kind to Annie. She may only have the intellect of a first grader, but she is a good judge of character. She liked you. That says a lot to me. You are different from the others who have come around her. Franklin didn't like you. He thinks you're a cop. At this point, I don't care. If you're a cop, you can help me get her back. If you're not, you care about her enough to help me get her back."

"Let me see her room and the rest of the house. But before we do that, I have a friend out front I'd like to invite in. He can help us."

Danny didn't hesitate allowing Rone to join them.

As the three searched the house, Danny explained he always allowed Annie to stay home by herself for a few hours during the day while he attended classes at East Los Angeles Community College. When he called Annie on his way home to see if she wanted him to pick up anything for dinner, she failed to answer the phone. Danny remarked it was unusual for her not to answer the phone and rather than stopping to pick up takeout, he came straight home. When he got to the house, she was gone. She was not allowed to leave the house without telling Danny, a rule she never violated. There was no sign of a struggle but a telltale smell of Xiongmao cigarette smoke. Even Jake could detect a slight odor. Since Michael was the only one of Danny's associates who smoked Xiongmao and because of his previous comments about Annie, Michael was Danny's primary suspect.

The search turned up nothing of value. In the few weeks Jake dealt with Michael Yang, he never had a cell phone number for Yang. While Yang had Jake's number, Jake only contacted Michael at the business.

Though Jake didn't tell Danny about the attack at the cabin or the murder of Preston Brookside, he and Rone concluded without even discussing it, that Franklin Lee was involved. Since Jake met Franklin only two nights earlier, he had no contact information for the Wah Ching member.

Without offering an explanation, Jake asked Danny for the cell phone numbers of Michael and Franklin. Danny quickly provided the numbers.

"Are you aware of any place Michael could have taken Annie?"

"No, but I know at the reception the other night at Michael's, I overheard Michael and Lin talking about something tonight. I never heard the details, but Lin asked Michael if his little friend was coming."

"Who was his little friend?"

"I'm not sure, but now I'm wondering if it was Annie. Jake, can you find her?"

"I can promise you this, we're going to try."

Danny hesitated but then asked, "Jake, one other question. Are you a cop?"

Jake looked at Danny and said, "Something like that."

"Jake, I just want Annie back. I think you need to know the truth. That Kimber I sold you was a gun Franklin gave me after he shot somebody. He told me to get rid of it. I was going to destroy it, but when I heard you were into guns, I thought I could pick up some quick cash. I'm willing to take my punishment, I just want to find Annie."

"Thanks, Danny. Let's find Annie."

Jake pulled out his cell phone, scrolled through his contact list and placed a call. Peter Newman answered on the second ring.

"Jake, good to hear from you."

"General, I don't have a whole lot of time, but I need your expertise. If I give you two cell phone numbers, can you find their real-time location? Obviously, the Bureau can do it but it's going to take too much paperwork. I don't think time is on our side."

"Of course, give me the numbers and I can get you the information while you stay on the line."

Jake provided the cell phone numbers of Michael Yang and Franklin Lee. As one of the Centurion Solutions Group analysts was running the numbers, General Newman said, "The technology today is beyond amazing. We have the capability to read private and group chats and recover the browser history of any cell phone. For many of our clients, we do geo-fencing. We can designate zones and if a phone goes in that zone, we know it and can identify the subscriber. Frankly, a smartphone is a surveillance device that makes calls. In our world, it is almost counterproductive to carry one. We can backtrack the GPS identifier for each number. It's called breadcrumbing. We can identify the physical location of each of these cell phones for the past month . . ."

The general paused briefly and said, "This is interesting. Both phones are in the same Beverly Hills location." The general provided an address.

"Thank you, General. I don't have time to give you the details, but I think we discovered who killed Brian Sullivan and we may even have the weapon used in the murder."

"That's great news, Jake. I look forward to hearing all about it when you have the time. Stay strong and safe out there. Semper Fidelis."

294 OLIVER NORTH — BOB HAMER